Becoming
Shamus

A Novel

Elizabeth Curtisse

DC Publishing House
– New York –

FIRST PRINT EDITION.

Cover art designed by Elizabeth Curtisse and id29 (thank you Doug). Thank you also to Peter F. for his advice.

Library of Congress Cataloging-in-Publication: 2012948038

ISBN: 978-0-9855940-0-8

This book is dedicated to my family for their abundant love, support, and inspiration; to the cherished friends (you know who you are) who told me I could do this and then made me believe; and to the beloved dogs that have stood faithfully beside me through our intertwined journeys.

~One~

"We won't be long," Mom said, bending down to kiss me good-bye. She tussles my ears and inhales deeply. She smiles and closes the door.

Her warm breath lingers on my cheek as I watch them disappear. The crunch of the gravel grows distant. The humming engine fades.

I stare beyond the dirty windowpane long after they're gone. Gazing beyond the smudged fingerprints and my dried nose juice. Looking out into the morning, watching the clouds weave slowly over and around the early sun. It hasn't yet hit the highest point of the sky. A couple more hours maybe.

A familiar form glides through the sky. It's the red tail hawk searching for food. I've heard the hungry cry of her young. High above where their mother's shadow grazes the treetops that gently sway to a beloved melody. A spirited tune that rouses me. *Our robins?* I wonder as they flitter past the window.

Late spring. The trees are full of leaves and the grass is rich and sweet. A soft lilac scent drifts through the opened window.

My muscles ripple in anticipation. *It won't be long before I'm out there. They'll be home soon enough and I'll rush out to greet her,* I tell myself. I've waited all week for her arrival. We all have.

Nerves mix with hunger and my stomach rumbles though I ate just two hours before. Anxiousness wraps itself around my insides. I feel the grasp of the gnarly fingers. The tightness is uncomfortable.

Breathe, I remind myself, pushing my wet nose into a sliver of screen. A deep inhale stifles the restlessness that stirs within my gut.

You've been sitting too long, my aching hind end tells me. *Move your vigil to the soft, worn pillow.*

The cushiony folds envelop my body, and I see the tattered towel resting inches from me. I pull it close and let the scents fill my nostrils.

"I thought it would help if you were familiar with her scent before we bring her home," Mom had said when she first laid the towel at my paws a few days earlier. But too many scents had mingled together, and even those scents had since started to fade.

No matter though. Because today's the day. The shelter called. Shelby's coming home.

I rub my muzzle against the dirty fabric. Soft, light pieces of fur tickle my nose. Soft, light and fuzzy. Her fur isn't dark and coarse as Lela's had been.

Lela. My teacher. My friend.

A familiar pang jabs at my heart as Lela's face flashes before me. Joy and sadness mingle as I recall the memory of our first meeting. A memory that's been tucked safely away.

My breath catches somewhere deep inside my throat. My body twitches. Hot, blinding tears seep into my eyes.

Five years ago, Lela waited for me. That was the day I came to live on the lane. I was only ten months old, naive and self-centered. But she had unlimited faith in me. She saw the dog I could become.

I've changed since then.

We've all changed.

Would Lela recognize me now? I wonder. There are certainly times when I don't recognize myself.

Yes, Lela taught me well. I carry her still in my heart.

I can't contain the sigh that pours from my chest. Its heaviness pulls my body deeper into my pillow.

How lonely I've been. How long the days and nights feel without her. Especially the nights. When there's no one to talk to or to share secrets with.

Lela said our paths would cross again. I've spent the last year looking for her. *Perhaps she changed her mind,* I think. The possibility makes me quiver.

"Where are you, Lela?" I whisper in a scarcely audible whine. "I've taken care of them. Wait till you see how they've grown."

I look to the clouds, but there's no answer. No one responds. Silence surrounds me. A yawn passes silently through my lips.

Time drags its heels and boredom creeps in. Another yawn sneaks silently into the daylight. My eyes begin to droop, and my paws absorb the weight of my head. My eyes slide slowly backwards, and my jowls flutter lightly. I glide in and out of consciousness. Images flicker on the insides of my eyelids. The snapshots fade in and out.

Back in time I drift.

Reflections.

Recollections of my life.

~ Two ~

Gwen shifted her weight beneath me. "Here we are, Shamus. This is our lane!" she said as we made the sharp right turn. Her voice was vibrant despite the strain.

Shamus. The name Gail gave me on the day I left my birth mother. "It's a fine, strong name," my mother said affectionately. "You'll grow into it." She rubbed her muzzle against mine and caressed my snout and head with her soft tongue. "Don't be afraid," she whispered in my ear. "Have faith. This is what you were bred for. A family of your own."

Gail was a schoolteacher nearing retirement. I was nine months old when I moved in with her. Ten months old when Gwen knelt in front of me that afternoon. "It'll be all right," Gwen said. She cupped my muzzle in her hands, and I looked deep into her eyes. "You don't have to be afraid." She stroked my back reassuringly. Compassion flowed from her strong fingertips. "What do you say?" She stood and pointed her head towards a truck she called Big Red. "Wanna come home with us?" I knew instinctively that she ruled her pack.

I turned my gaze toward Big Red. Her body was filled with laughter. The father's robust laugh and the kids' airy titters cascaded out the opened doors, spilling out into the early evening. *Maybe this is what I was bred for*, I thought. *This family.* My mother's words swirled in my head. *Have faith.* But I was only ten months old. I knew nothing of faith, and trepidation made my body tremble.

"It's all right, Shamus." Gwen walked slowly backwards. Her eyes locked on mine. I hesitantly took one step forward. "Good boy," Gwen said encouragingly, slapping her thighs to coax me along. She slowly let my leash fall to the ground. "Good boy!" Gwen repeated as the family's laughter spiraled around me. My muscles responded to the joyous sound. My legs pushed my body forward until suddenly, without thinking, I dashed toward Big Red and leaped into her arms.

The journey from Gail's was just under an hour. Anticipation made me anxious, and my insides were taut when we turned onto the lane. Big Red groaned, and her engine whined as we ascended the steep, long windy road. We passed several large houses with expansive, manicured yards as she climbed. There were trees. Lots of trees and boulders in between. And a pond. I caught a glimpse of a glassy pond in the distance. I hadn't roamed wooded trails or swam in water since leaving the farm.

My heartbeat raced ahead of us, and my quivering body pressed against Gwen. I felt the labored rise and fall of her chest when I leaned deeper into her. Her fingers searched blindly for the button that would pull down the glass. She struggled and strained under my weight. "You're no lap dog," she wheezed as I edged closer to the outdoors. Then the cool air rushed in without warning.

I eagerly thrust my head through the opening. I gasped as the wind shoved itself into my lungs. Its strength surprised me. I had never ridden shotgun before. I'd always been confined to my crate.

I braced myself against Gwen and the door, and craned my neck farther out the window. I let the powerful current wash over me. My ears and jowls thrashed madly around my face. The flapping sounds made me laugh, and I strained to control my tongue as it rolled about, lapping up the sweet evening air. I rejoiced despite my stinging eyes and the occasional insect that lodged itself in my teeth.

My body relaxed, and the knot in my belly eased. The tightness in my bowels loosened. A loud plume of gas burst into the air.

"Quick, Raj. Put the windows down!" Gwen cried as the fumes filled her nostrils. My ears filled with jubilant laughter and with the pounding my chest barely contained. I thought my insides might burst from eagerness, but then the lane ended suddenly.

Big Red stood in front of a grand house that boasted a large stone patio with an abundance of spring flowers already planted near its walls. The same flower beds that became the burial grounds for my half-eaten bones and chew toys. Each spring, rotted remains are unearthed as the beds are readied for new plantings. So many remain unaccounted for. I've lost track of where they're all buried.

Raj silenced Big Red's engine, and an enchanting melody drifted around us. A melody I hadn't heard since leaving my mother. It was an inviting chant. The frogs, katydids, and crickets raised their voices to greet us. They were welcoming us home.

Gwen opened her door, and I leaped out onto the gravel driveway. My paws sunk slightly into the loose pebbles that felt cool under-paw. I took a long, deep breath and surveyed my surroundings.

The house sat on top of the suburban mountain. A large yard flanked its front and sides. There was an abundance of grass, shrubs, flowers, and trees. But no other houses that I could see. I felt as though we were miles away from anything or anyone, though I knew the pristine village we'd driven through lay beneath us. I heard the cars whizzing by on the parkway below and a train pulling away in the distance. The sounds were muffled. Muffled and quieted by the forest's canopy that I looked down upon.

Sumptuous smells assaulted my senses. My nostrils were overcome by the sheer number. It was intoxicating sifting through them. Some were more pungent than others. Some familiar. Some new. Then the scent of a dog pricked my muzzle. A strong, fresh scent. Not long left behind. I followed the trail into the grass and surrounding shrubs. I lifted my leg and left my mark to introduce myself should she return.

"I'll go in and get Lela. We should probably introduce them outside," Gwen suggested.

Lela? Why does that name sound familiar? I wondered.

It didn't take long to remember. I'd be bigger than Lela when I was fully grown. That's what Gwen told Logan when I first met them. She knew from the size of my paws. *Lela is their dog*, I predicted. *The scent in the grass.* My stomach turned in excitement.

It was then that I felt the smoldering eyes upon me.

Lela looked at me with hard, narrow eyes from behind a curtained window. Her gray mask signaled that she was older. Much older than me. Even older than my mother.

I wanted to meet her.

I bolted toward the house, but Raj's strong hands stopped me before I reached the patio. "You're a strong one," he said, regaining his balance. "You better wait here, Shamus. Let's see what she does." He snapped my leash in place. But I didn't want to be held back. It'd been weeks since I played with another dog. I strained against my collar. My breath grew hoarse and ragged.

The front door opened, and Lela charged toward me. Her hackles were up, but I wasn't afraid. I sensed that she wasn't an aggressive dog. She was merely protecting her family, and I was certainly no threat.

I pulled to break free from Raj's grasp, but he held tight. Gwen and the kids waited near the front door. They all held their breath. Waiting to see what transpired as Lela and I circled around each other. Raj danced about to avoid getting tangled in my leash.

I wanted to play, but Lela snarled, "Settle down." She was older, ten years older, and she commanded respect. I crouched low and licked her muzzle. I rolled onto my back submissively. A trick I learned from my mother when the older dogs came around. I remained in that position, not daring to look her in the eyes, until she signaled that I could stand and face her.

Lela's beauty was inspiring. She was beautiful like my mother, but a black Lab like me. A striking black Lab. Her coat glimmered, and the light, aging fur around her eyes and mouth glowed in the twilight. A faint butterfly freckle donned her nose.

Lela of New York. That was her proper name. It suited her. She was elegant and composed. Not clumsy and awkward like me. She fit her paws perfectly, while I hadn't yet grown into mine.

"So you're Shamus." Lela's voice was cool. She was neither glad nor mad to see me. Her dark eyes inspected me from head to paw to tail. She watched me suspiciously. "I've heard Mom and Dad talking about you," she said. Her hackles remained slightly raised. She was on guard. Undecided as to whether or not she trusted me.

"Mom and Dad?" I asked. I'd never heard a dog refer to his or her humans as Mother and Father. It seemed a bit unnatural at the time. Hard for me to understand since I hadn't been with Gail long enough to develop a strong bond. She worked a lot, and I was often alone. Still I winced thinking of her.

"They're my family. They take care of me." Lela's eyes went soft when she gazed at Gwen and the kids. "They love me as humans love." She turned from me and followed the trio indoors. I'd been seemingly dismissed.

I leaped to join them, but Raj tightened his grip on my leash once more. "Let's wait a minute, Shamus." He stroked my back as we waited. My body grew increasingly impatient listening to them carry on inside. Then I heard the familiar sound of kibble filling a bowl. My stomach grumbled when the smell poured through the opened windows.

"Now?" I whimpered.

Raj looked down at me with his kind eyes and unfastened my leash. I raced ahead not waiting for him. Nose to the ground sniffing out my dinner. Oblivious to my surroundings. Oblivious, at least, until Lela's voice rumbled toward me.

"This is where I eat," she growled.

The ferocity of her tone startled me, and I skidded to a halt just a few short feet from her. She stood protectively near two bowls. My stomach gurgled at the sight of my kibble. I ignored its beckoning and remained frozen. Frozen until Lela rushed at me.

"Out," she snarled with incisors and canines exposed. I quickly turned and bolted from the kitchen with my tail safely stowed between my legs.

Lela and I never ate in the same room from that night on. I could drink from her water bowl, but she ate in the kitchen and I ate in the den. It was a good-sized room with a large desk and a baby grand. I could easily dash under either should Lela barge through the door. I always listened for the fast approaching snarls and scraping nails while I ate. She drew blood only once, and I milked that wound for all the attention I could get. Needless to say, I never learned the bad habit of begging. Lela always stayed close to food. Close to food and close to Gwen.

Nobody followed me from the kitchen. I

explored my new home alone. Free to wander and traipse around from room to room. There were five bedrooms and four bathrooms. A formal dining room, sitting room, laundry room, mudroom, and a large playroom stocked with toys.

It's a large house. Much larger than Gail's, I marveled, sniffing about the playroom. I looked around at all the lonely, discarded toys. I suddenly felt small and alone amid the clutter. There was nothing familiar. A chill ran along my spine, and my echoing cry chased me from the room.

I found Gwen and the others in the TV room. Nestled together on a big sofa. Lela lay on the plush area rug near Gwen's feet. She glared at me as I approached. Her hackles were raised slightly, and her low, steady snarl warned me to behave. She didn't want me pestering them for I was still an outsider.

I halted on the threshold and whimpered.

"Come 'ere, Shamus," Haley called in a soft, high-pitched tenor. "Shamus! Shamus!" Logan echoed. His voice too was immature and had a nasal, airy quality. They bounced up and down and patted the cushions invitingly.

Haley was five and Logan four. They had shiny, dark, almond-shaped eyes and dark hair and skin like their father, Raj, but they bore more physical resemblance to their mother. Gwen was pale in comparison to them. She had fair hair and those bright, round, pale eyes. And all those eyes were staring at me. I felt my ears flush in embarrassment.

As much as I wanted to run to them, I waited for

Haley and Logan to come for me. They scrambled off the sofa and raced toward me with outstretched arms and rosy faces. They were unafraid when I hurled myself at them. "Hi," they cooed in delectable voices. Apple juice tainted their breath, sweet juice and cheddar crackers. Their skin was warm and soft. I covered every inch of their faces in sticky saliva. They shrieked with delight. Never had I interacted with such small humans before. They were young like me, and energy oozed from them.

Lela stood and rolled her dark eyes. Her body tensed and her weight shifted back. I was afraid she might lunge.

"It's OK," Gwen said reassuringly. I wasn't sure to whom she was talking.

Another snarl tumbled from Lela's jowls.

"Shhh," Gwen said, placing her hand on Lela's back.

Lela reluctantly acquiesced. Her hackles lowered and her snarling quieted. Her body remained rigid and her steel gaze made me shiver.

Will she ever accept me? I wondered.

~Three~

I welcomed the nighttime hubbub. I was glad to be a part of it. It was my first night on the lane. My first night participating in the endless evening rituals. Rituals that haven't changed much over the years.

I busied myself with the kids. Because when Lela wasn't growling at me for overstepping one boundary or another, she simply ignored me. I wasn't used to the constant rebukes or rejection. I yearned for a companion and took comfort in the kids' presence. I followed at their heels as Gwen and Raj readied them for bed.

Lela waited in the hall while pajamas went on, teeth were brushed, potty trips made, and stories read. And when bedtime was near, Haley and Logan fell next to me and showered me with affection. "Night-night, Shamus," they muttered. My body succumbed to their soft, mesmerizing voices and delicate caresses. I slumped slowly sideways and then rolled onto my back. Four little hands, twenty little fingers, rubbed and tickled my belly. My tongue rolled onto the floor in ecstasy.

Haley and Logan were tucked into their beds, and the lights went out after prayers. Gwen and Raj headed downstairs, and soon after, the children drifted effortlessly to sleep. Lela was last to check on them.

My pillow rested next to Logan's bed. I was asked to sleep there. But the room was dark and still, and I missed familiar things. I missed Gail's soft breaths and my snug crate. I missed my mother.

My eyes misted over thinking of Gail and my mother. Remembering the day Gail led me from the farm. I was the last of my siblings to go. They had long since been adopted. It pained me to leave. It occurred to me then that while I looked like the father I never met, sheen and glossy black, I had inherited my mother's softer side. But I wanted to make her proud, and I shook the clouds away.

But the clouds hovered over me in Logan's room. *Why did Gail send me away?* I wondered. I thought back on the events of the day. Gail had said nothing as she affectionately stroked my ears. But her eyes carried the same sadness as my mother's when we parted, when I raised my paw in good-bye. Gail had pushed my paws from her fleshy thighs and turned her back on me. The front door shut tight behind her. The windows of the two-story condo were closed, and the curtains were drawn. I would never see her again. I understood and trembled. "Why?" I whined.

The despair in my heart was wretched. It was Logan's teddy bear that eased the ache. It toppled from the bed and plopped down next to me. Its eyes were nonjudgmental, and a smile stretched across the furry face. I pushed my muzzle into its belly. It squeaked in response, and the clouds lifted slightly.

There was a bumbling downstairs followed by hushed voices. Gwen and Raj. I heard them moving in the downstairs bedroom. I listened to their low sounds. I yearned to be with them, hoped they might settle my uneasiness.

I crept down the stairs and through the hall to

find reprieve from the aloneness. I cautiously poked my nose into their room, sensing Lela was near. I knew she slept with them. Her pillow lay next to the oversized bed. The side closest to the door. *Gwen's side*, I guessed.

Lela laid in wait. She had heard me coming. "This is where I sleep!" she snapped. She sprang and chased me from the room.

I sat at the end of the hall waiting for my courage to return. I took a deep breath and inched my way forward. I wouldn't be put off so easily. But Lela growled and lunged at me the moment my paws hit the threshold.

Over and over again I tried entering, and over and over again Lela denied me access.

"How about the kitchen?" Gwen suggested.

Raj obediently fetched my pillow and led me to the kitchen. "It's OK, Shamus," he said, gently running his hand from the top of my head down the length of my back. "It's going to take some time for everyone to adjust." He placed my pillow near the large picture window. He patted the cushion and coaxed me onto my bed. "Lela won't bother you in here, and we can all get some sleep." He scratched my side and left. Gates prevented me from following him. It was pointless to try.

The lights went out, and the kitchen filled with the moon's ghostly glow. The loneliness seeped in again, and the foreign sounds were scary. The rat-a-tat-tats on glass panes. The whistling wind and rustling leaves. The moans and groans of an old house. I was sure something unnatural was watching, and I pressed my body flat against my pillow.

I dared to breathe while the trees' eerie shadows scraped along the kitchen walls. The long limbs twitched and twisted, as if reaching out for me. I retreated into the darkness to escape their looming clutches. Oh, how I longed for the safety of my crate. The crate that cradled me while I slept. The door was always left open. Yet there was never a need to leave its protection. No need until nature called. But they had left my crate at Gail's.

I quivered against the gate and whimpered. My whimpering escalated into a sorrowful wail. Gwen and Raj then came for me. Lela lurked in the hall, eyeing me guardedly.

"Well, what now?" Raj asked gruffly. The hour was late and he was tired. Tired and frustrated.

"Let's see if he'll sleep on his pillow on your side of the bed," Gwen proposed. "I'll stay out here with Lela while you get him settled." She unlatched the gate and I jumped up and down with gratitude, nervously nipping at her T-shirt. "No, Shamus. Off," she commanded as Lela edged closer. I cringed and moved slightly behind Raj, keeping him between Lela and myself as we passed by.

I was tense, edgy, listening to Lela's clicking nails approach. Her low growl filled the room the moment she stepped through the doorway. She knew I was there, and she didn't like the sleeping arrangement. I sank lower into my pillow.

"Quiet, Lela," Gwen scolded.

I stayed very quiet and very low. I knew from where I lay that Lela was still standing, and she was ready to spring. I could see her pillow and legs when I peeked under the bed. I turned my head. Afraid she might catch me spying on her.

She struck swiftly and suddenly. There was little time to react. An incisor scraped my flank as I leaped onto the bed. I lay at Gwen's feet motionless, not wanting to be heard or seen.

Lela's deep, low, gurgling growl turned my blood to ice. She was annoyed. Very annoyed. Her growl was so low and so deep that it was nearly silent, but Gwen heard it.

"Go to sleep, Lela." Gwen's voice was firm. "Now," she commanded.

Lela reluctantly obeyed. She settled down with a "humph."

"It's OK, Shamus," Gwen said, sitting up. Her fingers grazed the top of my head. Raj snuggled deeper into the mattress, signaling his assent.

I allowed myself to breathe. Softly.

The silence returned and we all drifted into sleep.

Eventually.

~Four~

The sun was just beginning to rise when my eyes first fluttered. A light, rumbling snore drifted around me. An unfamiliar snore. Lela's snore.

My eyes flew open. I remembered then that I wasn't at Gail's.

My heart tightened as I thought about the previous night. How Lela forced me to find shelter on the bed. She didn't like me in their bedroom. She didn't like me so close to Gwen.

Where exactly was she? I wondered, lifting my head cautiously to survey the room. Nothing had changed from the night before.

I dragged my body slowly over the covers toward the source of the snore. Closer to the edge. Closer to Lela. She lay sprawled across her pillow. Her front paw twitched. It jerked up and down, then slightly to the side. Her jowls shook as another snore tumbled out.

Not so intimidating now with the slobber sliding down your jaw, I chuckled to myself. Then her lips smacked together, and her tongue mopped up the drool as if she heard my thoughts. My body recoiled instinctively. I shimmied away from the edge.

A foot bumped against my leg, and I felt a slight stirring deep under the covers. Steady inhales and exhales surrounded me. The house still slept. I lay patiently waiting. My movements were purposely slow and small. Careful not to disturb the silence. Careful not to awaken Lela.

The sun rose reluctantly. Even the birds were uneager to rise. I watched time pass. The clock's numbers changed painfully slow. 5:35. 5:36. 5:37. The restlessness stirred, and I grew bored. I hadn't yet learned to channel my energy.

My muzzle busied itself in the fluffy comforter. Poking and sniffing around the folds for anything interesting. A goose feather objected to the intrusive prodding and pricked my snout. I couldn't stifle the tingling sensation. A sudden sneeze burst from my chest. I held my breath, immobilized, until Lela's snore stirred the quiet. I was free to exhale. A long, slow exhale.

I glared at the feather that caused the ruckus. I tried trapping it between my paws. It clung stubbornly to the fabric, sneering at me as I uselessly scratched. It ignored my snorts and reprimands. Then retreated deep within the comforter's folds. I grabbed the folds between my teeth. Pulling, gnawing, searching for the offensive feather. I heard the ripping. A short tear followed by a longer, shredding sound. My head jerked back suddenly as the fabric gave way. Hundreds of goose feathers danced above my head.

A gruff "humph" resonated next to me.

I sunk deep into the covers, hiding among the feathers, avoiding Lela's gaze. She stood close to the bed. Her eyes bore into me and her breath was hot. I waited for the reprimand, a growl. But there wasn't any. She only grunted at the feathers gliding by as she left the room.

Probably shouldn't follow her, I thought as I

slid off the bed.

I stayed back several paces as she made her way to the kitchen. I listened as she lapped her water. My own throat felt parched, and my stomach rumbled unexpectedly.

"Go back to bed, Shamus," Lela directed.

I pulled back quickly and withdrew several steps. I listened safely from the hall. Her clicking nails grew louder. *I'm only a few shorts bounds from the bed,* I reassured myself.

I was about to bolt when the clicking ceased. I peeked around the corner to see Lela treading up the stairs. She moved gracefully in and out of the kids' bedrooms, just as she had twice during the night. When her rounds were finished, she retreated to the TV room. The big sofa squealed when she took her place on it.

Lela loved that sofa. As silly as it sounds, that sofa loved her too. When she couldn't easily jump on or off, the cushions gave way. They gently nudged her aging hips when she had difficulty getting down.

My body relaxed knowing the sofa was then enveloping Lela in its plush foam and feathers. My appetite returned, and I realized I needed to pee. Badly needed to pee. I was used to being up and out by 5:30 a.m. That was the schedule Gail and I shared. I couldn't go back to sleep.

I pawed at the bed to get Gwen's attention, but she wouldn't move. Only loose feathers responded. They floated silently to the floor.

My stomach was empty and my bladder was full. I grew increasingly impatient and uncomfortable. I tugged at the comforter, careful not to rip another edge. But it was big, and Raj had part of it wrapped tight under his body. I sunk my big paws into the plush mattress and pressed my cold, wet muzzle against Gwen's skin. She flinched from the chill and retreated deeper under the folds. I threw my upper body against the bed and pawed at the bodies buried beneath the cover. The pressure in my bladder swelled.

"Get up. Get up," I whined and pleaded.

"No, Shamus," Gwen said groggily. "Go back to bed."

I wasn't about to go back to bed. I was up and ready for breakfast, and I badly needed to pee.

"Get up!" I howled.

The covers shifted and bodies turned, but neither Raj nor Gwen was willing to get out of bed.

My bladder screamed. It was ready to burst. I flung myself onto Gwen's chest without any reservations. It became our morning ritual. A game we played for weeks until she bought me a crate.

"Oomph," she gasped when my weight bore down upon her. Her eyes flew open and she gulped for air. She shook her head fiercely and flailed her arms while my cold, wet nose and coarse tongue assaulted her face. Her body writhed beneath me as she struggled to free herself.

It was Raj who pushed me from the bed.

Gwen sat upright, panting. She was quite a sight. Drool-soaked hair stuck to her cheeks and forehead. She struggled for air. Her bemused face turned toward me. Her eyes fixed on mine.

I sprang up to greet her as she stood, tugging lightheartedly on her pajama bottoms. She fell back against the bed. A torrent of feathers spiraled around her.

"What?" she stammered. "Shamus?" she asked in disbelief, grabbing at the torn comforter. More feathers oozed from the gnarled corner.

"This is no! No, Shamus!" she scolded, pointing to the tear. I knew from the edge in her voice that she wasn't happy. Anger flickered in her bewildered eyes. She rested her hand against her forehead; her face shook from side to side.

Gwen wore the same expression Gail wore the day she caught me wrestling with toilet paper and toothpaste. It was an end piece of toilet tissue that caught my attention. It fluttered lightly in front of me. Trapped behind the cabinet's door. I crouched low and sprang upon it. It smugly watched the clumsy paws that scratched uselessly at the wooden frame. My ears grew hot along with my temper as it evaded my clutches. It was a quick, powerful jerk of my head that ended the ridicule. My muzzle caught an edge and the door pitched forward. The insolent roll of paper plunged to the floor, and I snorted jubilantly at the once-hidden bounty stacked before me. I dove in.

Roll after roll tumbled to the floor. Some fled behind the toilet while others sought safety behind the wastebasket. I seized each one between my jaws. Forcefully shaking them back and forth. I tore each roll apart, layer by layer. Bits of the mangled tissue stuck to my tongue.

Take that, I thought triumphantly, tossing crumpled paper high above my head, scampering through the fallen shreds that lay lifeless on the floor. I bathed in victory. Rested on the spoils of war until a familiar scent caught my attention.

It was the faintest of smells but one I knew. I pushed frayed tissue aside and followed my nose to a hard, tiny drop that lay just on the inside of the cabinet's door. I dabbed at the drop with my tongue. Tingling cool mint. Over and over again my tongue scraped against the hardened blob. I gnawed and pawed at the wood to release the dried paste embedded deep within the grain. Another lick, another gnaw. The cabinet door became my chew toy.

"Shamus!" Gail hollered. She'd come home early. I didn't hear the front door close or her footsteps on the stairs. "What on earth are you doing?" It was the same harsh tone she used when I chewed her new straw hat and knocked over the garbage can for the fourth time. Still I leaped up to greet her. But ruined tissue clung to my paws, and I stumbled forward as I leaped. My head knocked up against Gail's chin. Her upper and lower jaws collided, and her head snapped back ferociously.

"Owww!" she yelled, cradling her chin in her hand.

"I'm sorry," I whimpered with tail between my legs.

Gail massaged her chin between her fingers and slowly knelt down next to me. The softness returned to her eyes, and I battered her creased face with my tongue. On hands and knees, she scooped up the chewed wood and paper. She rubbed her hand up and down the sides of the gnarled cabinet door. She stood and shrugged her shoulders. A long sigh followed.

Remorse settled in my gut. I lowered my eyes and approached Gwen meekly. Careful not to catch her gaze.

Raj grunted and threw the covers over his head. Another wave of feathers shot up into the air. Gwen inhaled and blew the breath from her lungs while more feathers slipped to the floor. She turned on her heels and walked out of the room. A thud echoed from the TV room.

Now you've done it, I told myself cowering on the floor. I sank low into the rug, listening to nails scraping wood. This time the clicking didn't stop at the stairs. It grew louder until Lela stood over me, surveying the damage. She looked down her muzzle accusingly, but she didn't growl. She didn't have to. Her eyes said everything. I inched forward slightly, nervously catching her muzzle with my tongue. She responded with a disapproving shake of her head before leaving to find Gwen.

I followed at a safe distance and listened from the dining room. I peeked around the corner to see Lela brushing up against Gwen's legs. Gwen smiled. "Good morning, Miss Lela." She knelt down, taking Lela's muzzle between her hands. She planted the lightest of kisses on Lela's nose. Lela affectionately returned the gesture with a light flip of her tongue. A butterfly kiss. So soft and delicate. Unlike my rough, slobbery messes.

I yearned for such tenderness. The aching drew forth a whine.

Gwen spotted me spying on them. I thought, *I should just leave*. But the corners of her eyes lifted, and a broad smile followed. "Good morning, Mr. Shamus." The edge in her voice was gone. "It's OK." She reached for me. Her outstretched arms beckoned me. I slowly stepped forward.

"Don't be a nuisance," Lela warned. "You've done quite enough already." She blocked my advance.

"It's all right, Lela." Gwen's voice was soothing. Her hand smoothed Lela's fur. "Come, Shamus."

Lela looked up at Gwen and then back at me. She stepped to the side and allowed me to pass. I moved forward. Cautiously.

Gwen's playful fingers tousled my ears and scratched under my chin. She kissed my brow, and I accepted her embrace.

Overjoyed! I lapped at Gwen's face and fell into her chest. She laughed, stumbling backwards.

The coffee machine gurgled and giggled. Fits of steam burst into the air, and the strong smell of coffee wafted around us.

Lela rolled her eyes and strolled slowly from the room.

I sensed that perhaps, just maybe, a truce might be forged.

~Five~

It was a sunny, warm Saturday. My first Saturday on the lane.

Haley had a soccer game early that morning. Raj was her team's coach. They called themselves the "Gummy Bears." We left for the game shortly after Gwen cleaned up the feathers.

I'd never been to a soccer game, and I waited with Big Red. A shroud of young maple leaves protected us from the midmorning sun. A breeze whipped through the opened windows, carrying with it the laughter of little girls and the aroma of coffee and donuts. Glazed and chocolate-covered donuts. My favorites.

I braced myself against the dashboard and pressed my nose into the windshield. Nose juice trickled down the cool glass. My eyes followed Haley as she skipped up and down the field. Both teams huddled tightly around the soccer ball. A lonely girl stood in each goal. One played with her braid. The other scraped her cleat against the grass until a cloud of dust curled around her ankles. Giggling. Non-stop giggling as the gaggle moved around the field.

Logan followed his sister from the sidelines. He was eager to play. "Next year," Raj told him. "You'll get to play next year." A disappointed Logan shoved a powered donut into his mouth. Gwen brushed at the crumbs that covered his T-shirt, but he dashed from her grasp before she finished. *I'll clean the rest*, I thought happily licking my chops.

Haley paused to pick a dandelion while a teammate looked on. Raj cupped his hands around his mouth. "Go for the ball," he yelled. "Go after the ball, Haley." She tightly clutched the flower and charged ahead.

I howled playfully when her team scored. I cheered with Gwen and Raj and the other Gummy Bear parents. Logan too jumped up and down with excitement. Goals were far and few between.

"Is the game over?" Lela asked. Her head popped up from behind the rear seat. Only her eyes and the bridge of her muzzle were visible. I'd almost forgotten that she was back there.

"No, but the Gummy Bears just scored!" I exclaimed.

The corners of her eyes lifted when she grinned.

"Do you like soccer?" I boldly asked. I'd spent the morning treading softly around her. But her warm gesture was encouraging. She was tolerating my presence.

"I like playing," she yawned. "But we're not allowed on the fields during game time." Her joints creaked mildly when she stretched out her legs. "Darren started playing when he was five." The name fell affectionately from her lips.

Who's Darren? I wondered.

Lela rested her front paws on the backseat and looked beyond the dashboard. Her eyes scanned the field in front of us. She beamed proudly at Haley. "I've watched a lot of soccer over the years," she said. "A lot of soccer." She reminisced without taking her eyes off the game. She talked about Darren.

Darren was Haley and Logan's half-brother. He too played soccer when he was younger. Lela watched his games every weekend and practiced with him afterwards. She liked playing defense. Loved chasing him down the field and batting the ball away with her paws or muzzle. He lived with his mother and stepfather in a town not too far away.

"He's a great kid. You'll meet him one day." Her smile wilted. "We don't see him much anymore. He's a teenager now." Sadness seeped into her eyes and her voice faded. "Hasn't played soccer in years."

Applause sounded outside, interrupting her memories. The opposing team had scored. Lela grew quiet, and we watched the game in silence as the Gummy Bears rallied.

She's warming up to me, I thought confidently.

The Gummy Bears scored again.

A deafening cheer erupted.

The light returned to Lela's eyes.

The Gummy Bears jumped around enthusiastically.

Lela grinned at the spectacle.

The whistle sounded.

Game over.

The Gummy Bears won!

~Six~

I was tired when we headed in for the night. Fatigued to the bone. I should have napped during the Gummy Bear game. I wasn't used to being up and out all day, and I hadn't slept well the night before. It wasn't until after dinner that I had a chance to rest.

Cuddle time in the TV room. That's what Gwen called it. Family cuddle time after the kids were bathed. They cuddled on the big sofa, eating popcorn while watching a movie. Lela claimed the smaller floral sofa, and I was grateful to rest near Gwen's feet.

It wasn't long after the movie started that Lela's snoring began. Gwen turned the volume up slightly to drown out the rumbling.

I struggled to keep my eyes open. The popcorn smell began to fade. The movie and Lela's snores grew distant. I imagined what Gail might be doing. What she might have done during the day. Just as I started to drift off to sleep, a faint pitter-patter moved across the kitchen floor.

Am I dreaming? I wondered, looking around.

I sniffed the air and picked up her scent. A robust, dirt-like scent. I hauled myself up to investigate.

I headed quickly toward the dining room but stopped abruptly when I spotted the small tiger cat slinking toward the stairs. I tripped over my own paws as they slid out in front of me. My hind end hit the floor with a thud. The noise startled the little cat, and she dropped to a low, crouching position.

Her eyes were large and wild. They darted

nervously around the room before resting on me. Inquisitive eyes. Piercing. Distrustful. I didn't dare move. The cats on the farm had been vicious. They'd attack anything that wandered within three feet of them. I was about five feet from her.

She studied me and slowly transferred her weight to her back paws. Her tail twitched behind her. Just an itty-bitty thing she was. But I was sure she could pack a pounce, and it certainly looked as if she was ready to spring. I'd been on the receiving end before, and it was not an experience I wished to encounter again. A cat's claws stung. They could easily rip through fur and flesh.

I shifted my weight and used my front paws to push myself away from her. My butt slid easily, quietly across the wood floor.

I bumped up against Lela, and my breath stuck to the inside of my lungs. I hadn't heard her approach. I leaped to my paws, and the little cat fled up the stairs. Lela knew I wanted to follow.

"Leave her alone," Lela said protectively. The little cat paused to look back at us. Her eyes met Lela's, and she lifted her chin slightly before disappearing somewhere upstairs.

Interesting, I thought. *A dog protecting a cat.*

"Who is she?" I asked.

"That's Emi. She's very timid and scares easily."

"Why?" *I'm nothing to fear*, I thought.

Lela patiently explained that Gwen and Raj found Emi at an animal shelter. She'd been abandoned by her humans. She spent more than a year in the wild, scavenging for food and fighting off all sorts of predators. Then a kind human rescued her and brought her to the shelter. They gave her food and a warm, safe place to sleep. But so many animals needed homes. The shelter was noisy and crowded. Emi spent most of her time there in a cage. She wasn't allowed outside. Little by little, she began to lose herself as she distanced herself from the suffering around her.

I felt sad for the little cat. My heart ached for her. I couldn't imagine being caged or left to fend for myself. I was lucky not to have ended up in a shelter. *It could happen to any of us*, I speculated.

"Did you live in a shelter?" I asked.

"No, I was adopted from a breeder near Grammy's when I was a pup. I was only three months old when they came for me." Her eyes sparkled. "I'll never forget that day." She stared far beyond the dining room walls. "Years before Haley and Logan were born. But Darren was with them. He held me tight against his chest." Her eyes closed, and she inhaled deeply, savoring the memory. "He was only four."

Lela said that Grammy was Gwen's mother. I could tell from her voice that she was very fond of her.

"Why isn't Emi afraid of you?" I wanted to know.

"I've known Emi for many years. Almost six. Mom and Dad adopted her while Mom was still in law school. We lived in an apartment then. It was small, and we didn't have a yard. Emi stayed indoors and wasn't allowed out. She'd spend hours sitting in the window watching the birds flitter past. She missed the outdoors but was grateful to have a loving home. We had plenty of time to get to know each other."

Lela turned to face me. She looked deep into my eyes. "She's a good cat. Don't bother her."

I resisted the urge to look for Emi. Although I wanted to learn more about her, I didn't want to get sliced by her hidden daggers. I had looked into her eyes. Something wild stirred behind them. Maybe fear. Maybe distrust. I thought it best to heed Lela's advice.

It turned out that Emi didn't like me much. My sudden, awkward gestures made her nervous. She kept her distance and came indoors less and less. She didn't start coming in on a regular basis until after Lela died. That she did for the kids. Mostly for Haley.

~Seven~

It felt much longer than a two-day weekend. But neither Gwen nor Raj were ready for it to end. Monday would start another workweek.

It hadn't occurred to me that they both would head to work the next morning. I wondered who'd watch us. I was nervous about being alone with Lela despite the seeming armistice. Our relationship was still fragile. I had yet to find my place.

I worried about these things while Gwen and Raj cleared the dinner table. I turned to the kids for a distraction, but they were absorbed with their trains in the dining room. They'd built an elaborate track that weaved in and around the table and chairs. They were always building things. They used tracks, blocks, boxes, bags. Just about anything really.

I watched the trains loop around the wooden rails. Some moved automatically. The others Haley and Logan pushed along, crawling on all fours, trying not to let the chugging engines catch them. I joined in, pursuing a locomotive between chair legs. But the chair pitched forward, taking out a bridge and adjoining tracks.

The trains toppled from the dismembered rails. I grabbed an engine and playfully flung it into the air. "Shamus!" Logan yelled, stomping toward the fallen pieces. The train crashed to the ground in front of me. "No, Shamus," he grumbled angrily. His stubby fingers collected the fallen pieces. "No!" he exclaimed, wagging his pointer finger at me. "No!" He turned to reassemble the track.

I sulked in the TV room. Sniffed around for something to do. It didn't take long to find Raj's sneakers. They were wedged under the coffee table. His strong, zesty smell permeated the inside soles. The leather was supple, the tongue worn but chewy.

"I'd stay away from shoes." Lela's voice turned me to stone. She had a way of sneaking up on me. "I once chewed through Dad's work shoes," she chuckled. "He wasn't too upset because they were old. But, boy, was he mad when I got hold of his new pair."

I dropped the sneaker that had been dangling from my mouth. The soft thud echoed through the quiet room.

"Stay away from furniture too. They were mad when I chewed the chair leg. I was only a few months old and teething." Her voice grew firm, its lightheartedness gone. "I didn't know any better. You're older. Stick to your chew toys," she warned before leaving me.

I had a difficult time imagining Lela as a pup. I couldn't picture her getting into trouble. She knew exactly what was expected of her and what she expected of others. *Who was her teacher?* I wondered, shying away from the shoe. I nudged it back under the table and hoped Raj wouldn't notice the teeth marks or drool.

I snooped around the room and saw a familiar chew toy bunched up in the corner. I lumbered over and poked it with my nose. It still smelled like Gail's house. Pieces of her gray hair still stuck to it. I dragged the toy to the area rug to have a better look. An interesting tag stuck out from its side. One I hadn't noticed before. I grabbed it with my teeth and pulled. I pulled, tugged, and chewed until a piece of the toy gave way. The wet, ripped fabric fell from my jaws, landing delicately on the rug's corner.

I tasted the fabric and inadvertently nipped the rug. The rug was plush and something sweet was buried within its fibers. I gnawed at the fibers, row by row. A bite-sized corner of the rug disappeared. It was the first rug I had ever chewed but not my last. I liked the feel of a good, thick rug. The dense fibers satisfied my chewing urges much more than any chew toy. I couldn't resist the wool's feel.

Thank goodness Lela's barking interrupted my ruinous behavior. I don't know how much of the rug I would have devoured. She was barking at a car climbing the windy driveway. I ran to the kitchen and positioned myself next to her in front of the window. Our paws rested, side by side, on the sill. She didn't seem to mind. Either that or she just didn't notice.

A young woman emerged from the car with a bag in hand. She leaned over and kissed the car's driver before waving him off. Lela stopped barking. Her tail wagged modestly. She knew the girl, but I sensed Lela wasn't particularly fond of her.

Gwen tightly held my collar. I gagged from the strain against my throat.

"Hey, guys, Ana's home," Raj hollered. The kids raced into the kitchen screaming. Ana caught them in her arms and planted kisses on their cheeks.

"Hello, Miss Lela," Ana said with an unusual

accent. "And you must be Shamus." She grabbed my face with both hands and rubbed her cheek against my ear. Her skin was soft. Her long, wavy locks flowed down past her waist and smelled of honey. A mellow floral fragrance rested behind her ear. Her face and lips were round. She was shorter and fuller than Gwen. Not much shorter though. And the jewel stud in her nose sparkled like her dark, penetrating eyes.

That was the first time I'd met Ana. She was an au pair from Germany. It was her job to watch after us.

~Eight~

I grew to dislike Mondays just as much as Gwen and Raj. They were at work all day, and the kids had school. The house was quiet. Too quiet after a busy weekend.

Weekday mornings were always the same. Gwen silenced the alarm's high-pitched beeping, and I'd paw, lick, nip, and jump to make sure she was awake. Gwen and Raj had their morning cappuccino. Then they'd shower, dress, and pack their workbags while the kids slept. After Lela and I relieved ourselves and ate our breakfast, Gwen would wake the kids and make them breakfast. She'd lay out their clothes and pack their bags. Raj would always rush by, claiming he'd be late again and miss his train. Sometimes he'd miss the train or just give up and decide to catch the next one. Always in a hurry. But there was something comforting about their routine.

I loved the mornings. They were hectic, but we were all together. And that first Monday . . . well, that was the day I met the neighbors.

Gwen grabbed her hoodie, and I bolted into a sitting position. My leash caught my collar and I twisted playfully around to grab it. I loved gnawing leashes and had chewed through two Gail had bought.

"No no, Shamus," Gwen scolded. She tightened up on the leash, and I couldn't reach the supple leather despite my will and efforts. She stuffed her pocket full of treats, and we practiced the "sit," "stay," and "come" commands. She knew I'd stay close to those treats.

Liver treats.

"Ready?" Gwen finally asked. Lela let out a playful howl and stood patiently near the opened door. I beamed up at Gwen. My tail wagged furiously, and I charged ahead. Gwen strained to hold me when I yanked her across the threshold. I pulled her down the stairs and out into the cool morning air.

"Easy," Lela growled.

The sun hadn't been up long, and the dew stuck to the sweet new grass. I listened to the birds humming softly overhead. As we turned the first steep bend, Lela trotted ahead to a neighbor's back porch. Her paws left a telltale path in the dew. She sat at the back door, waiting patiently before calling out, "Ronan." I heard a stirring inside, but no one came to the door.

I wanted to join her, but Gwen tightened her grip on my leash as we passed. "Not yet, Shamus," she said, handing me a treat. Lela waited a few moments more before running to catch up to us. I made a mental note to ask her about Ronan when Gwen wasn't listening.

We walked in silence, the three of us. Enjoying the peace and quiet that hung in the air. Gwen loosened her grip so I could sniff the wet grass. I noticed the pond in the distance. The water was calm, and I longed to dip my paws into it. But a soft tug on my leash and another treat kept me moving forward.

We left the asphalt and stepped onto a dirt path. The path was moist under-paw, and my nostrils filled instantly with the pungent smell of skunk cabbage. A bullfrog sounded in the distance, and I could smell the deer that had recently walked the trail. Chipmunks scurried around, and the squirrels jumped from tree limb to tree limb. My muscles rippled.

Gwen sensed my restlessness and handed me another treat. "Should we try this?" she asked, kneeling in front of me.

Lela had already scampered ahead, unencumbered by a leash. I wanted to be free. I hadn't been free outdoors since the farm.

"Yes!" I pleaded.

Gwen dropped my leash and held up her hand. "Stay," she commanded while drawing back a few paces. She commanded me to "come," and I obliged despite my twitching muscles.

"Good boy, come," she praised, and my tongue snatched the reward.

"All right then." Despite the apprehension in her voice, Gwen leaned over and unleashed me. The leash hit the ground and I took off running. Dirt flew up from under my paws as I raced around her. She raised her arms to protect her eyes from the onslaught of earth, decaying leaves, and twigs.

The woodland air filled my lungs and fed my body. The dew that clung to low-lying limbs and ferns and shrubs bathed my fur. Clumps of wild grass tickled my underbelly. My legs felt weightless as they carried me high over fallen trees and boulders. Gwen called these woods the "sanctuary" and, indeed, they became my retreat.

"Good boy!" Gwen called out when I paused to catch my breath. She lured me toward her with those moist treats. Lela shot me a warning glance. I was careful to stay relatively close to them as we made our way through the woods.

My legs were weary and my muscles fatigued when it was time to head home. My body felt nourished, satisfied, when we exited the woods. My pulse slowed, and the breeze caressed my face. It carried to my ears the sound of canine voices.

Two dogs and three humans lingered close to a mailbox. Lela recognized them and jogged ahead. I pulled at my leash urging Gwen to walk faster. "Good morning," Gwen called out. Her friendly voice faded on the gentle wind.

Lela was the top dog among the canine trio. That was easy to tell by the way they interacted. Lela and the other dogs circled playfully around each other. The humans circled around as well, trying to unscramble leashes while holding their coffee mugs tight. Gwen urged me to slow down as we approached the group. All eyes were on me.

"Good morning," Gwen said to the group again. She reached down to pat a golden retriever mix. "Good morning, Miss Bridgette."

"Who's this?" a human holding an Irish terrier asked. Gwen scratched the dog under his chin. "Good boy, Ronan," she said.

So that's Ronan, I thought to myself.

"This is Shamus," Gwen answered, and the humans began talking among themselves. I learned that Owen and Nadine were Ronan's humans, and that David was Bridgette's. I didn't pay attention to them after that. I was more interested in their canine companions.

Lela began those introductions. She stepped slightly to the side so I could approach. Bridgette and Ronan were older dogs. Not as old as Lela but clearly they had several years on me. I approached them in a submissive position, crouching slightly, keeping my tail low, and wagging while I licked their muzzles.

Ronan spoke first. "So you're Shamus." I nodded humbly as he looked me over, circling around me. "Lela's told us about you." He finished his inspection and stood before me. I couldn't help admiring his appearance for he was a handsome breed. He was lean and muscular. His wiry coat was groomed perfectly, and his beard was neatly shaved. His ears stood erect. Just the very tips were precisely folded over. His stump of a tail was trimmed evenly. It stood tall, beating back and forth. "Welcome to the lane," he finally said.

Bridgette moved to his side. "Welcome," she chimed in. Her snout and ears were pointier than Ronan's, and her hair was long and light. Her coat was thick. Thick and shiny. She too was well combed and kept.

What do they think of me? I wondered, glancing at the matted fur that wrapped around my legs and midsection. I was covered in dirt and mud.

They turned toward Lela and nodded. Formalities ended. It was time to play.

Lela lunged toward Ronan and thwacked his shoulder with her paw. He returned the frisky gesture while Bridgette circled around them cheering. I dropped to my elbows, butt in the air, eagerly waiting for an invitation to play. My tail wagged high and fast.

It was Ronan who approached me first. He bowed before nudging me. I couldn't help smiling. I barked and bounced around playfully.

Ronan howled.

I dared to swat him back. He thrust his muzzle up under my chin. I reared and caught his neck between my paws. He tussled me to the ground, and I submissively yielded.

That was the beginning of our relationship. A cherished friendship that grew over the years.

~Nine~

Gwen was mad. Hot in the face, word-stammering, finger-shaking mad.

"I can't believe he did that to our new quilt. Lela has never acted out like that. He also peed again in front of the den. I get that. He marks his territory. The den is where he eats. But to pee all over the new quilt? Just because he's mad?" Gwen massaged her temples with her fingers. "I think we should have him neutered."

Raj cringed at the words, and I knew I was in trouble.

Lela and I had been banned from the dinner party. Punished before committing any offense. Banished to the bedroom. "How can they do this? This isn't fair," I barked.

"It's only for a couple of hours. Just relax." Lela stretched out across the rug.

I didn't want to relax. I didn't want to miss my first dinner party. The chattering voices. The tantalizing smells.

With the help of a footstool, it was an easy leap over the gate.

"Aren't you coming?" I called to Lela. She looked up from where she lay. "You'll be back," she said bluntly.

I lifted my chin and trotted defiantly into the dining room. I held my head high until Gwen's fingers clutched tightly around my collar.

"Oh no you don't," she scolded. Her grip was firm and she pulled me back to her room. She stowed the stool in her closet and placed a second gate on top of the first. "That should keep you," she said before turning her back to me.

But the top gate was unsteady, and with one swift push from my paws, it clattered to the ground. The noise brought Gwen running before I made it down the hall.

"You stay," she said firmly, blocking the doorway with her nightstand. She stacked the two gates behind it.

I grinned. *An easy escape*, I thought. *I can use the nightstand as a launching pad.*

My body twitched, and Gwen knew I was up to something. Her eyes darted from me to the blockade and back to me. She followed my gaze. "Oh no you don't," she said, waving her finger and head. She quickly moved the table behind the stacked gates. My hopes for escape foiled.

"Now stay!" Gwen called out as she walked away.

I grunted and hopped onto her bed. I laid there sulking. Hurt and humiliated, avoiding Lela's sanctimonious gaze. *Why couldn't I join the fun?*

My hurt turned quickly to anger. "She'll think twice about gating me in here again," I grumbled. I raised my back leg slightly.

"I wouldn't do that," Lela advised.

Her know-it-all tone infuriated me more.

I lifted my leg higher than I'd ever lifted it before, and I let my anger rain down on Gwen's new quilt. I deposited my anger on a velvet patch, then a silk patch, and then a patch with shimmering sequins. When it seemed that my bladder was dry, I squeezed out a few last drops. "That'll teach her."

The smell of urine filled the room, and Lela shook her head in disgust. The acidic stench infiltrated my nostrils while I gazed upon the mess I'd made. The once beautiful quilt was stained and stinky. I lowered my head, ashamed by my rash behavior. Regret gnawed at my guts.

Two weeks later, I was taken to the vet.

"Is he sick?" Haley and Logan asked.

"No. He isn't sick. He's going to have a little operation. Nothing serious," Gwen explained before we left.

"Good morning, Mr. Shamus." Kristen looked down at me from behind the reception desk. Her small, rectangular glasses magnified her cheerful eyes. Her fingers danced across the keyboard. The clicking sounds echoed through the quiet lobby. It was Lauren who came to get me. I wasn't scared. I'd been there before, just a few weeks prior for a checkup.

"Be a good boy, Shamus." Gwen hugged me and kissed my forehead. She didn't follow when Lauren led me away. I began feeling anxious. *Why isn't she coming?* I wondered, looking at Gwen's back as she walked away.

My muscles tightened and my stomach rumbled. Lauren choked up on my leash. "It's OK, Shamus." She gently tugged.

It wasn't OK. I didn't feel OK. "Will someone please explain what's going on?" I whimpered while my paws slid through exam room one and into a room I'd never visited before.

It was a cool room and my body began to tremble. A kitten slept in a cage, and a little dog lay in a small crate with a tube extending from his front leg to what looked like a bag of water. He wasn't asleep, but he wasn't awake either. His eyes stared at nothing in particular. His expression was blank. He was young but not well. I pitied him there alone without his family.

I was placed in a large crate and fed some pills. Lauren tried hiding them in a chewy treat, but I knew they were in there. They were crunchy and bitter.

"I'll be back shortly to get you. The doctor will be here soon." Lauren closed the door, and the latch snapped into place.

I was alone and my mind began to wander. Insecurity crept in. It crawled across the floor and climbed into my crate. *Would Gwen come back for me?*

I'd been a handful. Eating rugs. Chewing sandals. Wandering off. Marking my territory. Ruining comforters and quilts. *But surely she'd come back for me?* I questioned.

My heart filled with doubt, and my head grew heavy. Very heavy.

That's the last thing I remembered. My last thought with my balls still intact. *Would she come back for me?*

"How are you feeling, Shamus?" the doctor asked. I slowly lifted my cloudy head to meet him eye to eye. My throat was parched. I wanted to rise and run, but my wobbly legs wouldn't hold me. A sharp pain near my belly reminded me that I'd been neutered.

"Easy, Shamus. Lie still for a while longer. You're doing fine," Dr. Kagan said. He checked my eyes, mouth, heart, and lungs. He lifted my leg and peeked at my belly. "You're doing fine," he repeated.

I drifted in and out of sleep. It was hard to tell how much time had passed. My dreams were unsettling. Pictures of the farm, my mother, and Gail. Then Emi and I sat waiting in a cage. The cage was much too small for the two of us. Animals around us wailed. "Will they come back for us?" I had asked Emi. She looked sadly at me, shaking her head.

I was glad to wake up.

I grew more alert and hungry. I shook off the drug-induced dreams as best I could and eagerly ate the food Lauren offered. Cool water quenched my thirst. My legs were shaky but my senses cleared. The sun's glow told me it was late afternoon. *Would she abandon me as my mother and Gail had?* I fretted.

The kitten was gone, but the little sick dog remained. The same question swirled in my head, again and again, while I lay in the crate waiting. *Will she come?*

It was getting late. The sun dropped lower in the sky, and my spirits sank with it. Shadows moved eerily across the walls. Despair wrapped its arms around my chest. The pain was physical and intense. More intense than the pain between my legs.

Then I heard the far-off voices. Voices I thought I recognized. I jumped to my paws and listened intently. I ignored the jabs of pain. *Had I been dreaming?*

Familiar voices grew louder.

My gleeful howls ripped through the silence.

Mom, Haley, and Logan had come for me. Despite my flaws, they were waiting to take me home.

That was the day Gwen became Mom and Raj became Dad. They were more than my caretakers. Mom and Dad, Haley and Logan. They were my family.

~Ten~

Mom placed me gently into Big Red. The sluggishness had returned, and my groin ached. She stroked the top of my head and looked tenderly at me. "Feeling OK, Shamus?" Her voice was calm and soothing. I wagged my tail and licked her hands. She smiled and closed the door.

"What's neutering?" Haley asked. I heard the familiar click of her seat belt.

"The doctor took out Shamus's bullets so he can't make babies. To make a baby, a boy's bullet has to shoot a girl's egg. The egg cracks and a baby's made. Shamus no longer has any bullets." Mom tugged the seat belt twice and closed the door.

"Do I have bullets?" Logan asked. Mom grunted faintly as she hoisted him into the truck.

"Yes. Yes, you do," she chuckled.

"Where?" he wanted to know.

"They're inside your body. When you're older, your body will make them in those two sacs that you have by your penis. You shoot the bullets out your penis," Mom explained. Another click and another door closed.

"My balls?"

"They're called testicles. Don't call them balls, Logan. That sounds rude." Big Red shifted slightly when Mom took her place behind the wheel. A third click and closing door. The engine hummed. I felt the wheels and road moving beneath us.

"Daddy calls them balls," Logan giggled, "and

nuts."

"Yeah, well I'll talk to Daddy about that." Mom tried to sound serious, but her voice cracked as she suppressed a snicker.

I laughed lightly to myself as I lay there. Careful not to anger my throbbing groin. I recalled the pep talk Dad gave me earlier that morning. I would still be "a man" despite not having "balls." I didn't understand the association between my masculinity and my balls. *Why did it matter?* I wondered.

"So Shamus and Lela can't make babies?" Haley asked.

"That's right. Lela doesn't have any eggs. The doctor removed them when she was a puppy."

"Lela will never be a mommy?" Haley's words trembled. "Why would you do that?" she asked in a bewildered tone.

"Do you remember when we went to the animal shelter to look at the cats and dogs? When we brought in those old blankets and sheets?" Neither child answered. "Well," Mom continued, "those animals need homes. We decided to have Lela's eggs removed because too many puppies need homes. We didn't want to have puppies that we couldn't care for."

Haley and Logan stayed silent. I supposed they were processing the information. They'd heard a lot. *Maybe too much for their young ears?* I wondered.

Mom waited a few moments more before turning on the radio. She sang along to a tune I hadn't heard before. Her voice was light, upbeat. She was, I imagined, relieved that the conversation was over.

"You OK, Shamus?" Haley asked in a voice as sweet as a glazed donut. She twisted in her seat to see me.

"I'm fine," I woofed quietly, trying hard not to flinch when Big Red clipped a pothole.

My answer appeased her, and she turned back around.

The thought of not fathering pups didn't bother me. I'd never met my father. My mother never met my grandfather and so on. And based on what I'd recently learned, I didn't want to father a pup that could end up in a shelter.

The pain between my legs was a small price to pay for my own peace of mind.

~Eleven~

I was a bit unsteady when my paws touched the ground, but Mom was there to steady me. She knelt next to me while I regained my balance. The kids rushed ahead and opened the door. Lela stood there waiting. She knew I wasn't feeling well, and she stepped aside to let me pass.

Mom led me to the bedroom. The kids chattered endlessly behind us, but I didn't mind. I had missed them so very much.

My home. My family. My pillow. I smiled and dropped into the soft, inviting folds. The drowsiness returned and curled up next to me.

"Sleep, Shamus. The doctor says you should rest and stay quiet. Sleep now." Mom kissed my head. "Gentle," she reminded the kids when they knelt next to me. My tail thumped softly in response to their caresses, but I grew too tired to lift my head. My eyelids were heavy, too heavy to keep open. I heard the dog gate close, and Lela's clicking nails grew soft. The kids were talking. Their voices faded. Sounds grew distant.

It was dark outside when I awoke. I couldn't say for how long I'd been sleeping, but it was a good sleep. I awoke feeling hungry and somewhat refreshed.

Dinner's aroma hung in the air. I inhaled the smell of herbed chicken and sweet potatoes. My nostrils and taste buds tingled. My stomach growled furiously. I rose but a sharp pain pushed me down. I remembered then that my bullets were gone. I licked my wound to ease the ache. My stomach rumbled again.

"You OK, Shamus?" Lela whispered. Her concerned voice moved me. I lifted myself gently and eased slowly toward the gate that separated us.

"Your pain medicine must be wearing off." Lela's voice was full of sympathy. "You'll be back to yourself in a couple of days. For now you have to rest. And don't play with the sutures, those black pieces of string holding your skin together. If you pull them out, you'll have to go back," she warned. "Are you hungry?"

"Starving," I whined.

"That's a good sign." She let out a playful bark, and moments later Mom and the kids appeared.

"He's awake. He's awake," Haley and Logan cried out. They leaned over the gate to touch me. I covered their faces and hands with slobbering kisses.

"How about we bring Shamus his dinner?" Mom asked.

"Yes," I barked.

The distant sound of food filling an empty bowl made my stomach rumble. Drool fell to the floor like rain. I was eager to eat and ecstatic when Mom and the kids brought food and water. Lela let them pass without incident.

I devoured the kibble in seconds.

A burp hurled itself from my belly.

Fits of laughter filled the air.

"Where're my babies?" A voice called out. Dad's voice. He'd come home early from work. "In here," Mom yelled. His briefcase dropped with a thump, and his steps were heavy. He was wearing his work shoes. I knew from the sound. He greeted Lela then jumped over the gate.

"Daddy, Daddy. Shamus doesn't have any bullets. The doctor took out his bullets," Haley announced.

Dad's face scrunched up. He turned his baffled expression toward Mom. "I'll explain later," she said with a wave, grinning. "Let's just say we had a little lesson in baby making."

"And he has stitches on his belly." Logan pointed to my sutures as he spoke. I rolled slightly over to give Dad a better look.

"Does he now?" Dad knelt down and stroked my back. "Poor guy. Lost your bullets and your bal…"

Mom elbowed him. "Keep it up and you'll be next," she teased. He leaned over and pressed his lips against her forehead. The kids piled on his lap.

They sat there for quite some time the four of them. Watching over me.

I wished for a human voice. Human words to tell them how grateful I was. Grateful that they made me a part of their family.

Not a perfect family.

But my family.

I felt finally at home.

~Twelve~

June 26th. My first birthday. The kids said they were planning a surprise. Lela listened as they teased me. I'd never had a birthday.

We celebrated Dad's birthday two weeks earlier. Mom and the kids made a cake and decorated the dining room the night before. They ate the cake for breakfast.

"It's a family tradition," Lela said. "Birthday cake for breakfast. But we have to wait until after dinner for ours!"

Lela smiled as she spoke of her past birthdays. "At first I thought it was a silly ritual. But over the years, well . . . I look forward to my birthday. Each reminds me that I'm a fortunate dog." She turned ten earlier that spring, shortly before my arrival on the lane. She looked younger than her age, and she accepted my compliment with grace.

I too felt fortunate on my birthday. Mom and the kids crowded around the kitchen table later that afternoon. Each wielded a butter knife. Their eyes focused on a jar of peanut butter and a box of dog biscuits.

"Can we make our own for Shamus? I want to make my own," Haley insisted.

Anticipation rippled through every muscle as the smell of peanut butter and biscuits filled the room.

"Yeah, but not too big. OK? We don't want him to get sick." Mom knew my stomach was sensitive. It made me gassy.

"I'll make a small treat for Lela." Mom didn't

want to upset our budding camaraderie.

Two birthday treats. *I'm having two birthday treats*, I thought merrily. My tail beat loudly against the wall.

Lela patrolled the floor while I waited near the threshold. She too loved peanut butter, and her tongue scooped up any remnants that fell to the floor.

"Can I put sprinkles on mine? Rainbow sprinkles?" Logan asked.

"Yes," I whimpered and whined. "I want sprinkles. Lots of sprinkles."

Mom reached into the pantry and set a jar in front of him. He giggled as the sprinkles splashed over the tower he'd created. Some stuck to the peanut butter but most skipped across the floor.

"Shamus, look!" Logan held his creation only inches from my nose. A tower of biscuits and peanut butter. "And sprinkles, lots of sprinkles. Do you like it?"

I inhaled the tantalizing aroma and imagined the scrumptious taste. The thought made me dizzy and drool slid uncontrollably off my tongue. I would have snatched that cake then and there had Mom not grabbed hold of it first.

"Look, Shamus." Haley stood beside me with a plate in her hand. "I made you a birthday cake. See, it's in the shape of an 'S' for Shamus." I caught only a quick glimpse before she turned her back to me.

"Mom, he should have a candle. A pink candle," Haley demanded. "Pink is Molly's favorite color, Shamus. Wouldn't you like a pink one?" Molly had been Haley's best friend, her BFF, since preschool. Like

Haley, Molly was spirited and good-natured, and she loved to tickle my belly. The girls often had playdates during the week.

Mom rummaged through drawers looking for birthday candles. "I don't have a pink candle, sweetie. I have red, yellow, blue, and green."

Haley hollered out, "Yellow then," and Logan shouted, "Blue."

"Sorry, Shamus," Haley said. But it wasn't the candles' colors that wrinkled my brow as they jabbed them into my cakes. I am, after all, mostly color-blind. It was the candles themselves that concerned me. I wasn't sure I could blow them out the way Dad had once they were lit.

"Not to worry," Lela mumbled with peanut butter stuck to the roof of her mouth. "They'll help you," she managed to say. She looked comical scouring her palate with her tongue. Her head bobbed up and down with each scrape.

I doted on my cakes that rested on the counter next to Lela's. I smirked, noticing that mine were much larger. *I am the birthday boy!* I thought gleefully. Lela lifted her brow and looked scrutinizingly down her muzzle. I lowered my gaze. Surely she knew my thoughts. *How does she do that?*

"They'll be safe from Lela and Shamus over there," Mom said, wiping her hands against her pant legs. "Come on now. Let's get cleaned up. Daddy will be home soon."

As Lela had predicted, I had to wait. We both had to wait. The smell of peanut butter and dog biscuits drove me wild.

I circled around the kitchen island. My stomach grumbled, for the lick of my lips did little to appease my appetite. It'd been several hours since I'd last eaten. But kibble wouldn't quench my craving. Only birthday cake would mollify me. I wished I could be less obvious. Lela was much better at controlling her urges. She laid patiently on a pillow and waited while I paced and whined.

Dad came home soon after the kitchen was cleaned and the table set for dinner. Dinner lasted for what seemed like an eternity. Only after the table was cleared were the birthday cakes brought out. I whimpered as I waited. Mom stood to the side holding Lela, while my family sang me a birthday song. When it was over, Haley and Logan blew out my birthday candles and laid their creations at my paws. I was deliriously happy.

I dove in, nose first. Peanut butter and sprinkles lodged themselves in my nostrils. A good, stiff sneeze sent the gooey mass spraying across the floor. My tongue greedily found the flecks of biscuits that hid in my whiskers. A loud belch confirmed that I ate too much too fast.

My birthday. My first birthday. Filled with an abundance of peanut butter and dog biscuits.

Every birthday's special. Another milestone. A time for reflection. Sometimes the reflections are happy and hopeful. Sometimes they are bittersweet. That year, they were happy and hopeful.

Lela's fifteenth birthday. A few years later.

Bittersweet.

~Thirteen~

There are only a couple of things that stand out in mind about Ana. They aren't so much memories about her in particular, but more about what I learned of my new family because of her and about humans in general. If I had to choose a word that reminds me most about Ana, it would be deception. To deceive is to make believe that which isn't true. It's to mislead, trick, or fool. I didn't know then that Ana's deception started weeks before my arrival.

The truth began to emerge slowly. In subtle ways that only Lela detected. Like the first time I wandered off. I wasn't leashed or hooked to my zip line as I was supposed to be. Ana and the kids were playing on the trampoline when I picked up the scent of deer. It was a strong scent that I followed to the top of a trail leading from the house to the mailbox below. The kids called it the "secret trail," and I made my way carefully down the muddied path.

Two geese drifting in the pond grabbed my attention. I ran full sprint across the meadow. The grass was shin deep, and grasshoppers leaped out of my way. But before I reached the water's edge, the honking echoed through the woods beyond. I only caught a glimpse of tail feathers as they slid out of the water and lifted effortlessly into the sky.

Still the pond was inviting. Water bugs darted across its surface, and tiny tadpoles swam frantically around decomposing leaves. My front paws slipped in. I felt the spongy bottom beneath them, but I wasn't afraid. I glided easily through the cool water. My ripples raced ahead of me to the other side. I shook my sopping body until the last few unwilling drops begrudgingly flew from my tail.

Refreshed. I began sprinting, running round in circles, grinning from flapping ear to flapping ear. Zoomies. That's what Mom says when I start dashing around in frenzied circles. I kept running zoomies until my legs yielded to my winded lungs.

Haley and Logan's laughter drifted down the hillside. The trampoline chanted as the kids bounced up and down. Lela called for me, and a familiar engine purred in the distance. The sound grew louder and louder. I raced across the grassy field just as Mom's truck passed by.

"Wait. Wait for me," I barked. She couldn't hear me as I chased her around the bend. But our eyes met in Big Red's side mirror. Disbelief flashed across Mom's face and settled in her stare. I caught up to her at the lower parking level we called the "corral."

"Get down, Shamus!" Mom hollered. "You're all wet." She was annoyed, and Lela positioned herself between us so Mom could get out of the truck. The kids rushed over and embraced their mother lovingly. She stroked their heads and kissed their damp, sticky faces. Then she turned toward Ana.

"Ana, did you know Shamus was at the neighbors'?" I knew from her tone she was angry. "You can't just let him run around the lane unattended. He has to be leashed or on the zip line."

"I was playing with the kids," Ana retorted with

a dismissive look on her face. Her eyes challenged Mom. Yet despite the obvious tension between them, nothing more was said as we all walked to the house to get ready for dinner. Lela frowned, and Mom would not confront Ana in front of the kids.

Later that night Lela told me that Ana had convinced Mom and Dad that the time was right to adopt me. She told them she would help take care of me and train me. But she didn't do either. Ana's attitude began to change. She became more defiant.

Lela began to watch Ana closely during the weeks that followed. It was Lela who realized that Ana wasn't going to stay. Mom had been blind, like me. We believed the lies. Ana was so convincing.

Like the day of Haley's tea party. Molly and other girls from Haley's kindergarten class were coming over after school. Mom and Ana spent the morning setting up for the party. The floors had been vacuumed, the furniture dusted, and the dining room table had been set with sparkling dishes. A large rose-filled vase sat on the table, and goody bags were placed in front of each plate. The food smelled wonderful.

Mom told Ana the bus would be coming shortly. That's when Ana broke down in tears. She broke up with her boyfriend and turned to Mom for advice. Mom listened sympathetically, holding Ana while she wept. Mom handed her a napkin when she finished. "You have to be honest with him, Ana. Don't play games. Just be honest." Ana nodded and returned Mom's hug.

Yet Ana continued seeing her boyfriend on a regular basis. They spoke on the phone, and he came by to visit while the kids were in school. I thought nothing of it. Not until that Friday night.

It was the start of a long holiday weekend. The Fourth of July. The family cuddled on the sofa watching a movie. I drifted on and off, catching only glimpses of the animated race cars. There'd been no opportunity to nap that day. Ana spent her time frantically cleaning while the kids were at camp. Lela and I followed her as she rushed up and down the stairs with cleaning supplies, garbage bags, and boxes.

I rose to greet Ana and her friend, Klaire, when they walked into the room. Lela eyed the two girls warily. Klaire stood off to the side, her fingers kneaded nervously under my chin.

"I'm leaving now," Ana said when she entered the room. Anxiousness tainted the excitement in her voice. She was off to visit a friend. A childhood friend from Germany. A family friend who paid for her airfare. Ana needed to get away. She needed to clear her head and heart of her ex-boyfriend. She'd return Monday. That's what she told us all.

"Do you need anything? You have your phone and credit card in case of an emergency?" Mom asked. "She knows your flight number and will be there to pick you up?"

"Yes. Everything's all set. But could I have my pay now? I know you usually pay me on Monday, but I could use it for my trip. If that's OK," Ana added hesitantly. Lela's eyebrows shot up.

The tension in the room shifted slightly. A tiny bead of sweat rolled off Ana's temple, disappearing into the waves of hair that clung loosely to her cheek before plummeting down her chest. Klaire's palms turned moist, and the scent of her uneasiness emanated from her skin.

Mom and Dad exchanged wary glances before he reached for his wallet. He handed her the cash. "Do you need more?"

"No, I have enough. Thanks," Ana replied. She exchanged hugs with the kids. Lingering hugs.

"Just be safe and call us if you need anything. Don't forget to call when you land," Mom added, though she didn't rise up from under Dad's arm.

Ana's steps were slow and deliberate as she turned to go. Nervousness kept the feet that wanted to run anchored. I recognized the tension in her stride. Sheer will kept her moving steadily forward.

I watched the girls from the kitchen window. They said nothing to each other as they got in the car. Ana let out an audible sigh. Our eyes met when she reached to close the car door. Something in her gaze troubled me. It reminded me of Gail's gaze the last time I saw her.

My chest tightened as she drove away.

"Gwen, can you come up here?" Dad's voice raced down the stairs. I knew by its pitch that something was wrong. "I'm in Ana's room."

Lela and I followed Mom upstairs.

Mom's mouth dropped open when she saw Dad sitting on Ana's bed with a letter in his hand. The room was empty. Only Ana's cell phone and credit card lay on the dresser. "She's not coming back," he said, handing Mom the letter.

Mom held the paper tightly as she began to read. The color drained from her face.

"Why didn't she tell us she was moving and that her friend found her a job? It says here she needs to send money home to her family. I knew her dad was sick. But why wouldn't she tell us? I thought she trusted me." Mom continued reading. "She talked to me about her family, school, her friends, the problems with her boyfriend. We could've helped her find a job." She talked as she scanned the letter again and again for clues. "I don't get it. She said it wasn't anything we did. Was she afraid of being deported if the agency found out?"

Dad walked over to Ana's corkboard. Her family photos had been taken down. The only things left on the walls were pictures Haley and Logan had made for her. "What are we going to do come Tuesday?" he asked. "I can't believe she did this. Look. She didn't even take the pictures the kids made for her." He gently folded each one and placed them in his pocket. "What do we tell the kids?"

Mom looked up from the letter. "We'll tell them the truth. Ana was offered a good-paying job. She needed the money to send home to her dad. I'll call the au pair agency first thing tomorrow. Maybe you could e-mail some of our friends to see if they know of any sitters looking for work. Mary and Lara may know of someone. I'll call them after we get the kids to bed."

Mom looked suddenly exhausted sitting there.

"What did we expect? She came here and saw

what private nannies make. I'm sure she felt like we took advantage of her. I don't know what we could've done differently. I know I'm not always the easiest person to live with, but she knew our house rules before she accepted the position. We didn't hide anything from her." Mom shrugged her shoulders. "I don't know anymore. I really liked Ana and thought this was going to work." Doubt and frustration materialized in her eyes. She shook her head and handed Dad the letter.

"So Ana's now an au pair for someone else?" I asked Lela in a hushed tone.

"No, she's with her boyfriend." Lela kept her eyes on Mom. "I overheard Ana telling Klaire that she wanted to get married and get a better job." Lela sighed and shook her head. "She had no intentions of staying with our family, Shamus. She wanted to come to America. She told Mom and Dad what they wanted to hear so she could get here. Then, she waited. Mom and Dad paid for her driver's license and language classes. Ana saved up some money and found a mate."

It took a few moments for the truth to sink in. "She lied," I whispered. *How could she have betrayed them this way?* I thought. Ruthless and calculated. Her actions had been so carefully orchestrated. I'd been duped. We all had.

Lela sensed my dismay. "She cares only about herself, Shamus." She paused, studying me. "Yes, she lied. She couldn't risk being sent back to Germany. And I couldn't stop the chain of events." Lela was irritated. She had known but had no way of warning Mom and Dad.

"It's better this way. The truth would only hurt them more." Lela turned toward the stairs. "Let's go check on the kids."

~Fourteen~

I learned more about my family during the hours that followed Ana's departure than I had learned in the prior three months living with them. Before that night, I'd never asked about, and Lela wasn't one to divulge information regarding, family matters. But something had changed that night. Something inside Mom began to wane. It went beyond the obvious stress of having to find a new sitter. It was more than that. Deeper and more subtle. Intangible. I couldn't put my paws on it. But behind her eyes, I saw it fading.

"So now what?" I asked innocently.

Lela inhaled and exhaled deeply to gather her thoughts. She scratched behind her ear and her tags jingled, like a school bell summoning children. I scooted toward the edge of her pillow and waited. She eased herself more deeply into the bed before answering.

"Mom will find another sitter. Ana wasn't our first au pair. Before her there was Mira and then Ailene."

"What were they like?" I asked.

"Mira came to us from Italy," she began. "Although she liked our family, we all knew she was lonely and sad. She spent a lot of time on the computer corresponding with her family and friends back home. She didn't socialize much with other au pairs in the area. Kept mostly to herself. It wasn't until she met Erik that her disposition improved. He was a polite boy. Brought her flowers and took her to the movies and dinner. She started spending every day with him and then spending most nights at his house.

"Mom told Dad that things weren't working out as she had expected. She thought Mira would become part of the family. But there wasn't any connection, because Mira would arrive just before Mom left for work and she would leave for Erik's shortly after Mom got home. There was definitely some tension. Especially on the mornings when Mira would be late or the nights when Mom needed to reach her but couldn't because there was no cell phone reception at Erik's house, which was in a remote, rural area. But Mom and Dad hadn't set a curfew or restricted her use of the car. They felt that to set those restrictions after she had already arrived wasn't fair. And Mira was, after all, wonderful with the kids, and Mom knew Mira had found love." Lela paused for a moment.

"Mira was kind to me too. She cried the night Mom brought me home from the hospital."

My ears lifted. *Did I hear her right? She'd been in the hospital?* It would have been after her eggs were removed. Years after that.

"During the days that followed, Mira watched over me while Mom was at work. She made sure I was comfortable. I didn't want to be sick. I wanted to be strong for Mom because so many nights she'd cry after putting the kids to bed. She felt alone despite being busy all the time. And she was so tired." Lela's voice trailed off as she paused to remember.

"It was a stressful time. Haley and Logan were four and three. They needed constant supervision. Dad was traveling a lot for work, and Mom was working full-time for a law firm. She commuted in to the office three days and worked from home the other two. They were trying to sell our house, but the economy wasn't doing well after 9/11; and the United States went to war shortly after they signed the contract on this house." Lela's voice dropped again. She stopped speaking to shift her weight. I took the opportunity to inch closer to her.

"You were sick?" I asked.

"Cancer. The news devastated Mom. I was eight at the time. Neither of us was ready for me to die. So we fought the disease. The tumors were removed, and I began taking all sorts of medicines. I handled the chemo well, though occasionally I'd vomit and defecate in the house. I was mortified. But Mom and Mira didn't mind, and in time I got better. I tried telling Mom the cancer was gone, but she couldn't hear me. She's still scared and worries needlessly. Every bump or ailment calls for a trip to the vet."

"Doesn't that bother you?" I couldn't help asking. I was eager to hear more.

"No. She does it because she loves me. She needs to feel that she has some control over my well-being and my eventual passing. She doesn't expect me to live out a full life. She's scared. She's not ready to let me go," Lela added softly.

Lela had never feared death. Her concern had always been for our family. She was their protector. Their guardian. They needed her, especially Mom.

"Does she need me?" I asked, not wanting to

know the answer.

"She will. She's trying to figure out how to love you without hurting me."

I couldn't suppress my disappointment. Lela heard the sigh. "You being here doesn't hurt me, Shamus. Besides, I'm starting to like having you around. You're a lot of work, but you're a good dog. Give it time," she said sympathetically.

Lela felt my insecurity and knew I was hurting. Rather than using my pain against me, she told me not to worry. She knew I'd find my place.

As we laid there in the dark, surrounded by silence, the jealousy I harbored in my heart began to fade. The empty space began to fill with admiration, and I wanted to know more. I wanted to learn more about Lela, Mom, our family. I needed to understand their past if I wanted to be a part of their future. There was so much I didn't understand, so much for me to learn.

~Fifteen~

"What's a 9/11?" I asked ignorantly. I didn't understand its significance. But I had learned those first couple of months that Lela chose her words carefully. Nothing she said was without meaning or importance. A 9/11 was important. I could tell from the change in her voice it meant something to her and our family. But what?

She took a deep breath. "It's not a thing, Shamus. It's a particular day. A day I remember vividly." Her voice was somber. "Mom and Dad both stayed home that morning because it was Haley's first day of preschool. Haley was so excited. Her flowered backpack was bigger than her. The three of them had just left and Honey put on the news."

"Who's Honey?" I had heard the name before.

"Honey lived with us in White Plains for over three years before Mira came. Her real name is Sabeen, but the kids call her Honey. She lives in Queens now with her husband. You'll meet her. We see her when we go into the city, and sometimes she comes up to visit." Lela's voice filled with tenderness.

Another piece of the puzzle snapped into place. Honey was their first babysitter. She had been good to them, and they cared about her still.

"Now on that day, 9/11, Honey put the news on like she did every morning. Logan was upstairs taking his morning nap. He was only one." Lela breathed in and out slowly. "I sat next to Honey while she folded the laundry. Her sudden scream startled me. The shirt she'd been folding lay on the floor. Honey's hands covered her mouth. Her eyes grew wide, and fear filled her large black pupils. She slowly reached for the remote and turned up the TV's volume. I knew something bad had happened.

"We learned that two planes had crashed into the twin towers of the World Trade Center. Thousands of humans were trapped. The footage was raw and uncensored. We watched in horror as humans jumped from the towering infernos. Then the towers collapsed. I couldn't believe that mangled steel and piles of concrete were all that was left of those magnificent structures.

"Tears streamed down Honey's beautiful face.

"The TV showed thousands of humans running through the streets. Sirens blared and reporters screamed into microphones so they could be heard above the chaos. The sounds were deafening. Humans were covered in ash. Many were hurt from falling debris. We later learned that two more planes crashed elsewhere. They were all connected. The work of terrorists."

I shifted my weight to the side. I felt myself growing impatient. I still didn't understand what 9/11 had to do with our family. Lela must have sensed my irritation.

"It wasn't long after the first tower collapsed that Mom, Dad, and Haley came home. Schools and offices closed so that families could be together." Lela paused. "Mom, Dad, and Honey were scared. They were scared for those trapped, scared for family and friends who worked downtown, and scared of what the fall out would be. Cell phones were useless. They had to wait.

Their anxiety grew as each hour passed. There was nothing any of us could do."

Terrorists. It's a word I was familiar with. The news was filled with updates about the "war on terror" and public opinion about our country's involvement. I never paid attention. Not before that night.

"Mom needed to get out of the house and away from the news. So we took a family walk. It was eerie, Shamus. No airplanes flew overhead as they normally would. Not one. The air was stagnant, and the streets were quiet. Thankfully, Haley and Logan were much too young to understand.

"I sat next to Mom when she watched the late-night news. She snuggled close to me and whispered in my ear, 'Remember how simple life used to be?' I looked into her eyes and saw that she had aged. Her eyes told me she felt it too. She was no longer the young, carefree bride who took me, a four-month-old pup, to her wedding. She was a mother with two young kids who needed her. They now needed her more. She not only had to vanquish the monsters in the closets, but she now had to be alert for enemies whose attacks were unpredictable. 'How are we going to protect them?' she asked me. 'We will,' I barked reassuringly. My paw on her lap restored some of her confidence. Just like the monster-be-gone we sprayed in the kids' closets . . . we'd find a way. She understood my gesture. I knew she did by the way she stroked my paw."

The image of them huddled together on that horrific night moved me. They were connected by an invisible bond. A bond between souls that transcended their species. They would always be there for each other. They were companions. Best friends. An existence every dog aspires to.

"The days that followed were ominous. A sickening, metallic smell clung to the air. Our family grieved for the dead and for those that survived. They grieved for the innocence lost, wondering what kind of world Haley and Logan would grow up in.

"Never had such a devastating attack been made so close to home. The humans in our community carried their fear like heavy baggage. The foundation of their security cracked. It was hard for them to feel safe, and it was shameful to feel any happiness amidst the carnage. They were numb.

"Mom tried hiding her fears from the kids, but she worried about Dad's traveling and about public transportation in general. She was cautious about bringing mail into the house, because the news spouted on about anthrax scares and other possible means of attack. Mom counseled Honey on what to do should terrorists attack the nuclear power plant not more than an hour from our home. She was wary about our water supply and kept bottled water on hand in the event the reservoirs were targeted. She felt drained, but taking control over the things that she could restored some of her inner balance. But she changed after 9/11, Shamus. She's reluctant to travel, and she doesn't like to be separated from the kids. Deep down she's still afraid. I can feel it."

There was nothing I wanted to ask about that day. Nothing more I needed to know. I lay there trying to block out the images my mind conjured. My family had witnessed the war on terrorism's origin. They had to live with its repercussions, manage their fears.

Maybe that's what I had seen in Mom's eyes earlier that night. Her fragile sense of security was fading. The fear was creeping back in. On whom could she trust and depend?

Me, I wanted to tell her. But I wasn't yet ready. There was still so much for me to learn.

~Sixteen~

"How do you know all the things you know?" I asked Lela. She was smart and knew so much. I often felt small and insignificant in her presence. But she was willing to teach me.

"I watch and listen," she said, yawning. "We're born with two eyes and two ears but only one mouth for a reason." She smirked and the moonlight bounced off her incisors. I knew I had to work on my listening skills. "We should probably get some sleep. Morning comes early, and I need my beauty rest. I'm not a young pup anymore, Shamus," she said good-humoredly.

"But you didn't tell me about Ailene," I persisted. I couldn't sleep with the images of 9/11 still fresh in my mind, and I had heard Ana mention Ailene's name. Ana hadn't cared for Ailene. I didn't know why.

"I could go on all night about that one. Let's just say that she had a good heart. But when it came to common sense, she was . . . well . . . good sense was often lacking." Lela's tags jingled as she laughed.

"What do you mean?" I asked, leaning in closer. I could tell from Lela's tone and posture that there was much to be said about Ailene.

"She came to us from Ireland. She was older than Mira, an art history major, I think. She was chatty and friendly. Genuinely good-natured," Lela nodded. "Mom had thoroughly explained our house rules to her before she arrived, which then included a curfew on workdays and limited use of the car, and Ailene spoke in private to Mira and Honey. No secrets, no surprises.

Mom was hopeful that Ailene would become a family member.

"I suspected things might not go so smoothly. Ailene was loving, but she was headstrong and she certainly wasn't shy. She hadn't been with us for more than a week before asking Dad to replace her showerhead and insisting on a new mattress that wasn't quite so lumpy." Lela's tags jingled again. "She was a finicky eater and thought nothing of pulling Mom's good china from the hutch. Mom doesn't even use those dishes. She bought them in London and they're irreplaceable." Lela let out a light, airy sigh.

"Anyhow, a rift started when Ailene asked to take a couple of design classes. She didn't want to take classes that were offered locally while the kids were in school or when Mom was home. The classes she wanted to take were offered on weekdays in the city. She couldn't take them unless Mom changed her schedule and worked from home on those days. Mom wouldn't, and well, after that the relationship between them began to slowly crumble."

Ana had taken language classes before abandoning our family. They were on the weekends. Mom and Dad paid for the language classes so Ana could pass an English fluency exam. She had gotten her test results shortly before she deserted us. She'd done well.

"Ailene was certainly passionate. 'A fiery redhead,' Dad would jest. She wore her emotions openly, and the kids adored her. But Mom began questioning Ailene's judgment as the weeks passed.

Something gnawed at her. She paid for Ailene's defensive driving class and first aid course, hoping to get some peace of mind. Still she began losing confidence in Ailene as Haley and Logan's caretaker."

"Why?" I wanted to know.

"It started with little things. Like always leaving the lights, TV, and radio on when she left for the day or leaving the car windows down during rainstorms and snowfalls. Four times she left the car lights on, and Dad had to jump-start it the next morning. She even left a bucket of frogs the kids had caught on the front steps. Half of them baked to death in the sun. It was gross. She'd forgotten Mom's 'catch and release' rule." Lela stretched her legs and her joints creaked. "I could go on and on about the little things. But the little things turned into bigger things. Bad luck loomed over Ailene and that worried Mom."

"What bad luck? What do you mean?" I asked.

"Well, she ran into a mailbox for starters. She was driving the kids to school one day and turned around to yell at Logan. She wasn't paying attention, and she veered into the mailbox cracking the windshield. I say 'crack' because that's what she told Dad. She'd come back to the house and called Dad to ask if she should still drive the car. Dad said it was OK to take the kids to school if it was just a small crack. But it wasn't small and it wasn't just a crack. I saw that the mailbox scraped and dented the hood of the car before penetrating the windshield. Broken glass was everywhere. Luckily, no one was hurt. She was truly mortified and offered to pay for the damage."

I could only imagine how mad Mom must have been and how frightened the kids were.

"She lost her wallet one week and the car keys the next. She ran out of gas in Connecticut and left her cell phone at the library twice. She tripped the house alarm at least three different times and even managed to lock us in Haley's bedroom for a couple of hours. She stood on the roof outside Haley's window yelling for help. Luckily Ronan and Owen eventually heard her and let us out." Lela snickered. "Logan certainly liked peeing out the window."

The image of Logan peeing from the bedroom window stuck in my head. He's always peeing outside. Mom's told him that if he's gonna pee outdoors, to sprinkle it around the flowers to keep the deer and rodents away.

"Ohhh! And that first snowstorm." Lela shook her head. "It snowed heavily that night. Mom called Ailene and asked her to bring the car home because it wouldn't make it up the lane if she waited much longer. But Ailene sat at the local coffee bar with her friends. Sure enough, the car got stuck. It sat at the bottom of the lane all night creating a hazardous condition for any vehicle that dared venturing up or down the road. Now I don't think she deliberately defied Mom. She claimed to have simply lost track of time. But Ailene was always losing track of . . . well . . . things."

Lela let out another yawn. "So many stories." She paused to peruse through her mental directory, trying to determine which tales were worth telling. "She was accused of cheating on a college exam, and a classmate claimed she swiped his phone. Mind you, she didn't cheat or steal anything. She wasn't like that, and Mom helped her prove her innocence. But Ailene somehow managed to always end up in the wrong place at the wrong time. I felt sorry for her. So much drama!"

"Why did Mom let her stay if she was worried about the bad luck?"

Lela drew in her breath. "It was Dad really. He thought Mom was overreacting when she complained. So she tried overlooking the smaller things until safety became a real concern. That was the day Logan told Mom the car's tire was gonna blow up. Dad asked Ailene to get the car inspected and have its oil changed. Apparently the mechanic noticed a bubble in one of the tires. He explained to Ailene that she needed to have the tire replaced. The bubble could cause the tire to pop while she was driving. But Ailene never told Mom or Dad about it. Logan did. I was there for the inquisition that followed.

'Oh, right. I forgot about that,' Ailene had said sweetly in her thick Irish brogue. 'I'm so sorry. It escaped me mind.'

"Mom was livid, not understanding how Ailene could forget something so important. She called the au pair agency the next day. But the agency couldn't find us a replacement, nor could they find another position for Ailene. Mom and Dad knew Ailene would never intentionally hurt the kids, so Ailene was allowed to stay.

"But Mom curtailed Ailene's responsibilities those last couple of months, and it really hurt Ailene's feelings. She wasn't allowed to drive the kids anywhere. Mom dropped them off at school in the mornings and had trusted friends bring them home."

I understood then why Ana wasn't fond of Ailene. Ana and Ailene were opposites. Ana was smart, too smart. She was mature and responsible. She would have had difficulty tolerating Ailene's carelessness.

"Mom opened a bottle of vintage champagne the night we learned Ailene was safely back in Ireland," Lela recalled.

"Was Ailene angry at Mom?"

"Yes. Some of that anger was justified. Mom can be controlling and abrasive, especially when she's tired. She had grown very, very tired of Ailene.

"Mom's made mistakes with all of them, Shamus. Honey, Mira, Ailene, Ana. She knows it. Maybe that's why she chose to overlook some of Ailene's actions. As atonement for what she didn't or couldn't do for Honey or Mira. But she wouldn't risk anything bad happening to the kids. Enough was enough.

"Mom isn't perfect. I'm sure you've heard her tell the kids that no one's perfect except for God. Being perfect is an impossible, unrealistic expectation. Haley and Logan need only to do their best and learn from their mistakes. That's what Mom tells them."

I nodded in the dark. I'd heard Mom talk to the kids about perfection and God and mistakes. *I've certainly learned much from my own mistakes*, I acknowledged to myself.

"Mom's learned from all of them. She never

tries to hide her faults. That's why she lets a prospective sitter talk to her predecessor. Mom figures that the girls should know exactly what they're getting into. She never asks what's been said between them. If they don't like what they hear, they can choose not to come."

"And Dad? What does he think?"

Lela remained silent for a moment. I couldn't tell if she was drifting off or just pondering the question. A few more seconds passed before she continued.

"He's often stuck in the middle. He loves Mom and the kids, of course, but he hates confrontation. He avoids it, hoping the issues will just go away. This doesn't always go over well with Mom. She often feels that he doesn't support her. But I sense that he does. He listens to her, and he's pretty good at knowing when she just needs to vent. He's definitely better at letting the little things go.

"Mom looks at a given situation in the context of a bigger picture. Her instincts told her that Ailene's bad luck was attributable to a character flaw that could create a dangerous situation for the family. But Dad, well, he tends to look at events in isolation. A light on, no big deal. A car window left open, so what. The kids locked in a room, that's funny. A broken windshield, an accident. Accused of cheating, an honest mistake.

"Maybe Mom acts strict to compensate for Dad's leniency. I can't be sure though. But she looks out for this family. Always has our best interests in mind. I don't think she always goes about it the right way, but her heart's in the right place." Lela sighed, then rose and circled around on her pillow. "I really

need to get some sleep now. I've stayed up too late."
Her body plopped down with a light thud. "Good night,
Shamus."

I laid awake that night thinking about Lela. The
stories she told me and the things she didn't need to say.
I envied the strength of her character. Her unyielding
loyalty and commitment to our family. She spurned
death and battled monsters, both real and make-believe,
for them.

What monsters lay in wait for me? I wondered.
Would I rise to the occasions so eloquently?

I inched myself close to her as she slept
soundly. Her breath was light and warm on my fur.
There was comfort in her shadow. A shadow that
seemed less imposing than it had just a few hours
before.

I listened to her steady breathing and reflected
on the events and people that shaped her life and our
family. Honey's love, Mira's compassion, Ailene's bad
luck, and Ana's ruse.

*Who'd take Ana's place, and what would the
repercussions be?* I contemplated the possibilities long
after the tree frogs retired for the night.

Mom's instincts about Ana had been wrong.
Would she lose faith in herself? I wondered. *In her
ability to protect our family?* But Mom didn't know the
depth of Ana's betrayal.

Lela was right.

It was best none of them knew the truth.

~Seventeen~

"Hey, hon, have you seen my BlackBerry?" Dad called from the hallway. "I thought I left it on the table last night, but it's not here."

I glanced around the corner. Dad was on all fours looking under the kitchen table. I hurried over to see what he was looking for. My wet nose brushed up against his rough cheek. He flinched slightly.

"Why do you call it a BlackBerry?" Haley asked, walking toward us. Milk dribbled from the cup that dangled from her fingers. "It's blue. You should call it a blueberry." Five small fingers dove deep into my fur.

Dad and I looked at her simultaneously. A smile stretched across his face, and he swept her into his arms. "It's just what it's called. But you're right. Have you seen my blueberry?" he asked her.

A bright grin glistened on her face. "Shamus had it. In the TV room this morning." I stopped lapping at the spilled milk. "He was playing with it. But I took it away." Her face beamed with pride.

Dad turned and faced me.

"What? Shamus had it?" His puzzled gaze met mine.

I had an inkling I was in trouble. My head sank between my shoulders.

Panic filled his eyes. He set Haley down and hurried to the TV room.

I approached with caution.

"Oh my God! What the . . . " Dad stuttered. His

eyes grew wide and black. His pupils fully dilated. He held the mangled BlackBerry in his hands. The same object I'd been playing with earlier that morning. It beeped and buzzed and vibrated. It was the vibrating that caught my attention. The way it rattled on the table when the screen lit up. The small rubbery and spongy buttons were irresistible and felt good against my gums.

"I can't believe it. He ate my BlackBerry. He actually ate my BlackBerry." Dad studied the disfigured object intently, turning it over again and again with his hands. "I can't believe it," he repeated. "He chewed right through the corner." He shook his head in disbelief.

"It's a blueberry," Haley corrected him. But only anger filled his ears.

"This is no, Shamus! This is no!" Dad hollered. He shook the chewed blueberry in front of my nose. I cowered behind Haley. Oh, how I wished to disappear into the rug.

Mom ran in. She stifled a gasp with her hand. She too shook her head and waited for her voice to return. "Will your company replace it?" she stuttered.

"I don't know. They just replaced the one that you sat on. How am I going to explain this?" he wondered aloud. "My dog ate it?"

Dad turned his bemused eyes toward me. Haley reached around and rested her hand protectively on my head. Her stance turned rigid. She was protecting me.

"Well," Mom stammered, clearing her throat, "it is the truth."

Mom's mouth began to quiver. Then snickers

sputtered from her pursed lips. The color of her face deepened.

Haley suppressed a giggle, and the corners of Dad's eyes softened.

A fit of laughter burst into the room. Mom doubled over as the joyous spasms poured from her body. Her amusement consumed us all as it freely flowed.

There was nothing to do but join in.

~Eighteen~

Mom and Dad never quite figured out why Kat had left her previous host family. But the au pair agency raved about her and assured Mom and Dad she was quite a find. Kat was older and more experienced than Ana. She was CPR certified and her driving record was clean.

Mom was hesitant. Her guard was up. Yet she needed a sitter and the kids liked Kat.

Haley and Logan were drawn to Kat the first time they met her, when she'd come to visit during the interview process. Lela speculated it was because Kat looked and acted a lot like Honey. Both had dark, short hair, cut just above the chin, and each had a bright, warm smile. They shared the same fluid body movements, and their lovely sharp, pointy features were similar. Kat doted on the kids and had brought them chocolates. *The chocolates won them over*, I thought pleasantly.

We later learned, however, that Kat wasn't quite the actress she hoped to be.

Mom worked from home that Monday, spending most of the afternoon getting things ready for Kat's arrival later that day. The new sheets, comforter, and towels lay neatly on Ana's bed. A vase filled with flowers the kids picked rested on the nightstand. But it was no longer Ana's bed or Ana's room. Kat would be the new occupant, though Ana's scent still lingered.

The kids talked eagerly that morning about Kat's impending arrival. It was the topic of conversation until they bustled out the door for summer camp. While Kat seemed friendly enough, I thought it odd that the kids weren't the least bit sad about Ana's sudden departure.

Ana was gone from their lives, and I doubted they would ever see her again. Ana had cared for them and truly loved them. That I knew. They loved her back, oblivious to her deception.

"Why aren't they upset that she's gone?" I asked Lela.

"Ana was their sitter and they knew she'd leave one day. Just like the others. But she isn't gone. They can choose to carry her in their hearts," Lela explained. "The people they love never leave them because they're always in the heart. That's what the kids have been taught, and it empowers them."

I remembered my own mother. The smell of her breath and the feel of her warm tongue when she cleaned my fur. The rise and fall of her chest when I snuggled in close. The tears that misted her eyes when Gail and I drove away. My mother lived in my memories. She was forever in my heart.

"I just thought they'd be upset," I said. I remembered missing Gail, and I'd only lived with her for a few weeks. Ana had lived with our family for more than six months.

"The kids are confident and happy because they feel safe and secure," Lela replied patiently. "Mom and Dad's love is constant and they've set boundaries for them, rules and limitations around being polite, respectful, tolerant. The rules stay the same even when sitters change. So there isn't too much disruption or confusion when one sitter leaves. That's why Mom works from home two days a week. She stays close as a physical reminder but also to make sure the sitters consistently enforce our family rules."

There was more to it though. More to Mom working from home. I'd seen it. Mom carried it sometimes in her eyes, other times in her tone. Never intentional but it was there. The resentment. She resented having someone else take care of her kids.

Lela knew it too. "She's made a choice though. She has to work for us to live here and to maintain this lifestyle," she explained. "And she sometimes resents them," she said of the sitters. "She sometimes resents herself."

I looked hard at the rich fabrics, dark woods, plush area rugs, and fancy fixtures that surrounded us. The concept of lifestyle was foreign to me. But Lela pointed out how important it could be to humans. The colleges they attend, the jobs they have, the towns where they live, the houses they buy, the cars they drive, the clothes they wear, the vacations they take. Lela's list went on and on.

I was surprised to learn that Mom was an artist. Her artwork hung on our dining room wall. But she traded her passion for financial security. She hadn't grown up with money. Poppy was a truck driver and Grammy worked in the school's cafeteria. Mom's childhood wasn't easy. Poppy died when she was young. Whereas Grammy relied on her God for strength, Mom decided early on that she wouldn't rely on anyone. She stopped drawing and painting long before the kids were born.

Lela watched sadly as Mom placed a premium on lifestyle.

But then Haley and Logan came along, and Mom returned to the values Grammy held dear.

Mom struggled to balance work and family. Yet the balance shifted as the law lost its luster. Long hours. Late nights. Mom wanted more time with the kids. But there's no such thing as part-time work in the legal profession.

"She's able to work more from home and prorate her billing requirements and pay. But she can't prorate the workload or stress and making partner's out of the question," Lela clarified.

Mom began questioning the choices she made. Lifestyle became less important.

Lela and I watched her slowly unwind.

Perhaps the relationship between Mom and Kat was doomed before it began.

~Nineteen~

The ceiling fan hummed. Its breeze provided welcomed relief as it stirred the muggy night air. The tree frogs and katydids were well into their evening chorus. Their soothing melody drifted in through the opened windows. It swirled around the room in tempo with the ceiling fan's whirr. The blended sounds made a poignant composition.

Mom propped her head against the sofa's lush pillows and tucked her feet up under her. Wisps of hair blew gently across her face. Her eyelids closed. Lela's head rested lightly on her lap, and the children slept quietly upstairs.

Mom listened to the concert and sipped her freshly brewed iced tea. The zesty smell of lemon lingered on her fingertips. I drew in its freshness when her hand grazed my muzzle.

I stretched out on the rug beneath Lela's dangling paws. The rug I'd marred a couple of months before. Mom was livid when she found the tangled mess. The superglue she swiped across the rug's backing kept it from fraying further. She'd hidden the disfigured corner behind the couch. Still I saw the jagged silhouette from where I laid.

I'm an addict, I confessed in silence.

I had since chewed the corner of two rugs upstairs. Mom hadn't yet noticed. It was only a matter of time. My belly filled with remorse when I thought about the repercussions. Yet I couldn't ignore my chewing urges.

I despised this lack of self-control. My inability to turn away from the alluring feel of coarse, wet wool massaging my gums. *Could I ever resist the impulse?* I wondered.

Kat entered the room during the midst of my self-loathing. She carried in her hands a stack of photos.

Mom swiped the hair from her forehead and placed her tumbler on the end table. The ice cubes clicked against the glass, and condensation rolled slowly down the side. I could still smell the lemon. "Are you all unpacked?" Mom asked in a caring tone. She wanted to like Kat. I knew she did despite the bruise remaining from Ana's abrupt departure.

"Just about," Kat answered in her soft Russian accent. "I have some photos to share if you'd like to see them. Is now a good time?"

"Of course," Mom said, lifting Lela's head up slightly. She liked looking through photos. "Raj and I have been to Europe. Several times before the kids were born. Haven't been to Russia though. Maybe when they're older." She patted the cushion next to her.

Lela didn't budge when Mom gently scooted over to make room for Kat. She lay still and pretended to sleep. I knew she was awake despite her closed eyes. She was always listening and watching.

Kat sat down and the sofa grunted. She passed the stack of photos to Mom. Mom sat back, and Kat leaned slightly over her shoulder as she thumbed slowly through the heap. Mom looked attentively at each photo until Kat finished her narrative.

The first few photos were of Kat's family.

They'd been taken before her mother's death. Kat was sixteen when she died, and four years had since passed. "I'm so sorry, Kat," Mom said sensitively. She knew the sting of losing a parent at such a tender age.

"I never used to be fat," Kat blurted. "I used to dance. Ballet. But I put on a lot of weight after she died." She pulled her T-shirt off her big breasts and smoothed it over her protruding stomach. She tucked her loose hair behind each ear and straightened her back.

Lela's eyebrows lifted, but her eyes remained shut. Mom's lower jaw dropped slightly. Kat seemed more concerned about the loss of her figure than she did of her mother's passing.

Mom shook off her surprise. "You're not fat, Kat. You're beautiful," she remarked. Mom was careful to avoid using the word "fat" around the kids. She didn't want them judging themselves or others by outward appearances. "Besides, what matters is how beautiful you are on the inside." A line she'd used often on the kids. "You're both," she added with a smile.

I didn't know what Kat looked like on the inside. I hadn't yet formed an opinion. She had just arrived earlier that evening. But her outward appearance was pleasing. *She's plump*, I thought. *Not fat. Not skinny. Plump.*

Kat disregarded Mom's comments and pointed to the flowers and tiara she clutched in the photo. It was taken at a dance performance. Her last performance before her mother died. I lifted my head to catch a glimpse. Kat's mom held her proudly. She had her mother's bright, bold eyes.

"Your English is very good, Kat. Did you study it in school?"

"Yes. English was taught in my school. My mom thought school was important. We had to walk. Nearly two miles one way."

"You'll have to tell Haley and Logan. They complain when they have to walk up our driveway," Mom chuckled.

Mom thumbed through dozens of pictures. They were all of Kat. Dancer Kat. No pictures of plump Kat. No pictures of her country, her home, or even her prior host family. Nothing to suggest who Kat was currently. Just a few older photos of her family and a recent photo of an au pair she'd befriended, Randi.

Randi lived with her host family two towns over. She and Kat sang in a local church choir. Kat loved to sing and her voice was lovely. We didn't know at the time that Kat aspired to be an entertainer. She'd come to New York for a chance to fulfill her dreams, despite telling Mom she'd come for the work experience that would help her get a job when she returned home.

The night wore on.

Kat reminisced and Mom patiently listened. I kicked my legs out in front of me and flexed my paws to release the tension. It felt like hours had passed before Mom eventually laid the final picture on top of the stack. She made sure all the edges were perfectly aligned. She kept them a safe distance from her glass and the pooled condensation that had, at that point, just about dried.

Kat at last grew tired of talking and turned in for the night. She left with her photos, gripping her sense of worth in her hands.

"Good night," Mom said. She gazed toward the doorway even after Kat disappeared upstairs. Mom picked up her glass and slowly finished its contents. She emptied the remaining ice chips into her mouth and deliberately crushed the fragments between her back teeth. It was hard to tell what she was thinking.

Lela extended her legs and slipped her head slightly over the sofa's edge before making her bold prediction.

"This one's not going to last," she whispered.

What does she know? I wondered.

~Twenty~

Lela was right. She was always right. Kat was back in Russia by early November, three months ahead of schedule.

No incidences had arisen during Kat's first week in our home. The kids were happy, which made Mom content in return. *This one will last,* I naively thought. *She'll stay until her scheduled departure.*

Lela quickly tempered my optimism. She'd seen the cycle before. We were still in the honeymoon phase according to her. A time when neither Mom nor Kat could do any wrong.

"But the novelty will soon wear off," she warned. "Reality will set in, and expectations will have to change for the relationship to work. Kat's personality will eventually determine how long each cycle lasts. She knew before she came what Mom expects. Although Mom did her best to determine if their expectations were compatible, she never really knows until after an au pair settles in. I have a hunch Kat wasn't honest with Mom, and she has a strong, self-centered personality."

Lela's hunch came to fruition. The kids liked Kat. That wasn't the issue. They sang and danced and jumped on the trampoline together. They colored and read and played hide-and-seek. They enjoyed their time together, and Kat never put them in harm's way. But Kat neglected her other responsibilities, like the kids' laundry and cleaning up after them and herself.

"Housecleaning and laundry aren't part of my

job," Kat objected shortly after arriving.

The reality that Kat duped Mom began to settle in. It weighed heavy on Mom's shoulders. The kids' laundry and cleaning up after them *were* part of Kat's job, and she had plenty of free time. Kat was paid to work forty-five hours a week despite both kids being in camp until late afternoon. Yet Mom knew the relationship was doomed if she nagged Kat into submission.

The honeymoon phase came to a screeching halt. Lela and I waited with bated breath because we knew Mom had grown weary of au pairs.

Mom surprisingly held her tongue and asked our housecleaner, Marta, to come once a week. Marta usually came every other week, but Mom found it impossible to keep up with all the dishes, cleaning, and laundry. She did insist, however, that Kat encourage the kids to pick up their toys at the end of each day. Mom ignored the insolence in Kat's rolling eyes.

Outwardly Mom adjusted her expectations, but inside she fumed. She tried concealing her anger. "This one has to last," she told Grammy.

As each week passed, Lela and I knew Mom and Kat's relationship grew untenable. The fabric that held it together was already frayed, and Mom hadn't yet discovered that Kat was neglecting another responsibility. She neglected Lela and me.

Kat didn't walk us as she said she would. On rainy days she expected us to urinate while tethered to the porch rail. Sometimes she'd simply forget to let us out until the kids came home. Those were the days she stayed in her room, singing and dancing and scanning the computer for open auditions. She wanted to be famous and spent her days dreaming of her big break.

Lela and I did our best not to urinate in the house, but there were a couple of times we just couldn't help it. Mom began to suspect that she'd been lied to. Kat said she would look after us, but she only said what she knew Mom wanted to hear.

"I don't like getting wet," Kat retorted when Mom asked about my latest accident.

Mom's body stiffened. "You can't expect them to urinate if you leave them tied to the porch on a three-foot lead," she reprimanded. Her tone was loud and condescending. It was the first time she raised her voice toward Kat. Kat turned defensive, and Mom's disappointment swelled. Her manner toward Kat turned brusque, and she paid Marta to walk us afternoons.

"At least the kids are safe, and Marta is now looking after the dogs," Mom rationalized. She eagerly waited for February though the new school year had just begun.

She waited and watched.

Mom silently scrutinized Kat's obsession with weight and outward beauty. The makeup, new clothes, and designer bags and shoes. She didn't object to Kat's passion for fashion. Not until Haley asked, "Why does my belly stick out? Am I fat?" Mom reminded Kat that she couldn't use the word "fat" around the kids or talk about being overweight. "Only inner beauty matters," she'd repeat when she was sure Haley was in earshot.

"Whatever," became Kat's standard response. A

response that made Mom's blood boil. But Kat had grown tired of the perceived nitpicking, and she too began counting down the days. She hung a sign in her room that read, *Wake Me Up When February Ends*. A parody of a hit song Mom knew well.

Mom found the sign offensive.

Dad thought it was funny.

The resentment Mom harbored festered and made me anxious. I grew nervous and edgy. Only chewing soothed me. Rhythmic chewing. Repetitive grinding. I spared nothing left within my reach. Toys, clothes, throw pillows, shoes. Yes, shoes. And my rug addiction worsened.

Mom was beside herself when she saw the gnarled foyer runner. The one she purchased earlier that week. It was ruined. Superglue couldn't mend the shredded corners.

I tried apologizing, but my jumping and licking only annoyed her more. My nails ripped her hosiery, and she pushed me away. Tired and frustrated, she dropped down to her knees and cried.

"You wanted another dog," Dad said as Mom fingered the tattered edges.

The tension was getting to him too. Every night Mom complained about something Kat did or didn't do that day. Still. His harsh tone surprised me. His voice sounded cruel.

"Go away!" she yelled when I approached to comfort her. Her forceful shove sent me stumbling. She'd never before raised a hand against me.

"Did I make a mistake, Shamus? Why do you

destroy everything? Why do you always jump on everyone?" Anger swelled in her eyes.

I lowered my gaze. My shoulders and tail sank with my spirit. "You mean why can't I be more like Lela?" I whined.

Mom turned away from me. I felt alone and scared. My old insecurities began to resurface.

"It isn't just you, Shamus. Mom would never deliberately hurt you." Lela's body brushed gingerly against me. "Kat's holding Mom hostage, and you know Mom's job has become more demanding," she sighed.

There was no consoling my bruised heart.

"Just give Mom some space," Lela offered. "She's trying to figure out if all the added stress is worth it."

I sought refuge in my pillow's embrace. The foam cradled my aching heart until I felt the stirring beside me. "I'm sorry," Mom whispered next to my ear. I licked the salty wetness from her cheeks. "Me too," I whimpered.

That weekend she bought me a crate.

Mom never crated Lela because she thought it was inhumane. But my crate was extra-large and kept in the den. I felt safe inside it, and I could eat my treats free from fear that Lela would ambush me. In fact, I felt safe enough to stand up to Lela when she did come poking around. I wasn't shy about scowling back at her if I knew the latch was secure.

Mom felt better about my crate once she saw how comfortable I was in it. Yet still she worried that Kat would neglect me and leave me in it for too long of periods. But I didn't mind being left alone in my crate, especially since Marta came in the afternoons. And if the truth be known, Kat didn't pay much attention to whether I was crated or not. She left the door open, and I wandered in and out of it as I pleased.

Only Lela seemed bothered by my crate. Some nights she'd grumble when she passed by. Maybe it was the treat I kept buried under my pillow, or maybe she was jealous she didn't have a crate of her own. I never knew for certain, and I certainly never asked. In time she simply let me be.

I was safe in my crate. It restored my sense of balance. I became more settled and less destructive. Though I still liked to jump and lick, I did so less often. I turned to my chew toys to satisfy my cravings. Mom was indeed less harried without my ambushing her every morning. Our relationship flourished, and a sense of calm filled the house despite Mom's escalating resentment of Kat. For Kat grew more bold and disrespectful. She thought that as long as the kids were happy she wouldn't be asked to leave. That's what she told Randi.

Mom played along and held her tongue. Yet the cost of keeping Kat happy was beginning to outweigh the benefits. How much Mom was willing to take was uncertain.

"It's the calm before the storm," Lela warned.

I found solace in my crate while the storm brewed, and I watched the days grow shorter. The autumn breeze cooled heated temperaments and ushered in Halloween.

My first Halloween on the lane. Mom and Dad's favorite holiday. It was a time for celebration, and our house became a haunted mansion. Tombstones and carved pumpkins, ghosts and mums were strategically scattered around the yard. We all dressed for the town parade. Lela wore a Dracula costume, and I was dressed as Spiderman. Logan and I wore matching costumes. Haley was a stunning mermaid and Dad a king.

"Sit still, Shamus. I want to take a picture," Mom pleaded in her Geisha costume. I couldn't help scratching. My mask was itchy and it bothered my ears.

"You're lucky," Lela teased. "I wore a large, fluffy tutu my first Halloween. Before we moved from the city. All the dogs from the run were in costume. I kept tripping over it." I laughed with her and the image of her in a tutu. She didn't look or act the tutu type. I indeed felt lucky to have been thrust into a Spiderman suit.

The gaiety didn't last long however.

Kat took the kids to Randi's house without Mom's permission two days later. She gassed up the car before realizing she'd forgotten her wallet. She and the kids waited at the gas station for over an hour before Mom was able to get to them with cash.

A week later Kat left for Russia.

"Consider it an early wake-up call," Mom said under her breath as Kat's livery service drove away.

~Twenty-one~

While Kat and the au pair agency made final arrangements for her departure, Mom called nanny agencies and scanned the newspapers for a live-out sitter. Mom worked mostly from home, so she could interview the parade of women that applied for the job. Some were young and some were older. Some had light skin and some had dark skin. A couple were in college and one even brought her daughter to the interview.

Lela and I listened as Mom went through her laundry list of questions. Each night she reviewed her notes with Dad. The ages of the candidates, years of experience, driving records, references, starting salaries, general first impressions. Mom sensed Dad wasn't paying attention to the details. "They're your kids too," she said tersely. They narrowed the candidates down to two. Dad liked Ruth best.

Ruth was a young grandmother. She reminded me of Grammy, short and petite but with dark skin, coarse, long curly hair, and an uplifting accent. She was from Jamaica, and she lived with her daughter and grandchildren in a neighboring town. She previously worked for a local family and had her own safe and dependable SUV. She was willing to do light cleaning and cooking, and let Lela and me outside during the day.

If Mom knew that Ruth sometimes slept while the kids were at school or that she watched a lot of TV when she could have been cleaning or doing laundry, Mom didn't let on. She was glad to have found someone responsible to look after the kids. Dad was glad not to hear any complaining.

Marta went back to cleaning every other week, and she no longer came for our afternoon strolls. Though Ruth was good about letting us out to potty, she didn't take us for the long afternoon walks I'd grown accustomed to. I grew restless and wandered more as autumn entrenched itself on the lane. The wild turkeys, geese, and deer were too tempting to resist. Chasing them made for good exercise. I never wandered too far from our property, but still Mom didn't want Ruth chasing after me.

It was Dad who unpacked the wireless canine containment system. Lela looked on suspiciously when he took one of the collars and started walking a perimeter around the house. When the collar beeped, Mom stabbed a flag into the ground. The shrill beep stung my ears. Lela quivered from the noise. I followed her as she hurried to the porch.

Another beep. Another flag added to the periphery.

Lela trembled as she looked on. "Are you OK?" I asked her.

"I remember that sound, Shamus. If you pass through those flags when your collar's on, you'll feel a burst of energy on your throat that will leave you breathless. Trust me. I've wandered through the flags before."

I had no idea what she was talking about.

"Mom and Dad installed a similar fence at the old house in White Plains. Not long after Haley was born. We lived close to a main road, and Mom worried that I'd get hit by a car. Every now and then I'd see a squirrel or a cat taunting me, and I'd break through the flags. That's when I'd get zapped."

My ears stopped listening when she mentioned Haley's birth. I didn't know Lela saw Haley being born. "What was it like?" I wanted to know. I heard the story of bullets and eggs but never of a baby being born.

"It startled me more than it hurt because Mom kept the stimulation low."

"No, not that. I mean Haley being born. Did you see it?"

"What?" Lela's eyes refocused. "Oh no. No," she said, shaking her head excitedly. Her body relaxed as she continued speaking. "Haley was born in a hospital. Mom went into labor the night before we moved to White Plains. She writhed in pain for hours that night. I knew it was going to be a long labor. Haley decided to come into this world two weeks early but decided she would take her time doing it. The movers were coming early the next morning. Grammy and Aunt Abbey helped us move. Boxes were lined and stacked up against every wall." Lela paused to catch her breath.

"Dad asked Mom if they could go to the hospital after the movers came. I thought she was going to rip the hair out of his head when the next contraction hit." Lela laughed heartily. She'd forgotten about the electric fence.

"So then what happened?"

"Well, Mom and Dad left for the hospital while we stayed to wait for the movers. The next time I saw

Mom was in White Plains. The hospital sent her home because Haley wasn't ready to come out. Problem was, we didn't have a home yet. They sold the apartment but hadn't yet closed on the house. The movers arrived before the attorney. Mom paced around the yard, squatting with each contraction. They were getting closer and stronger. There was nothing I could do for her. Grammy timed the contractions. I remember her hollering, 'They're a minute apart.' Then Mom and Dad drove off. The attorney finally came with the keys, and I stayed out of the way while the movers hauled our belongings into the house."

"Were you scared?"

"No. I knew Mom would be fine. Birthing is natural, and Dad called early the next morning to tell us that Haley finally arrived. I waited at home while Grammy and Aunt Abbey went to the hospital. They came back with one of Haley's diapers. That was my first introduction to her. It was a weak but sweet smell. But nothing could have prepared me for the changes that followed."

"They were busy with Haley?"

"Yup. And they bought a fence to protect me. The freedom was wonderful. I could go in and out when I wanted. But I had to learn my boundaries." She looked up at the row of flags Mom planted in the ground. "Those flags there are your boundaries," Lela warned. "Don't go beyond them unless you're told it's OK." The nervousness returned to her eyes.

I was either stupid or stubborn. Maybe a little of both. I had to test the boundaries for myself. Lela and I knew where every flag was located. Mom and Dad walked us around the perimeter endless times over a number of days. They made sure we knew our boundaries before letting us out unattended. We could only cross over if they said, "It's OK." That was our safe command.

Despite Lela's warnings, I had to try. I had to test just how far I really could go. *Maybe it won't hurt as Lela warned*, I told myself that Sunday afternoon. *Maybe she's just trying to scare me*, I thought while boldly stepping toward the flag. The little piece of plastic snapped in the wind. Then came the familiar beep, and I inched my way closer to the flag.

A steady beeping followed. I closed my eyes and froze but nothing more happened. *Maybe the fence doesn't work,* I speculated.

I ignored Mom's voice and the gravel's sound under her swift footsteps. "No, Shamus!" she hollered when I pushed my two front paws daringly ahead. My body moved well beyond the flag.

The beeping intensified and a quick zap followed. The sudden sting shocked me, and I bolted toward the house with my tail planted firmly between my legs.

Mom caught me in her arms and tenderly stroked my side. "Are you all right, Shamus?"

My tongue fell from my parched mouth. I could scarcely catch my breath. "Yes," I managed to yelp. Only my ego was battered. I was otherwise fine.

Mom attached my leash and led me toward the flags. I eyed them nervously as I drew nearer. My lesson apparently wasn't over. Five feet from the boundary, I sat back and dug my front paws into the gravel. "No," I whined, trying to wriggle free.

"Come on, Shamus. Come on," Mom said in a sappy voice. Lela looked on from the safety of the porch.

I wouldn't budge. I planted my butt and front paws deep into the gravel.

Mom dangled a juicy treat in front me. The smell was overpowering. My willpower quivered. Drool pooled and spilled off my tongue.

"Come on, Shamus." Her words fell sweetly from her lips. The treat's scent was arousing. My resolve fled, skipping down the lane. Just as I was about to snatch the temptation from Mom's fingers, she cleverly tossed it close to the flag.

"Come, Shamus," Mom coaxed. She upped the ante with another, larger succulent treat. I smacked my lips and swallowed the excessive saliva.

"Come on, Shamus. You can do it. Come on." Mom's words were encouraging. She slapped her knees. "Come on."

I drew in a deep breath and eased slowly toward her to consume my reward. Hot dogs. Juicy, sweet hot dogs! I love hot dogs just as much as Logan. Only he doesn't eat the bun.

"What a good boy!" Mom patted my sides in praise.

The flags crackled in jest, and I glared at them with disgust. They mocked me. I was sure of that. But I'd learned my lesson. I didn't follow Mom when she dropped my leash and walked well past the flags. I watched her from my perch on the rocks. I could see the corral below and the smile on her face when she turned back to look at me.

Lela was waiting for us near the porch steps when I'd finished the day's session. I approached with my eyes lowered. Embarrassed. Ashamed of my stupidity.

"Are you all right?" Lela's voice was full of concern. I lifted my head and met her caring gaze.

"Yes," I said humbly. "I should have listened to you."

~Twenty-two~

Fall turned to winter. The bitter cold slipped in after Thanksgiving, and then the snow came. That was the winter we traded Big Red for Commander.

"They've named their cars and trucks for as long as I can remember," Lela said as we basked in the oversized rear end.

Big Red had been big, but Commander was much more spacious, and Lela thought it performed better in snow. This was good because winter on the lane was both beautiful and treacherous. The steep climb of the driveway made it perilous to drive until the plows came. Since the lane was a private road, the hired plows usually didn't get to our driveway until the early afternoon. Mom and Dad worked from home on those days.

They took turns entertaining the kids so the other could tend to calls and e-mails. It was hectic, but there was always time for sledding or skiing down the driveway. Lela and I would chase after the kids, encouraged by all their hooting and hollering. The air was fresh, and the smell of smoke from neighboring fireplaces drifted around us. And when the kids were chilled to the bone, Mom would make hot chocolate and Dad would start a fire.

Lela was still stable on her feet those days, but the cold gnawed at her hips. They'd stiffen if she played too hard. But her medicine eased the pain, and she felt remarkably jolly that Christmas Eve. We both did. The kids' giddiness was contagious.

They couldn't sit still through dinner. Not that they could on most other nights either. But that night they were exceedingly fidgety.

"How much longer till Santa comes?" they wanted to know.

They chattered endlessly between themselves about the gifts he might bring. Mom and Dad listened inconspicuously and sighed with relief when the kids whispered their latest desires. The kids had changed their minds several times over those past few weeks about the gifts they wanted most. Mom and Dad were right to have waited to make their final purchases.

The purring dishwasher signaled that dinner was over. The kids begged to know where Santa was. Dad led them to the den, and they found Santa with the Santa tracker. The kids crowded around the computer screen. The blinking lights reflected off their smooth faces and wide eyes. They stared in awe at all the places Santa had already been.

"How does he deliver all those presents?" Logan asked with wonder-filled eyes that watched a Santa-sighting video. Mom and Dad exchanged nervous glances. They needed a quick diversion.

"Look!" Dad suddenly exclaimed. His voice filled with gusto and contrived alarm. "Santa's just about to cross the Atlantic." He pointed fervently at the monitor. "You best hop in the shower. You know he won't come if you're still awake," he warned, but Haley and Logan had already scampered up the stairs. I could hear their animated voices and scurrying footsteps above. They sounded much like the mice who sought shelter in our attic.

"They get so excited," Lela said. "Just wait until tomorrow morning." Her eyes too sparkled with merriment, and she licked her lips anticipating what her own gift might be. Santa left her a large cookie and chicken chew toy the previous year, in addition to the powdered chocolate and marshmallows she had helped herself to during the night. A gift that wasn't meant for her as it later turned out.

Mom announced it was time for bed just shortly after a Christmas cartoon ended. Santa's sleigh was positioned somewhere over the Atlantic. It pointed toward New York. The kids rushed to the monitor to see for themselves.

"Ohhh!" they gasped in awe. It was true. Santa was on his way. Their fixated eyes remained frozen on Santa's sleigh until Mom's voice broke the spell. I heard their spry steps bouncing up the stairs.

"Quickly! Let's get ready for bed." Mom rushed up the stairs chasing after them.

I'd never seen them get ready for bed so fast. They brushed their teeth, tidied their rooms, and hopped into bed without being begged. Prayers were said and the lights went out. I could feel their excitement as they wiggled and squirmed under the covers. They fought hard to stay awake, and they strained to hear the distant sleigh bells. But exhaustion swiftly found them and carried them into sound, peaceful sleep.

I knew there was no living Santa. Lela told me weeks before about Mom and Dad's role in the charade. "Christmas has an energy of its own," she explained.

"The legend of Santa embodies it and makes the season magical. Mom and Dad want the kids to believe in that magic and the uncensored happiness it brings." Lela spoke with sincerity for she believed in Christmas magic.

I didn't comprehend what it meant to believe. I couldn't grasp the essence of what she spoke about. Christmas. Energy. Magic. Not at first anyway. But gradually, as the month of December wore on, I began to understand. I felt the growing force as each day passed. The warmth consumed me. Its presence caressed my soul.

The enchantment began with the transformation of our home. The splendid decorations, the fresh, airy tree, and strings of dazzling lights captivated my senses.

Right after Thanksgiving, as it had always been since Lela could remember, Mom and Dad hauled the holiday decorations from the attic. Santa figurines and reindeer, candles and ribbons, snowmen and angels were merrily strewn about our home. Christmas poinsettias flanked the fireplaces. Seasonal towels and placemats replaced the fall linens, and the spicy smell of autumn gave way to winter's cool peppermint and pine fragrances. But in the midst of the frivolity, Baby Jesus looked down upon us from his perch on the big fireplace mantle. "We celebrate his birthday at Christmas," Mom reminded us as she arranged the farm animals around the manger.

It was Haley and Logan who picked out the tree. Lela and I watched from Commander while they ran through the church parking lot searching for the fullest, tallest tree. Many were too short, some too bare, and one was much too wide. There was a large selection that Black Friday, and they eventually settled on an enormous Douglas fir that Dad strapped onto our truck. It hung off either end, and Mom grabbed its top through the opened sky window as we drove home. Dad lugged the oversized pine in through the rear door. Beads of sticky sap clung to its moist bark and seeped from its bottom. The fresh, woodsy scent filled the TV room.

"Look out!" Dad yelled when he cut the twine that bound the branches together. The unleashed boughs flung open wide, and a flurry of pine needles rained down on us. I shook hard to dislodge the coarse needles from my fur. Haley and Logan skipped deliriously around the tree until Dad positioned it in front of the large arched window.

Dad weaved the lights around the branches, while Mom and the kids carefully unwrapped the ornaments. Each ornament represented a snapshot in time. A cotton ball angel from a southern plantation. A ceramic sled from Philly. A mermaid from the Caribbean. An elephant from Africa. Haley's cradle and Logan's teddy bear. The growing collection convened annually. The memories mingled and reminisced. The newest was a turtle from Mexico.

"We need to get one for Shamus," Mom said to no one in particular as she placed Lela's ornament near the tree's top. It was a small doghouse frame, and Lela's face peeked through the door. It was a face not yet aged by the passing of time.

"I was close to your age when that picture was

taken," Lela said. "Not one gray fur in my muzzle."
Despite her age, she was still strong and youthful. *I
hope I'm as lucky*, I marveled, looking at her.

The ornaments were gingerly placed among the
tree limbs. A velvet and silk tree skirt was draped
majestically around the base, but the coronation wasn't
complete until Mom placed the angel on the tip-pity top.
The angel's perfect porcelain face smiled lovingly at us.
Her feathered wings moved ever so slightly in the air.
She held a single candle, a steady beacon a top the
blinking hullabaloo.

Yes, the Christmas lights sparkled inside and
outside our home. They beamed bright all over town.
The flashing colors bounced off the walls and sky and
icy snow. Illuminating the deepest, darkest, coldest
nights.

Christmas music played nonstop. Lela and I
hummed and swished our tails in rhythm with the tunes.
I learned every one of the songs that played over and
over again. Toes were constantly tapping, and singing
filled our home. Bad moods were swept up in the
melodies and carried away.

Peace flooded our home, and Mom and Dad
encouraged the kids to spread holiday cheer. "Christmas
is about giving," they said, and they helped the kids
purchase toys for needy children and collect donations
for a local food bank. They sponsored a family who
lacked basic necessities and prepared meals for the
infirmed. The kids participated with compassion, but
they were still young. Their primary focus was on Santa
and the gifts he might bring them.

They dreamed of Christmas morning and anxiously counted down the days. They kept an eye on Mom's "Naughty and Nice" chart. It was kept conveniently in the kitchen as a reminder that Santa was always watching. "You don't want to end up on Santa's naughty list," Dad threatened throughout the month. But the nice deeds always outweighed the naughty ones.

I laid next to the kids as they excitedly scanned magazines and listened intently to television commercials. Every day a new magazine came in the mail. Every day a new commercial aired. Haley and Logan kept indecipherable lists of the toys they wanted most. A week before Christmas, they scrawled letters to Santa telling him how good they'd been and what they wanted in return. Logan taped pictures to his letter so there would be no misunderstandings.

Mom and Dad wore their joy openly that Christmas Eve as they bustled about filling stockings and arranging the ornately wrapped gifts under the tree. They had spent countless hours planning and wrapping those presents. Hiding them in places the kids would never look. On Christmas Eve, the culmination of their endeavors lay beneath the tree. Big presents in the back and smaller packages toward the front.

"I hope they're happy with what we picked out," Dad said, sitting on the couch admiring their handy work. "Do you think we bought enough?"

"Raj. It's not about the presents," Mom playfully scolded.

"At this age it's all about the presents," he taunted. "It's quantity and how big the packages are to open." He greedily wrung his hands together in jest.

"You better not talk like that in front of the kids." Mom kicked his shin lightly as she passed, carrying three small gifts in her hands. Peanut butter and fish smells emanated from under the decorated wrappings. A faint "yum" filled my ears, and I knew Lela caught a whiff of them too.

"We haven't forgotten about you," Mom teased.

She carefully buried the packages deep within the tree branches and well beyond our reach.

"No repeats of last year, Miss Lela. Stay out of the tree and gifts. You hear me?" Lela donned an innocent expression and thumped her tail against the carpet.

Peanut butter for Lela and me, fish for Emi, I presumed as the drool gathered. I licked a loose drop from my chin and let out an impatient whine.

Mom's fingers tickled my chest and stilled my eagerness. "You'll just have to wait till morning like the rest of us. Quiet now so you don't wake the kids."

When the stockings were filled and empty boxes and bags discarded, Mom plopped next to Dad holding two glasses of wine. Drops of the dark, spicy-smelling liquid toppled over the rims and trickled onto her hands. She lapped them up before they hit the sofa. "I can't believe it's Christmas again," she sighed, leaning into him.

Lela's rhythmic breaths floated around us.

Dad put an arm around Mom's shoulder and brushed his lips against her hair. The sofa moaned, and the two became one in the shimmering light.

I averted my gaze, looking out into the darkness at the glistening night sky. Stars danced in front of me. It was hard to discern the stars from the village lights below. The skyline and village merged splendidly in the shadows. Then a distant sparkle caught my eye. The steady glow glided across the sky.

Maybe, I wondered, staring through the frosted windowpane.

Just maybe, I thought while listening for the bells.

~Twenty-three~

"Santa came! Santa came!"

Haley and Logan's loud voices roused me from a deep, heavy slumber. From a dream filled with running waters and cool grass. Plenty of chicken and chew toys too. It was a good dream, and I wasn't ready to wake.

"He came! He came," their voices sang. Thundering feet moved across the floor.

Who's here? I wondered, rising slowly to shake the sleep from my body.

Lela's tags jingled somewhere in the distance. They jangled merrily in harmony with mine.

The cloud around my head began to lift. My senses stirred.

A bright light pierced the darkness, and the kids came bounding in. They threw themselves on to their parents' bed. "He came! He came! Come on," they hollered. Their energy and exhilaration filled the room.

Logan grabbed Mom's arm and dragged her from bed. The clock on her nightstand read 4:55. She steadied herself. The sleep hadn't yet left her body. "He did? Are you sure?" Her voice feigned wonder and disbelief as she wrapped her worn, faded bathrobe tightly around her.

Logan gazed up at her with mammoth eyes, grinning ear to ear. He stood nodding, his body bathed in mystical wonderment. It enveloped them all. Radiated from every pore. Glowed brightly on their faces.

Christmas snuck in under night's cover.

The revelation snatched my breath. Joy rushed into my body. The magic consumed me too.

"I thought I heard something on the roof last night!" Dad shouted out. His slippered feet shuffled across the rug. "I hope he left me a cookie." He amusingly raised his eyes and praying hands toward the ceiling.

Visions of cookies and treats swirled in my head. *My treat*, I remembered. The one buried deep within the branches. I imagined the fragrant peanut butter and the smooth, creamy texture rolling over my tongue. My heart raced and I pranced on my pillow, licking my lips.

"It's Christmas!" I barked joyfully.

The kids screeched and sprinted from the room. I followed at their heels and tripped over them when they stopped suddenly before the tree. Their jaws fell open and their eyes grew wide. The illuminated tree looked more beautiful than it had the night before. The twinkling lights sparkled bright. Reflections danced around us. Presents encircled the tree's base and more spilled across the floor. The kids jumped up and down and all around, clapping their hands and cheering.

I too was captivated. *My treat's in that tree*, I thought excitedly.

Lela looked on amused. "I never grow tired of it," she whispered above the Christmas music that floated in from the kitchen. Mom sang along as the coffee machine cheerfully spewed out its cappuccino. The smell was exceptionally strong that morning.

"It's chilly in here," Dad said, blowing warm air into his cupped hands. "Let's first light the fire." The flume creaked open, and the wood hissed when the starter log ignited. Lela left the room when the first crackle rang out. She was always leery of loud, sudden noises.

"Looks like you kids were awfully good this year." Dad focused the video camera he set up the night before. "Merry Christmas," he said, scanning the room through the small lens.

"Merry Christmas," the kids hollered back, not looking up from their endeavors.

Haley was vigorously shaking a box. The shiny bow once carefully taped to the corner dangled haphazardly next to her ear. Her forehead crinkled and her nose scrunched up. Her puzzled eyes narrowed on the mysterious package she turned over in her hands.

Logan was on his knees and elbows scanning the presents farthest beneath the tree. "That one's mine! That one's mine!" He pointed to the largest present buried beneath the boughs. He was just about to tunnel his way back when Mom sashayed in with two steaming mugs.

"Merry Christmas," she said pecking Dad's cheek. She swayed past him and set the mugs on the table. She reached tenderly for her children. "Merry Christmas," she said, bending over each of them and kissing their brows.

Dad gulped his coffee and placed a Santa cap on his head. *He looks nothing like Santa*, I thought. His cheeks and chin were shrouded in a dark, coarse scruff not a snowy beard. His nose wasn't round like a cherry, and his belly didn't shake like jelly. His skin and hair were dark, not fair, but he was certainly jolly.

"Ready for presents?" Dad wore a cheeky grin.

An affirmative chorus rang out, and he passed out the gifts, one by one.

Logan's fingers tore easily through the wrapping, but Haley was much more deliberate. She meticulously lifted each piece of tape, taking great care not to rip the paper.

Mom and I grew anxious watching. "You can rip it, Haley. Just grab a corner and pull," Mom said, yanking animatedly at an imaginary present. Haley laughed and mimicked her mother's gesture, sending waves of shredded paper high into the air.

The kids' energy was infinite and infectious. It sent me spinning around in circles. My zoomies were small and tight. Discarded wrapping paper flew around me. Boxes and bags crumbled under my paws. Mom clung to Dad when I flew over her outstretched legs. I landed with a thump and skidded toward the dining room, nearly taking Lela's paws out from under her.

"Whoa," she grinned, stepping to the side. She'd been laying near the door listening to Christmas morning. The fire had died down, and she was just about to join us.

"Lela, come on," I whined, circling around her and stamping my paws.

Her smile grew broad and her body braced for impact. She shifted her weight back, and I boldly lunged forward. Her front paw playfully slapped my shoulder, and I rolled to the ground laughing. Our lighthearted snarls and growls echoed through the house.

"Would you two like your presents?" Mom asked, hovering over us. We jumped quickly into a seated position. Our chests heaved greedily in and out as the air refilled our lungs. Mom's hands dug deep into the tree's branches, and Lela and I eagerly licked our lips.

"Here you are!" Mom exclaimed, laying our gifts before us. Lela trapped her present between her front paws. She expertly used her teeth to remove the wrapping. It was obvious she had done this many times before.

Haley knelt beside me while I clawed helplessly at my gift. "Aw, Shamus." Her small fingers gently removed the wrapping. "Here you go," she said, handing me the bone. I carefully took it from her hand and sank my teeth deep into the peanut butter-filled core. The rich, velvety filling flowed through my mouth, over my tongue, and between my teeth. The smell and taste made me dizzy.

I retreated to the playroom to consume my Christmas present. I eased my way past Lela. Slowly. Not wanting to raise suspicion. I made a quiet dash for the stairs only after I'd turned the corner. I clenched my bone tightly and plodded carefully down the cool, dark stairway. I found a safe place just beyond the futon to dine.

It was a perfect blend, a decadent masterpiece, of texture and taste. The crunchy, grainy bone. The silky, sweet but salty peanut butter. I licked, nibbled, and chewed my way through it all in a few short minutes. I cleared every crumb from my muzzle and the carpet. I lapped up the soft, nutty goo. Careful not to taste the rug's fibers. I was still a rug addict, and though I hadn't chewed through one in weeks, I didn't want to provoke my impulses. I'd come such a long way.

I laid back when my belly was full. I felt its shifting contents, and a burp interrupted the silence. The faint smell of peanut butter scattered around me. The savory aroma teased my wits and stirred my sensations.

All the edible and inedible joys of Christmas, I thought gleefully.

An insatiable thirst swelled inside my body. I was hungry for more.

I skipped up the stairs to rejoin my family. To partake in the revelry. To satisfy all of my cravings.

~Twenty-four~

I hadn't always listened to my inner voice. The small, quiet voice that stirred deep inside me. It started as a whisper. A gentle calling I often questioned. A subtle, cautionary nudge I frequently ignored. Lela told me to trust the voice, and that night I listened. The voice grew big and bold, and I heeded the warnings. That night, the voice became my ally. A sacred advisor and trusted friend.

It wasn't long after New Year's Eve. Mom and Dad were meeting friends for dinner. Neither Marta nor Ruth could baby sit, so Dad asked Seth. Seth was sixteen and he lived in a neighboring town. He was always respectful toward our family when he visited, and Haley and Logan adored him. They had met him at church school, and he'd been their camp counselor.

Still something about Seth troubled Mom. Something she couldn't articulate. Her inner voice had spoken, and I felt her apprehension building that night.

"Quit worrying. They'll be fine," Dad said reassuringly. But his words could not quell the tugging in her gut or mine.

Lela knew Seth had a dark side. I felt it too the night Mom and Dad first went to meet Kat. The kids were already asleep in bed, and Mom and Dad were only gone for an hour. But an hour was enough time for me to discern that there was something troubling about Seth. There was a faint, foul aura about him. Something malignant stirred inside his young soul. I saw it in his eyes as he snooped through drawers, fingered personal items, and made himself comfortable on Mom and Dad's bed.

I couldn't explain what it was that bothered me about Seth. It was a feeling that agitated my insides. Nothing concrete. Nothing I could directly speak to. Like Mom, I wanted to believe he was of moral character. Nothing he did or said indicated he would harm our family.

Surely they wouldn't entrust him with the kids if they think there's a threat? I thought nervously. But still, something nagged at Mom, and it made me edgy too.

"Keep your eyes alert and focused on Seth," Lela instructed me shortly before he arrived. "Stay close to the kids. Raise your hackles and show your teeth if he does anything suspicious. I'll be watching too."

What does she mean by suspicious? I wondered to myself.

"Do you understand?" Lela asked sternly. I nodded because I trusted her. I trusted her instincts better than my own.

"Listen to your gut, Shamus. Allow yourself to feel what it's telling you," she advised. "Trust it."

OK. Listen and feel. I can do that, I reassured myself. *I can do that*, I told myself over and over again. My insides knotted up and I felt queasy.

"Shamus, you all right?" Mom rubbed my belly. "You're not acting yourself." Her comforting touch loosened the knots and settled my stomach.

Then Seth came.

His mom's minivan rattled up the driveway a

little after 7 o'clock. The kids had already showered and were in their pajamas. Their hair was still wet and they smelled fresh, clean.

"Bedtime at eight," Mom told Seth. "They can watch some TV and fall asleep in our bed, but lights out by eight. We'll be in town, and you can reach us on our cells. The numbers are on the fridge."

Mom and Dad kissed the kids good night. "Listen to Seth. He's the boss while we're out." The kids laughed and ran around the dining room table. "He's the boss. He's the boss," they mimicked as they ran. Their angelic voices soared into the air.

"Good luck with those two," Dad said to Seth, chuckling. "They're all set for bed, and the dogs have already gone out. Help yourself to anything, and call us if you have any questions. We'll be home by ten."

At first, nothing seemed unusual. The kids and Seth watched Sponge Bob in the TV room and ate goldfish crackers and pretzels. Lela and I stayed close, watching them all. It was close to 8:30 p.m. The kids should have been in bed.

Seth began shifting on the couch, and Lela inched closer to the kids. Her eyes were focused and alert. Her hackles were partially raised.

Concentrate, I told myself. *What do I feel?*

I listened with eyes closed, and I felt the energy in the room change.

I opened my eyes and studied Seth. The way he ate his pretzels and the way he watched the kids. He wasn't watching Sponge Bob. He was watching the kids with the hardened eyes of a predator stalking its prey.

Waiting for the precise moment to strike.

He wouldn't hurt them. Would he? I questioned myself.

A prickle ran up my spine.

"Let's play hide-and-seek," Seth suggested. Haley and Logan jumped up off the couch. "You're it. You're it," they cheered.

"All right. But take off your clothes. I'll hide them. You have to find them and put them on before I count to ten."

Haley and Logan danced naked around Seth, waving their pajamas high over their heads. He stared at them, smirking. A sinister smirk. I was too stunned to move.

Lela circled around the kids who were blind to the danger. They always ran around the house naked, and Seth was their friend. He brought them his old toys and movies. They trusted him as did Mom and Dad.

A wave of nausea hit. My inner voice became loud and strong. *Protect the kids!* it screamed.

Seth grabbed their clothes and raced out of the room. "Wait there," he called out.

His voice ignited my senses. The peril throbbed in every strand of my fur, and the smell of danger roused my latent instincts.

"Come and find them," Seth called to them from upstairs. "I'll give you a hint. They're in your rooms."

The kids bounded past me. They skipped up the stairs with Lela and me following close behind. Seth waited in the hall. Lela and I pushed past him and positioned ourselves in front of the kids' rooms. Our hackles were up and ears pulled back. Our wide, round eyes glared at him, daring him to move forward as Haley and Logan searched enthusiastically for their pajamas.

He knew we were watching him, and he was nervous. Tiny beads of sweat formed on his brow. He chewed his lower lip, the end of his tongue was visible. He took a half step toward Haley's room.

A low, slow snarl resonated from Lela's taut lips. She drew back her muzzle and exposed her canines. Her weight shifted over her hind legs.

The show of aggressiveness startled Seth, and he slowly stepped backwards. He was edgy. His fingers drummed on the stair rail behind him.

I smelled his fear. The smell bolstered my own courage. "Get back," I growled, moving towards him. "Back," I warned with wrinkled muzzle. My own canines glistening.

Seth turned and quickly fled down the stairs. "I'll be in your parents' room." His voice trailed behind. My eyes followed him until he was out of sight. Only then did I exhale.

"I got 'em! I got 'em!" Logan ran past me, flailing pajamas in hand, and barged into Haley's room. The kids were safe and happy.

"I knew you had it in you," Lela said softly as she smiled upon the kids. I stored her accolade within my heart.

The kids dressed, and the four of us made our way to Mom and Dad's room. They bounced along cheerfully, unaware of what had transpired.

Seth looked uneasily at Lela and me when we entered. His voice cracked when he spoke. "Good job. You found them. Now here's a quarter for each of you. So don't tell your mom and dad we stayed up late playing our game. OK?"

The kids toppled into bed. They'd played hard, and the fatigue quickly set in. Seth waited until they settled under the covers before turning out the lights. The kids fell asleep not long before 9:30 p.m. Lela laid with them, and I kept watch by the bedroom door. Adrenaline kept me alert, and I heard Commander's engine before I saw the headlights bouncing off the walls.

I greeted Mom and Dad by the kitchen door. Seth avoided my scowl and slinked out into the darkness. Dad drove him down the hill and out of town.

I didn't sleep well that night. I shuddered at the images of what might have been. But I knew my inner voice would protect my family if I trusted it. *But how will I warn Mom?* I wondered. There may be a day when neither Lela nor I could intervene. *What then?* I worried. Perhaps I would have slept better that night had I known Haley and Logan would warn their parents themselves.

"We have to tell," Haley whispered to Logan the next morning. "We're not supposed to keep secrets."

Logan shook his head. Doubt shone in his eyes.

"Yes, tell," I barked, stomping my paws trying to get them to listen. "Tell," I barked again.

"What's going on? What are you two chatting about over there?" Dad asked.

Haley and Logan looked down at their feet. Neither would look Dad in the eyes.

"Tell," I howled insistently. I pawed at Logan's leg.

"But Seth paid us twenty-five cents not to tell you about our game," Logan stammered.

Dad looked puzzled. "What game?"

I pushed Haley forward, and the story tumbled out. Logan joined in, and fear settled in Dad's eyes as the details unfolded. His brow wrinkled and his posture became rigid. I sensed he wanted to know more, needed to know exactly what happened, but he resisted the urge to pry. He didn't want to frighten them.

When they finished their tale, Dad knelt down and swept them both into his protective embrace.

"I can't breathe," Haley gasped. Dad gave another quick squeeze and released his hold. Logan blew an exaggerated breath from his lungs.

"You did the right thing telling me. We don't keep secrets. I know you like Seth and you don't want to get him in trouble, but you shouldn't have stayed up so late playing that game, and he shouldn't have paid you to keep a secret like that." Haley and Logan slowly nodded, and he pulled them back into his chest. "I'm glad you told me," he reassured.

He smiled a strained, tight smile. "All right then. Go play with your trains. I need to talk to Mommy." He stood and steadied himself against the wall. I followed him from the room.

"Gwen, where are you? We need to talk."

Mom was in the den checking her e-mails when

he found her. She turned to face him and knew instantly something was wrong.

Dad told her what happened.

She said nothing while he spoke, but the color drained from her face. Her shoulders and head sank into her chest. Her hands covered her mouth and nose. She looked as though she was praying.

"Oh my God," she wailed when he finished. Tears flowed uncontrollably. "Did he hurt them? Did he touch them?" She rocked slowly, back and forth, in the chair. Her arms wrapped tightly around her stomach. She leaned forward and retched.

"No," I barked. "He didn't touch them," I told her. But she didn't understand my words. Ambiguous howls were all she heard.

Dad reached for the phone. "Neal's an adolescent psychiatrist. Maybe he can tell us what to do. I don't want to scare the kids. Right now the only thing they think Seth did wrong was tell them to keep a secret. They're not otherwise acting differently."

Mom worried as she waited for the call to end. Seconds felt like hours. Minutes like days. I placed my chin on her lap to comfort her. Her tears ran down my muzzle. "I wish you could tell me what happened." She choked on the words.

"Me too," I whined.

"Neal said to remain calm and see if we can learn more about the game without asking for specific details. Let them do the talking. He said we could try asking if Seth tickled them and then just see what happens. Watch them for any behavioral changes."

Mom nodded numbly.

"Gwen." Dad drew in his breath before continuing. "He also said we should consider reporting it to the police." He stepped gingerly toward her.

"The police?" Her puffy, swollen eyes shot up at him. He froze next to her. "But they're going to ask the kids all sorts of questions and make them feel dirty. Like they did something wrong. I don't want them to feel like that." She gagged on her sobs. Her breathing grew hoarse.

Dad placed his hands firmly on her shoulders so she could regain her balance.

"No, Raj. You don't understand. I sensed something was wrong with him, and I did nothing. I let him into our home. I did this!" she cried. "I did this. I'm supposed to protect them."

Her physical pain engulfed me. I backed slowly away.

"No, Gwen. We let him into our home." Dad grabbed her hands between his. "Honey, I really don't think he touched them. The kids are acting fine. They're worried about staying up past bedtime. Not the game." His voice was convincing. He was the source of strength she needed him to be.

"Thank God they told us, Gwen." He kissed her hands. "We must be doing something right." He swallowed hard and brushed her tear-streaked cheeks.

She looked deep into his eyes. She wanted to believe him. But she knew there was no way of ever knowing for certain. She knew she'd have to find a way to live with her suspicions. To assuage the guilt she felt for ignoring her internal voice.

Yet more than suspicion and guilt consumed her. Something else smoldered inside. Just below the surface it hovered. She strained to control it. The exertion made her tremble, and the tears flowed again. Quiet tears. Her body slumped in resignation.

Lela walked in and I turned to her for answers.

"Later," Lela said in a hushed voice as she passed by. Mom reached for her.

"It's all right," Lela whimpered softly. "It's all right."

~Twenty-five~

"I don't understand. There's something else. She's hiding something. Something bad. I can feel it. And when Dad mentioned the police, I felt her panic. You must have seen it. She had that wild, almost crazy, look in her eyes." I paced back and forth.

"Lay down and I'll explain," Lela said sadly.

I plopped down, not caring where I lay. I could tell from Lela's posture that whatever was troubling Mom was serious.

Lela lay down across from me. She closed her eyes and thought hard about what to say and how to say it. Her head bobbed slowly, and her breathing was slow and deliberate. When she opened her eyes, she told me that Mom had been molested as a child. I listened, horrified, as Lela spoke about the betrayal and the emotional scars it left.

Lela explained how Mom grew up feeling dirty and betrayed. Mom figured that if she got too close to someone, they just might find out the ugly truth. She buried the truth and kept people at arm's length. She blocked the memories of her childhood from her mind. She pretended her life was perfect. That lie became her reality. She had to be perfect at everything. School. Sports. Work. Perfection became her obsession. Awards, plaques, titles, and certificates of accomplishments littered the attic. Yet this strength became her weakness. It made her fragile, susceptible to breaking, and falling apart.

"I wasn't there when it happened, of course. But

I was there when Mom went into therapy. It was before Haley was born. Mom needed to make sure the past was behind her before she had children. It was a painful process but something she had to do. Mom had to confront her past. Move beyond it and accept that she didn't have to be perfect. She needed to know that it was all right for her to make mistakes. She didn't want her children believing that they had to be perfect. She couldn't do that to them. It was too great a burden."

"So that's why Mom and the kids say that no one's perfect except for God."

Lela nodded slowly.

These revelations explained so much. I knew it was hard for Mom to trust people. She was still coming to terms with her own limitations. The Seth incident exposed the scars. The insecurities she suppressed over the years began to bubble and blister. They mixed with new betrayals and guilt. Mom was close to snapping.

She needed to watch the kids. She needed to look for any sign that might indicate the unthinkable had happened. She wouldn't entrust that responsibility to anyone but herself. She had to protect them. She had to protect them from everything that she possibly could.

An outsider would have thought she acted unreasonably. But Dad said nothing when she fired Ruth and told her boss, Phillip, she couldn't leave the kids anymore. Lucky for Mom, Phillip needed her and agreed she could work from home three days a week. The other two days she commuted but was home before the kids' school bus arrived. She cut back to a thirty-hour workweek.

"I don't know who to trust anymore," she shared
with Lara, her dearest friend. "I can't keep doing this.
It's not worth it. In the last two years we've had three
sitters. I let these strangers into my home. God only
knows what happens when I'm not here. Now Seth. I
can't believe I was so stupid."

For the first time since their births, she was both
mother and sitter. She drove the kids to school and
picked them up afterwards. She took them to their after-
school activities and packed their lunches. She washed,
folded, and showed the kids how to help put away
laundry. She arranged their playdates and monitored
homework. She read to them and they read to her. The
kitchen filled with arts and crafts projects. All the things
the sitters had done she now did for them while
watching over them. She hovered over them like a
hawk.

Each night, after Haley and Logan were safely
tucked into bed, Mom would check her e-mails and tend
to anything her boss needed tending to before Dad came
home. Often, she'd work well after he'd gone to bed.
She was tired. But tired was good. She was too tired to
wrestle her demons. In an odd way, the exhaustion
restored her stability. She slowly regained control.

The effects of the Seth incident faded gradually
as the weeks passed. Time confirmed what Lela and I
couldn't tell Mom in human words. Haley and Logan
were fine. In fact they were better than fine. They
flourished under Mom's watch and care.

Mom listened as they chitchatted endlessly from
the bus stop to home, telling us who did what to whom.

The kids packed their snacks and helped decide the next night's dinner menu. They were responsible for picking up their toys, clearing their plates from the table, and getting themselves showered and into pajamas. Their favorite games were butt bump on the trampoline and nighttime tag. Mom, Lela, and I would chase them from room to room. Their jubilant screams filled the house as they tried to evade the tickle monster. We'd end the day collapsing on Mom's bed, listening to her read aloud from a favored children's series. The thought of human-sized ants frightened me.

Lela and I certainly enjoyed having Mom around too. There was little time for long walks, but we did manage daily jaunts down to the mailbox during her lunch break. If we were lucky, we might run into Bridgette or Ronan. While Mom worked, I lounged under the desk. Her toes mindlessly kneaded my ribs and flank. Lela sprawled out on the carpet just to the right of Mom's chair.

Winter and spring slipped away, and Mom realized she'd need to find someone to help with the kids during their summer vacation. But who? Mom's friends worked. She wasn't about to hire another au pair. The thought of turning to a stranger frightened her.

It was Dad who suggested she talk to Marta.

Marta had been coming on a regular basis to clean the house since my family moved to the lane. Occasionally she would house sit and take care of Lela and me when our family went away. Mom thought Marta was reliable and friendly. A level of trust already existed. She also felt Marta understood children and was confident Marta would know what to do in the event of an emergency. After all, Marta had raised her own son. He was then twenty-one.

Marta picked the kids up from summer camp and watched them for a couple of hours the two days Mom commuted into the office. Marta was full of energy, and the kids liked her. They colored together, played on the trampoline, and made various arts and crafts projects. Marta was always kind to Lela and me, and she made a point of coming early enough to take us for a brief walk before picking up the kids.

After three weeks Mom asked Marta if she could work a couple of extra hours. Marta agreed, and Mom was able to stay at the office longer. Mom was noticeably more relaxed when she came home from work. She was less haggard, and her trust in Marta grew stronger. It was a good thing. Yet Mom didn't want to be separated from the kids. Not unless work demanded it. And work had started to demand it more.

By the end of the summer, Mom contemplated returning to a forty-hour workweek; three full days in the office and two half-days from home. Mom planned on discussing the arrangement with Marta when the family returned from the island the following week. Lela and I weren't allowed at the vacation rental, so Marta stayed with us while our family was away.

~Twenty-six~

The aromatic chicken, rice, and beans simmered on the stove. I hoisted myself up on my hind legs, wondering if I could sneak a taste before Marta came back. But the heat from the range stung the tips of my nose and paws. The fire glowed under the pots. The flames skipped along the bottoms, reaching up the sides.

I was scrounging the floor for any scraps Lela may have missed when Lela first noticed the smell.

"Do you smell that, Shamus? It's a strong, sharp smell and it's getting stronger."

I stopped scouring the floor and turned toward Lela. She stood near the front door. Her stance was strong as her nose combed the air looking for the source of the odor. Her muscles were taut. Concern filled her eyes. She was protecting our home. Protecting Marta and me. My chest swelled with admiration.

I concentrated, inhaling deeply, forcing myself to smell beyond the meal simmering on the stove. Yes, there was an unfamiliar odor. I inhaled again. "I think it's coming from the mudroom."

An old wooden ladder was propped up against the doorway where the stairs leading down to the mudroom would later be. I peered over the edge. Copper and plastic tubing littered the newly cemented floor. I barely noticed the paw prints I left embedded in the cool, coarse mixture days before. Andrew, our contractor, was planning to tape the walls once the plumbing was in place. He'd been at our home just about every day since early spring. He planned to finish his work before Mom, Dad, and the kids returned from vacation.

I stuck my nose through the doorway and inhaled. The acrid smell was definitely strongest in the mudroom. "I wonder what it is?" I asked aloud.

"I don't know. But I started smelling it soon after Marta turned on the stove. It was faint and familiar. But it's definitely getting stronger. Much stronger."

Marta's footsteps echoed above our heads. The shower door rattled open, and then the water surged down. We listened as she pulled the shower door closed. The glass doors clattered back into place. Lela left to check on Marta and to see if the smell permeated the upstairs.

That's when I heard it. A rumbling from the mudroom. Then the mighty BOOM!

There was no time to think. No time to react. I thought I was dreaming. I could feel my body being hurled across the kitchen by an invisible force. *But this can't be real. This can't be happening,* I thought.

The force of the explosion engulfed me. It stole my breath. The entire house lurched. I lay frozen on the cool slate as glass rained down around me. Smoke bellowed from the mudroom. My ears were ringing.

I slowly rose, shaking my head, trying to clear my ears and vision. My breath escaped my chest in ragged gasps. "What's happening?" I howled. The story of 9/11 flashed through my mind.

A scream. I heard Marta screaming. The thick smoke burned my eyes. I squinted trying to focus. My ears were still ringing. A form rushed by.

Was that Marta? Follow Marta, I thought. She was running outside. She stumbled. She grabbed her leg. She was on the phone. I circled around her. Terror clung to her as the smoke clung to my fur.

"Where's Lela?" I barked at her. I circled around her, trying to get her attention. But she couldn't hear me.

"Lela," I barked. "Lela. Where are you?" A shard of glass penetrated my paw pad. I yelped in pain.

"Yes. Yes. The lane. Explosion," Marta yelled into the phone. Panic tainted her thick Latino accent. I smelled the blood. I smelled it flowing from her foot. She cut her foot pad too.

Sirens. Loud sirens roared in the distance. They got louder, much louder. Marta moved away from the house. Glass littered the patio and driveway. The big picture windows were gone. Their busted frames lay mangled. Large broken pieces of wood and glass and debris were strewn across the yard.

Marta and I called for Lela. "Lela. Lela," Marta was calling as she backed away toward the corral.

My heart tightened. I had to find Lela. I turned toward the billowing smoke.

"No, Shamus. You stay here. No go inside," Marta said to me. She held my collar tight as I struggled to break free. Her petite frame veiled the strength that prevented me from finding Lela.

A siren screamed as it raced up our driveway. I broke free from Marta's grasp. "Shamus," she yelled after me. But the approaching siren drowned out her voice. The siren's scream swelled in my ears. Lights flashed around me. More sirens followed. The earth trembled under my paws.

Another explosion? I feared. *Run. Run to the woods. It's safe in there,* my inner voice yelled. I ignored the beeping in my collar and charged past the flags. My body trembled from fear and pain. I was alone and frightened. I barked for Lela, but she didn't respond.

I watched from the safety of the woods as huge fire engines plowed up our driveway. An ambulance and a police car followed. So many lights. So much noise. *Lela must be terrified*, I thought. I needed to find her. I needed to make sure she was safe.

Cautiously, I crawled from under the brush. I was about to emerge when a large fire truck screeched to a halt in front of me. It blocked my exit. I inched back. Slowly. Not wanting to be seen. I found shelter behind the woodpile. Firefighters jumped from the engine. They grabbed their axes and began unwinding a fire hose.

"No fire. I extinguished it. Looks like a gas explosion. Started in the mudroom. This way," a man called from the patio. I heard him but I couldn't see him. The engine blocked my view. I watched the firefighters as they headed for our home. I was certain they'd find Lela.

I paced back and forth as more trucks and people came. I cowered behind bushes and trees. I watched as police, firefighters, and news reporters invaded our home. I barked. But no one heard me. I inched my way closer, careful not to get too close to the flags. My body had felt enough pain for one night.

I perched myself on a rock ledge overlooking the corral. The same ledge the kids sled down in winter. From there I could see above the fire trucks and emergency crews. I saw Owen and Ronan. They were with Seth's mom. Then Seth emerged from the shadows. He stood behind his mother. He placed a large flashlight in his sweatshirt pocket.

My hackles stood erect. A low, gurgling snarl escaped my parched throat. *Seth shouldn't be here*, I seethed. *He isn't welcome.* For the first time in my young life, I felt the urge to lunge for the jugular. My body shuddered at the thought of acting on my primal instincts. Instincts that had supposedly been bred out of me.

"They're on vacation. Yeah. I have their number." Owen spoke to a police officer about my family. The police officer moved off into the distance. He talked to someone else, but I couldn't tell who. I couldn't make out what they were saying. My eyes still burned. My body ached. The ringing in my ears remained.

I saw Marta. Marta was in the ambulance. She was sitting on the edge while a woman tended to her wounded foot. A police officer questioned Marta. I saw her shaking her head. He was writing in a notebook. Then the ambulance took her away.

The throbbing in my own paw pad intensified. The glass shard moved deeper into my pad with every step I took. I had to get it out before it got wedged too far in.

My hind end stung when I lowered my weight onto it. My shoulders screamed when I lifted my paw to inspect the wound. The bleeding had stopped long before. Mud and dried leaves had mixed with my blood to form a scab. I licked the dirty, crusty blood. I peeled away the dirty scab, layer by layer until fresh, warm, sticky blood began to flow. The pressure in my pad eased. My tongue and flowing blood worked together to dislodge the broken piece of glass.

A familiar face made me pause. Winston, a stock English bulldog, pulled his human along. We didn't see Winston often. He and his family lived at the other end of the lane. "Has anyone seen the dogs?" his human, Nate, asked Owen and a police officer.

"One's in the woods," the officer told him. His flashlight scanned the property. It was a blinding light. I crouched close to the earth. I didn't want to be seen. I didn't want to be taken away. I wanted to remain hidden until Lela or Mom came for me.

"The female's inside. A firefighter found her wedged under a couch," he told Nate.

The dread inside my body lifted. Lela was safe.

"Let me take her. She and Winston can hang out until Raj gets back. I talked to him. They're catching the first ferry out tomorrow. They should be here around noon," Nate said.

That's when I saw her. Lela. A firefighter led her down the stone pathway. She carried her head and tail low. Nate went to her. He knelt beside her and gently stroked her head. She lifted her chin up towards him and waved her tail slightly. Winston moved close to comfort her.

Lela was alive. Shaken up a bit but seemingly unscathed.

"I'm here, Lela," I barked. But she couldn't hear me. She was too far away. I watched her glance nervously around the yard. She was looking into the woods. She was looking for me when Nate attached a leash to her and led her away. Owen and Ronan joined them.

"I'll come back and look for Shamus," Owen said. "He'll probably come out once things settle down." The five of them disappeared down the driveway. I was too frightened to follow. Drained. Exhausted and spent.

Time stood still. The surrounding scene felt surreal. Like I was a spectator in someone else's dream.

People invaded the broken home. They ran in and out carefully avoiding the shattered glass. Pounding. Lots of pounding. Sheets of plastic. They hung sheets of plastic over the empty window frames.

"We've secured the premises. All utilities have been shut off," one officer reported to another. I could smell their sweat and fatigue.

"OK. We're done here. I've spoken to the owners. They'll be here sometime tomorrow afternoon. Any sign of the other dog?"

"No. But I heard him barking in the woods earlier. One of the neighbors said he'll come back up once we clear out."

"Poor guy."

Voices echoed down the lane. They realized they were trapped. There was nowhere to go. Nowhere to turn their vehicles around. They were forced to wait.

Voices faded in and out over radios and walkie-talkies. The officers talked into their shirts.

Truck doors banged. An idle engine awakened, then another, and another, and another. A rumbling resonated down the lane. The engines bellowed as they backed slowly down our driveway. The eerie glows grew dim. One by one the trucks disappeared. One by one the lights went out.

The large plastic sheets rustled lightly in the summer breeze.

The cool, soft moss welcomed my weary limbs.

Everything began to fade.

~Twenty-seven~

"Shamus. Come here, Shamus."

Soft, distant voices beckoned me.

Wake up. Wake up, I told myself. But my eyes refused to open.

"Shamus."

The voices grew louder. My eyelids fluttered as they adjusted to the light. Soft light. Soft moonlight filtered through the trees.

I stretched out my legs and licked my dry lips. I listened to the rustling leaves aware of the stiffness that plagued my body.

"Shamus," a tiny voice whispered in my ear. The gentle purr lulled me.

A warm breath of wind brushed past my muzzle. I thought I might be dreaming.

"Shamus," the little voice uttered again. My heavy head turned toward the soft, tranquil sound.

Two small sparkling eyes met mine.

My breath raced ahead as I jumped to my paws. The creature stepped gracefully to the side. My eyes hadn't yet adjusted fully to the moon's light. They throbbed with the beating of my heart. Still burning from the smoke.

"Don't be alarmed. It's me, Shamus. Emi. They're looking for you."

"What?" I stammered, catching my breath. But she dashed off into the night before I could speak another word. Her tail flicked the dangling leaves as she skirted under the low laying limbs. She disappeared into the shadows.

She's safe. Everyone's safe. My heart lightened and the aching in my limbs eased.

"Shamus," a distant voice called. A beam of light stretched up the driveway. It wiggled its way around the bend.

"Shamus. Come here, Shamus." I recognized Owen's voice.

"Up here," I barked excitedly.

Ronan heard me. "Over there," he barked, turning in my direction.

Nadine's flashlight followed Ronan's gaze. The beam silently scanned the woods looking for me.

I paced around, back and forth, side to side. A twig cracked under my paw. A small flag staked in the ground warned me that my boundary was near.

"Here," I barked again.

The bright beam blinded me.

"Come on, Shamus. It's OK. You can come out now." Owen's voice was calm and steady. His silhouette advanced slowly, carefully making its way up the embankment. The light radiating behind him reminded me of Grammy's God. The God who stood with opened arms, wearing a halo, surrounded by a luminous light. It was Grammy's favorite picture, and it hung in her dining room.

I smelled liver biscotti. Nadine made the best liver biscotti. My stomach growled. It'd been hours since I'd eaten. I tiptoed closer toward Owen and the biscotti.

The small flag snapped to attention. My body

tightened, anticipating the warning hum and the electric pulse that would stun my body. I hesitated.

"Shamus, it's safe," Ronan barked.

The biscotti's smell hung in the air, and I began feeling light-headed. I thought about Lela and my family. My legs grew weak.

"It's OK, Shamus. It's OK," Owen assured me with extended arms.

I took a deep breath, gathered my strength and lunged forward into the light.

"Whoa!" Owen yelled as our bodies collided. The air sprang from his lungs, and we tumbled down to the corral. I lay sprawled across his chest when the night above stopped spinning.

No hum, no electric pulse. Only Owen and the liver biscotti he still clenched in his hand.

I lifted myself up over him and licked his soiled face. The biscotti tumbled to the ground, and I helped myself to it.

"Are you all right?" Nadine asked, rushing forward.

"Fine. Fine," Owen said, wiggling himself out from under me. He reached for his cap and brushed the earth from his jeans. I jumped and circled around him. He held me steady under Nadine's light and moved his hands gently over my body.

"I don't feel any injuries," he said patting my side. "Let's get him home and call Raj. They'll be glad to know he's OK."

The moon's light bathed us in its soft glow as we headed down the driveway. My laden steps led the

way, guided by Nadine's beam of light. All was
peaceful around me. Tranquility filled the lane. Fireflies
danced above us, and the frogs and katydids resumed
their mating choruses. The evening breeze felt good.
The fresh air cleansed my lungs and spirit.

I greedily ate the food Nadine offered and
quenched my thirst with cool water. My tail sounded out
my gratitude, and I licked her kind hands. The ringing in
my ears grew less noticeable. My vision cleared and the
burning faded.

"What a night for you," Nadine said as she
stroked my back and checked my body for visible
injuries. Her touch was delicate and soothing.

"That doesn't look so bad," she said, inspecting
my injured paw. She carefully tended the wound. The
ointment relieved the throbbing. "Come on. Let's go see
what Ronan's up to."

We found Owen and Ronan stretched across a
bed with the TV on in the background. Owen rubbed
Ronan's side, and Nadine took her place next to them.
The scene sparked a deep aching. It was more than a
physical pain. It was a profound emotional longing, and
the intensity astounded me.

I searched the room for a place to hide. A small
quiet corner where I could curl up and wait out the
night. But Ronan was a keen dog. He sensed my
suffering and hopped off the bed to console me.

"Everyone's OK, Shamus. You'll be reunited
with your family tomorrow." Compassion poured from
his eyes, and he faintly patted my shoulder. His light
touch and concern released the strain from my body. My

mood lifted, and the tension slipped slowly away.

"Lela's at Winston's. She's fine and knows you're OK. She was worried about you."

I breathed in, feeling comforted and secure. I exhaled, releasing the worry.

"What happened?" I wanted to know.

"A gas explosion. It was the propane tank." His eyes looked deep into mine. "You were lucky. Both of you," he added.

I nodded my head. *I am lucky,* I thought to myself. Lucky indeed to have a loving family and good, kind friends.

Thankfulness smothered my lingering anxiety. My bruised muscles grew nimble. A smile stretched across my face, and energy returned to my body.

Ronan sensed my risen spirit. He felt the joy that stirred my being.

"You get to stay here tonight," he said, prancing around playfully. "You don't snore, do you?" His eyes sparkled with mischief.

"No, but I fart in my sleep," I teased. My strength and resolve restored.

"Guess we can't let you sleep then!" he howled invitingly, leaping onto the bed. Owen rolled quickly out of the way.

I sprang into the air filled with elation. "Guess not!" I called chasing after him.

"It's gonna be a long night," Nadine speculated as we sailed over her.

~Twenty-eight~

"Ready to go home?" Dad asked Mom, stretching out next to her. The old bedsprings squeaked beneath him. The night was otherwise void of recognizable song.

"Yes," she muttered drowsily, sinking deep into him. He pulled the covers around them both, and his arms engulfed her protectively.

I quietly cheered as they slipped into slumber. The schlepping back and forth was over. We were moving back to the lane after spending two weeks with Dad's parents. It'd been a long, unsettling two weeks since the explosion. I was eager to return to the mundane routines that grounded me.

It was the first time I'd met NuNu and PaPa. Lela said they didn't visit often, and she warned me to keep calm in their presence. Though they were fearful of the dogs that ran wild in India, Lela had patiently proved herself a trusted companion. NuNu and PaPa were fond of her but wary of me during our first encounter. I heeded Lela's advice and kept my paws anchored, and they grew more comfortable with me as each day passed.

NuNu was a short, round woman whose bangles clattered when she patted my head. Her wrists smelled like sandalwood and her oily black hair like coconut. PaPa was a tall, lean man with a gentle touch. I recognized their faces from the photos Mom kept in the den. I couldn't understand their thick accents, so I wagged my tail and smiled when I thought they were addressing me.

Their house was large and filled with the pungent smells of exotic spices and incense. The sharp scents filled my nostrils and permeated my fur and skin. I could taste the distinct, foreign aromas, but they became less noticeable with time. And there was room for all of us. Plenty of room to wander and play. Haley and Logan practiced their soccer skills in a large finished basement.

Only Emi stayed behind. I often wondered how she was coping, but I knew she was fine. Her food dish was empty when we arrived at the lane each morning. Haley always inquired about Emi, and she was happy knowing that Emi was safe at home.

Though NuNu and PaPa were caring and jovial, I missed the comforts of my home. We all missed home. Logan wanted his train and race car tracks, and Haley wanted playdates with Molly.

Mom took an unpaid leave of absence from work to tend to our family and to mend herself. The culminating stress from the events of that year proved too much. She wasn't able to juggle work, family demands, and the cleanup, so she took a leave despite her boss's efforts to keep her engaged. He called no less than three times each day. Unsympathetic to what our family was going through. He had his own ring tone, and Mom cringed each time it sounded.

School had resumed and Mom drove the kids in each morning. She then began the painful process of restoring our home. Lela and I stayed out of her way. We kept watch on the patio.

Members from Owen's church had joined Andrew and his men in cleaning up the broken glass before Mom, Dad, and the kids returned from the island. So it was, for the most part, safe to wander about. But we had to be careful. Splinters of glass lay buried under the gravel. Shards would surface for years to come.

Mom spent her days cleaning and organizing. The firefighters had left holes in the walls, and the contents of our closets lay scattered around the floor. The attic door lay propped up against the hallway wall. Sooty footprints crisscrossed the floors and carpets. Dust covered the furniture and walls.

Tears rolled down Mom's face when she hung the fallen wall hangings and tapestries. She wanted our home restored as quickly as possible. She didn't want the kids to be afraid. She didn't want to be afraid. Our home was their place of refuge.

"The insurance company will pay for cleaners," Dad told her.

"Yeah, but not until after all the utilities are on and inspections finished," Mom answered. "Besides it's good for me."

Cleaning was therapeutic for Mom despite the absence of water and electricity. Every day she armed herself with her Swiffers, broom, rags, trash bags, and other cleaning supplies. Cleaning centered her, and she drew strength from the visible accomplishments she made each day. She was upbeat and positive when she picked the kids up at school. The hour-long car ride to NuNu's didn't feel so long.

One by one the inspectors came. Water and

electricity were restored, and it was time to move back in.

The kids were unafraid when we returned. Ignorant of all the damage and details. They slept soundly in their own beds. Surrounded by all things familiar and cherished.

It took more time for the rest of us though. Lela made extra rounds during the night, and Mom and Dad inventoried the work remaining. They relaxed more as the items on the list dwindled. As they relaxed, so did Lela and I.

Mom placed my new pillow next to Dad's side of the bed and left my crate open. My sanctuary had stayed on the lane while we were at NuNu's. I missed it terribly at first but found comfort sleeping near Dad. Lela welcomed my nighttime presence, and I felt safe. I relied less on my crate when we returned to the lane. It no longer steadied me as it had before. It seemed small and confining.

I chose my new pillow.

"He's graduated from his crate," Mom praised. Lela too looked pleased. My second birthday had come and gone. I'd be three in the spring. I hadn't chewed a rug in months, and I'd tempered my other compulsions. I couldn't quell the pride swelling in my chest.

I relished my new independence. It settled me. The new dog door and fenced-in run allowed me to sun myself during the day and fill my lungs with the crisp night air as I pleased. The day was vibrant and alive. The night was quiet and calm. I immersed myself in the two different worlds. Found delight in their distinctions.

The outdoors was rejuvenating.

Mom worried less about Lela and me. Our freedom liberated her too.

She worked side by side with Andrew to repair the visible lesions the explosion had left. Windows were replaced, cracks were filled, the roof repaired, and the house repainted inside and out.

The restoration left Mom exhausted, but Lara's company renewed her energy. Her presence was always uplifting. That day was no different as the two friends glided back and forth on the outdoor rocker. Their children ignored them. Content to jump on the trampoline. Haley and Logan were happy to have Alisa and Teo with them. Their laughter brought life back to the lane.

"What caused it?" Lara wanted to know. She had missed her dear friend. I saw it in her eyes as the two of them conspired over their mugs of steaming tea.

"A leak. A small leak. A spark from the hot water tank ignited the gas." Mom's voice was tinged with anger and frustration.

"No flips, Logan!" she hollered out.

Lela's head shot up from the grass. She looked around with startled eyes and wrinkled brow.

"Everything's all right," I reassured her. "Logan was about to flip on the trampoline." Lela's hearing wasn't the same since the explosion. An intermittent ringing plagued her ears. Some days were worse than others.

"He's gonna break his neck," Lela mumbled.

It was something Mom would say. Something

Mom said numerous times before. She never wanted the trampoline. Dad did.

Lela snorted when I chuckled and stretched her lean legs out in front of her. She yawned and rested her head gently on the cool grass. A soft snore escaped her lips moments later, and her tongue rolled out of her mouth. It slipped through the empty space where her canine tooth used to be. It broke during the explosion when her body was thrown against the hallway wall. The vet couldn't save it.

I lounged in the warm gravel, watching and listening. Playing sentry while Lela rested.

"What did Marta have to say about it?" Lara asked.

"She doesn't recall smelling anything unusual." Mom exhaled noisily before continuing. "She was pretty shaken up. But still . . . I don't know why she would leave food cooking on an open flame while she went upstairs to shower. What if the gas had infiltrated the main floor and hit the flames? What if the kids had been with her?" Mom shuddered. Lara remained silent, watching Mom shake her head disapprovingly.

I felt sad for Marta. She would never hurt our family. She'd always been kind. The explosion was an accident. No one was to blame. Still I knew Marta was gone from our lives, and I'd never see her again. Mom no longer trusted her.

A familiar ache returned to my chest.

"What about Haley and Logan? Are they all right?" Lara asked. The steam from her soy chai latte circled around the long strand of silky dark hair that cascaded down the side of her cup.

Laughter resonated around the yard, drowning out Lela's faint snores. Only the sporadic gaggles of honking geese that flew above us obscured the hysterical fits and screams of glee.

"I think they're fine. We're watching them, and we've asked their teachers to let us know if they see any changes in behavior." Mom's mood lightened and she cracked a grin. "They're both writing about the explosion. It's a hot topic!" She laughed with Lara at the joke. My spirits lifted too.

Yes, the kids were fine. Mom shielded them. They remained blissfully unaware of all the peril. They were delightfully naïve, filled with youthful resilience and optimism.

I quietly thanked Grammy's God and breathed in the crisp, cleansing air. The late afternoon sun bounced off the leaves that had already changed their hues in preparation for winter. A stirring breeze snatched dying leaves from limbs and dropped them on the yard. The potted mums stood hardy and rigid. They would not bend or sway.

Mom and Lara shuddered and cupped their warm mugs tighter against their chests. "And you?" Lara asked her friend. "How's work?"

"Oh fine. Phillip's Phillip and Valerie's Valerie. Phillip could care less that my house blew up, and Valerie's disappointed I'm back." Mom chuckled and sipped from her mug.

She resumed working a few days after we returned to the lane. She became more edgy and irritable. Phillip's reaction to the explosion left her bitter. He focused his attentions on making the department more profitable, yet he failed to see it was falling apart. He failed to see that Mom was falling apart despite her best efforts to keep everything together.

Phillip had unwittingly betrayed Mom, and Valerie waited patiently for her to implode. Valerie wanted to make partner. Only Mom stood in her way. But Mom was too tired to spar. Drained by months of fatigue. Paralyzed by her exhumed insecurities.

Immediate change was unthinkable.

Concealed wounds needed to heal.

~Twenty-nine~

The radiators awoke earlier than usual. They hissed at the cold morning air. A clink in one room was followed by a clank in another. I listened to them moaning. They warned that winter was near. I snuggled deeper into my pillow. I waited for the warmth that would soon radiate from the heater behind me.

I listened to Mom and Dad stir. They rustled under their covers, burrowing themselves into the plush feathered comforter. Their soft, rhythmic breathing let me know they were still sleeping. I chuckled when I remembered the first comforter they had to replace. I could still see the feathers floating above their heads.

It was an auspicious morning, as NuNu might say. The stars had faded and the morning sky prepared itself for the day. The hues turned from dark to gray. The lighter hues slowly nudged the darker, colder hues from the sky. The heat and light vanquished the frigid night. An owl hooted "good day" in the distance. But there were no other sounds outside. The world still slept.

Lela still slept. She lay curled up tightly on the pillow Mom placed near the radiator. Lela favored that spot when the nights grew cold. "The cold settles in my lower back and hips," she told me. But the radiator's heat soothed her aging limbs.

Behind her the steam sputtered. Lela stretched her legs out in front of her. Her muzzle twitched. She snored, then whimpered. She was dreaming. I wondered what she dreamed about. Her front paw bobbed up and down. The suddenness of it startled me. Then I noticed the abundance of light fur that padded her paws and shins. Her aging face glowed in the dawn's light. The light furry mask wrapped farther around her face than it had the year before. Her muzzle and eyes were now almost completely covered in the white fur. I had sprung into adolescence, while Lela slid further into her senior years.

An unexpected boom bellowed from the radiator behind me. The floor beneath me shivered. The warm steam hissed as it coursed through the heater's thick, iron veins. I stretched across my pillow, bothered by my revelation. My body welcomed the radiator's warmth. The heat eased my hurting spirit.

The last bang awakened Mom. I heard her before I saw her head pop up from under the covers. She sat facing her clock. It read 6:25. She yawned and stretched and peered over the edge of the bed. Her eyes scanned the floor. She spotted Lela asleep near the heater. Mom's eyes turned to me, and she returned my smile. "Morning, Shamus," she whispered. My tail thumped against my pillow. Its tip grazed the warm radiator.

From the corner of my eye, I saw Lela's body shift. I glanced over to see that her eyes had opened. She smacked her lips and pushed herself up over her front paws. Her butt stretched high into the air. She kicked her back legs out, one at a time. Her joints and the wooden floors creaked in unison. She yawned and then trotted over to Mom. Mom accepted Lela's butterfly kiss. "Morning, Miss Lela," Mom said tenderly. Her hand moved slowly around the soft muzzle.

"Ready for our morning walk?" Mom asked us. We smiled and shook our heads and tails approvingly. She let out a quiet laugh and discarded her pajamas for more suitable clothing.

We started our early morning jaunts after the gas explosion. The same time every day while Dad and the kids still slept. Mom liked to jog through the woods while Lela and I meandered about. The exercise cleared Mom's head and strengthened her body. The quiet, morning woods brought her much-needed solace.

That morning was no different. I took the lead as we moved down our driveway. Our breath was visible in the cold morning air. Just as I passed the steepest part of our driveway, I heard Lela stumble behind me. Her nails scraped loudly against the asphalt. I looked to see her hind end dragging. She struggled to lift herself up, but her rear leg was stiff and unyielding. I cried silently for her.

Mom rushed over and gently lifted Lela's rear legs. She positioned them carefully under Lela's hips and gently massaged the aching hind end. Lela's face was stoic, but Mom's eyes captured the pain.

Lela caught me staring. Her eyes commanded me to keep walking. My legs felt heavy as I moved forward slowly, reluctantly, but still watching. I saw the tension in Lela's hips respond to Mom's fingers. Mobility returned to the aching joints. Relief washed over Mom's face as Lela's rigid stance softened.

Lela's wagging tail showed her gratitude. But

her tail hung low. *When did that happen?* I wondered. Lela could no longer raise her tail. It wagged slowly, its tip only inches above the ground. Another pang.

Mom smiled a tight smile as she watched Lela trot down the driveway. The sadness lingered in her eyes, and her smile faded. She started a slow, steady jog. Much slower than usual.

"She needs to accept my aging," Lela said softly.

I knew Lela was right and that I too needed to accept her aging. There was nothing I could do, so I turned and followed her into the woods. Mom hung back. I felt her eyes upon us. Her stride was heavy and her breathing labored. I suspected she was crying, but I didn't look back. That morning I stayed near Lela and she stayed ahead of Mom.

When we returned, Mom told Dad about Lela's stumble.

"I think they dislocated her hip when they extracted her tooth. Her hips haven't been right since she came back from the vet. It's as if her hip came out of its socket because once I steadied her and massaged it, she was able to keep on trotting. It can't be from her arthritis alone," Mom sighed. "I think I'm going to start taking her to Dr. Kagan. He's been very good with Shamus, and it's easier than taking her to White Plains."

The pain returned to Mom's eyes. She couldn't bear watching Lela's body yield to its maturity. I couldn't help wondering who was hurting more, Lela from the arthritis that she lived with for years or Mom's heart from having to watch her beloved Lela grow old more quickly than she could bear.

Dad reached out for her. "She's getting older, hon. She's twelve now. If you think Dr. Kagan is just as good, then I agree it makes sense to start bringing her to him. He's definitely more convenient, and things may not get better for her. We knew these things would start to happen eventually," he said compassionately.

"I know. I know. I never thought that she'd be with us this long, and I'm grateful for every day. I just hate watching her slow down." She choked on the tears that gathered in her eyes. Dad leaned in close and hugged her. Lela rubbed her muzzle against Mom's thigh.

"Look at me. How silly is this. I'm crying when you're right here, alive and well." Mom knelt down to embrace Lela. "I'll call the office and see that Lela's files are sent to Dr. Kagan." Mom wiped her eyes and stood to face Dad.

"Hey, what do you think about spending Thanksgiving in New Hampshire?" she asked. "Nadine said we could bring the dogs."

"Won't your family be upset?"

"I just need time away from all of this." She looked pensively around the room. "No drama. Just quiet, family time."

~Thirty~

"You should get some rest, Shamus. It's gonna be a long weekend," Lela warned. "There won't be any time for napping."

I'd been much too excited to sleep. I stayed awake watching the clock's numbers change as the night dragged on. We were leaving first thing in the morning, yet morning felt so far away. It wasn't until the early hours of dawn that I drifted off. But it was not a fitful sleep. It was plagued by dreams that I'd been left behind.

"Come on, Shamus. Out of the car," Dad griped. His arms loaded with baggage. "I need to pack up the back," he strained with winded lungs. His breath was visible in the frosty air.

He'll just have to pack around me, I thought, inching farther back into Commander. I wouldn't be left behind. It was, after all, my first family vacation.

"Aw, let him be." Mom reached in and played with my ears. "At least he won't get into trouble if he stays in the car," she teased while laying my pillow next to Lela's. They fit nicely in Commander, nestled side by side.

A mighty heave and grunt sent bags spewing. Commander shifted under the extra weight, and Dad arranged the bags behind me. His elbow shoved my bottom to the side. I avoided eye contact and nudged over. The pressure in my bladder swelled.

The kids dashed back and forth with their belongings. Logan stuffed the seat back with books and games and whatnots, along with special snacks Mom had bought. Logan had always been a hoarder. A collector of unusual objects like screws and Snapple caps, broken electronics and old remote-controlled cars. He was a master at repackaging and spent hours using duct tape to piece together his inventions. Mom was convinced he was going to be an engineer.

"What on earth are you packing?" Dad huffed and puffed while tightening the dog gate. The bags were barricaded behind it. "We're only going for three nights," he hollered after Logan as he scampered back towards the house. Dad shook the gate to make sure it would hold. He hopped out the back and disappeared into the house.

I grew anxious waiting. My bladder was more than full and the increasing pressure excruciating. I tiptoed to the tailgate and peered around to make sure no one was near. Relief streamed from beneath my lifted leg. The warm urine steamed when it hit the cold air and splashed against the pebbles below. I hurried back to my pillow and eagerly waited.

Dad returned shortly carrying Lela in his arms. She looked uncomfortable when he set her on the pillow. Self-conscious of her aging hips. Still she never complained. She accepted Mom and Dad's help graciously. I turned my gaze toward the kids to avoid embarrassing her further. They jumped in their seats and buckled in. Their excitement was palpable, and I knew it was time to leave.

The car ride to Freedom was long. I envied Lela who slept through the journey. She was skillful at snoozing during any trip, long or short. I wished I could sleep, but I was too excited.

I passed the time watching the buildings grow fewer and farther apart. I counted dogs in cars and pretended to know where each was going. I marveled at the tall mountains and imagined myself running through the vast forests that stretched on either side of the highway. I could almost smell the pine and feel the soft needles under my paws. I listened as the kids played a game they called "twenty questions." My muscles grew stiff and sore.

"Feel that chill?" Mom asked the kids when we stopped to stretch our legs. "You may want to put your jackets on. It's only gonna get colder."

I drew in the chilly air and stretched my spine and neck. I shook each leg and felt the tension in my joints and muscles ease. My stomach grumbled, and Mom offered Lela and me fresh water and chicken treats. I felt refreshed.

Haley and Logan pretended not to hear Mom, but she ignored the silent protest. Her mood was light, and her body relaxed as the kids counted down the miles to Freedom. The changing odometer ushered in relief. Mom was glad to leave the lane behind. She was, for the weekend, free of the stresses the year had brought.

"I think this is it!" Mom called out when we pulled alongside a large log cabin. Nadine's family had built it as a summer home decades before.

"Where's the snow?" Logan asked, bouncing in his seat. His energy matched my own. Neither of us wanted to be contained.

The locks clicked open, releasing a flurry of excitement that rippled through my body. My legs quivered as Dad lifted the hatch. I dug my back paws in and launched myself up and over the tailgate. My nails scraped loudly against the paint. "Shamus!" Dad scolded, dropping the tailgate and reaching in for Lela.

I inhaled deeply. I never knew air could taste so sweet and pure.

"To be young again," Lela murmured as Dad gently placed her next to me. I nuzzled up against her and she grinned. She was stiff, but as she stretched and inhaled, the miles fell from her aching limbs and she trotted into the woods to relieve herself.

The house was just as Ronan had said it would be. Plush area rugs adorned the floors. Floral paintings decorated the walls. Richly upholstered furniture crowded the rooms, and a huge wood-burning stove stood at its core. The stove heated the house, and Dad quickly fired it up. The surroundings stimulated my senses.

"Is this where we're staying?" Mom asked the kids as she dropped two bags next to a chair. Although the fabric seat was faded and the wood worn, it was a sturdy chair that welcomed a third bag without creaking. Haley and Logan had already scouted out the cabin and chose a bedroom that would fit us all. They liked sleeping near Mom and Dad.

"I'm sleeping here!" Haley exclaimed while jumping on the bed's mattress. The squeaking springs joined the merriment. "Logan wants that bed. You and Dad can sleep over there." Her words surged out intermittently between ragged breaths.

"All right. But how about we not jump on the beds? We don't want to break anything," Mom warned as she and Lela headed down the hall.

The three of us listened as their steps drifted off. Lela's clicking nails grew quiet, and Logan hurled himself on to Haley's bed. The two of them laughed while spinning and jumping in circles. I didn't wait for an invitation to join. I jumped up next to them, and we bounced around kicking up covers.

"Guys, off the bed!" Mom's firm voice startled us for we hadn't heard her coming. Lela shook her head reproachfully when she saw the condition of the beds. I knew better but, oh, what fun!

"Come on, off," Mom repeated. She laid my pillow between their beds. "You too, Shamus," she added. I lowered my gaze and hopped down, though I knew from her demeanor she wasn't angry. It was Thanksgiving and there was so much to be thankful for.

The right side of Lela's lip lifted and the crack of a smirk appeared.

Mom's eyes shone bright as she mustered the kids. "Come on now. Daddy's waiting. How about we do a little exploring in town and find a place that serves turkey dinner?" The mention of dinner rallied my saliva. Drops pooled on the floor.

"Sorry, Shamus. You and Lela have to wait here." My disappointment was short-lived however. It disappeared with my kibble. Mom dressed it with canned turkey and vegetables and dribbled chicken gravy over the top. The combination was scrumptious, and she waited outside the bathroom door while I devoured every piece. I lapped at my bowl until it was shiny clean. It thwacked and clanked against the cabinet door.

Lela and I settled by the wood stove to wait for them. The thick iron door concealed the flames and quieted the crackling, but the heat poured over us as we laid at the hearth. My muscles yielded to the warmth, and I gave in to the weariness housed deep in my body. I drifted effortlessly into deep sleep while my Thanksgiving feast digested.

I never heard Commander pull into the driveway. It was the cold gust of swirling air that roused me. My senses were dull, and I laid there disoriented momentarily while Mom and Dad deposited the kids in their beds. I was about to rise when I heard their approaching footsteps.

"Do you think we should bring the dogs? This trail looks steep." Mom and Dad spoke in hushed tones. A map rustled in Mom's hands. She sat close to Lela.

Dad's hand rested lightly on Mom's shoulder. "Maybe we should just bring Shamus." He shrugged his shoulders as he spoke.

Lela's face remained expressionless, but I knew she was listening. She was close enough to hear what they said. The muscles around her jaw tightened.

"I couldn't leave Lela here," Mom insisted. Lela's body relaxed and a faint smile appeared. "It'd break her heart." Mom reached over and stroked Lela's back. "She'll let me know if she needs to take it easy, and I packed her medicine if she needs it." Lela's tail thumped lightly against the thick rug. "I can't leave her here alone." Sadness and gratitude comingled in Mom's eyes as she stared down upon Lela.

Dad opened the stove's door and silently stoked the fire. He shoved four more pieces of wood into the flames. "Well that should keep things burning through morning," he said, rubbing Lela's side. He didn't realize then that he took her presence for granted. He'd wept silently with remorse after she died and vowed he wouldn't repeat that mistake with me.

"You ready for bed?" Dad asked. His heavy, bloodshot eyes turned to Mom, and he stretched his arms high overhead and then brushed his hand tenderly against her cheek.

Lela rose slowly. Her laden steps moved her toward the pillow that called to her from beside Mom's bed.

"Yeah. I'm beat . . . and stuffed. I shouldn't have eaten that pie." Mom rubbed her stomach, and then her fingers found my side. She shut off the light, and we followed Lela to our beds. We moved quietly around the bedroom so as to not awaken the kids.

Lela eased into her pillow. Her satisfied sigh filled the quiet night. It wasn't long before I heard the beloved hushed snores.

"What did you wish for?" Dad asked softly, pulling the blankets up and under Haley's chin. She clutched the covers unknowingly.

Logan's head dangled off the side of his bed. I buried my muzzle in the wave of his dark hair. The smell of dirt, sweat, and fruity shampoo lingered in it.

"Let him sleep, Shamus." Mom carefully straightened Logan's body. She spread his fuzzy blanket over him and brushed his hair from his face. She looked down at me and kissed my brow. "Night-night," she whispered.

"What?" Mom softly asked when she turned toward Dad.

"The shooting star. What did you wish for?" Dad yawned and climbed into bed. He shuddered when his naked toes hit the cold sheets.

Mom caressed the top of Lela's head and tiptoed lightly around her. "Wasn't that something?" She pulled the covers back and slipped gingerly beneath them. The mattress springs exhaled, and she melded into Dad. They clutched and shivered under the covers. Another yawn floated into the air.

"Peace," rolled quietly from Mom's lips. "Just peace." Her breathing slowed.

The night swaddled us in silence and the sky outside was black. A million radiant stars danced above me. Transporting me to an earlier time. Time I'd spent with my mother. Her face appeared before me. Her warm breath filled the room. "I have a family of my own," I whispered to her. "They found me." The apparition smiled and wrapped its loving paws around me. Gratitude consumed my heart, but a mournful whimper broke the spell.

Logan's cry roused me. He was talking in his sleep, but his words were incomprehensible. His body trembled from the night's chill, and he clenched his small fists tightly. His favorite blanket lay in a heap near his exposed feet. I grabbed the soft cloth between my teeth and pulled it across his body. He stirred under its weight and another whimper followed.

"It's all right, Logan," I reassured.

I huddled next to him and placed my head lightly on his leg. His body responded and began to loosen. He exhaled the fiend that disrupted his sleep. His fists uncurled, and his soft fingers found the top of my head. They kneaded my fur without thinking until we drifted into peaceful sleep together.

Nighttime. The only time to sleep in Freedom for the weekend was full of the outdoors and adventure. An adventure that began midmorning with a hiking trip to White Horse Ledge.

The trails were heavily traveled despite the time of year. They were steep in parts, and ice had begun to form. Lela maneuvered the rocks and ice carefully. She was nimble despite the arthritis housed in her joints. We enjoyed the eclectic scents that lingered on the fallen leaves, while the kids scrambled forward. Mom watched us all carefully, making sure we stayed on the designated paths.

My breath froze in my chest the first time I peered over the steep cliffs. The sheer rock faces fanned out on both sides of where we stood, and the valley below seemed endless. I was instantly humbled and felt very small. Even the kids were quieted by the beauty surrounding us. We stood in silence taking in the majestic display.

Lela's eyes closed and she held her breath. A light wind lifted her ears slightly. A smile crossed her face as the air floated from her lungs. She looked young despite her fur's aging color. I didn't dare disturb her.

Mom's story of creation came to mind. *All this and more in seven days,* I marveled.

Our explorations that day ended at a lake that rested below the cliffs. The sun retreated beyond the peaks, and the beach was deserted. The sand was chilly and the crystal water was cold. Ice cold. Colder than any water I'd felt before. Lela told me of an icy stream she once hopped in. "Before the kids were born," she said with chattering teeth. Her story occupied my mind while Commander's heat drove the chill from our bones. The warmth and opportunity to lay eased aching muscles.

We all slept soundly that night and woke well rested. Stiff but rested and ready for Thompson Falls.

Thompson Falls was a series of waterfalls along a brook at a local ski area. I'd never seen such a spectacular waterfall. The water was frigid and the rocks were slippery. Higher and higher we climbed. I was surprised at how agile Lela was. Her heart and spirit still strong. It was her hind end that gave way. Mom saw Lela topple and suggested we head back. She knew Lela was stubborn and would keep going. "How about some sledding?" she suggested. There was snow at the base of the ski lodge, and the kids were anxious to test their new toboggan. I chased after them down the steep slope. Unable to keep up with the new sled.

The fresh air and the abundance of exercise were good for us all. We submerged ourselves in nature and accepted the gifts it offered. Warmth from the sun. Humility from the mountains. Energy from the wind and freshness from the icy waters.

Mom's cares slipped from her shoulders. One by one she left them on the trails. They fell among the autumn leaves, and the earth took them in. She left Freedom with a rekindled spirit. She was ready to return to the lane and tackle the unknown challenges that lay ahead.

~Thirty-one~

Fall turned into winter. Just like that it was Christmas again, and the new year nipped at its heels. I couldn't recall where the time went or what we did. The days rolled by, and we stuck to our daily rituals until Mom realized it was time for her to give up some control and get back into the office. Valerie was on maternity leave. Twice the work needed to get done, and there wasn't any one to whom Mom could delegate or seek assistance.

Mom enrolled the kids in an after-school program following the Christmas holiday. It was staffed by trained adults, and the kids were supervised at all times. The schedule allowed Mom to work three full days in the office and two from home. She felt guilty at first but found comfort knowing the kids were safe and happy. They were surrounded by friends and engaged in playful activities.

Yet Mom became more irritable as the winter months wore on. She tried to leave work at work and closed the den's door when it was dinnertime. But there were always e-mails and voice mails that she needed to address, and Dad was seldom home early enough to help.

"Do your homework. Eat your dinner. Clear your place. Take a shower. Brush your teeth. Bring your clean laundry upstairs," she barked. The stress she fought so hard to manage had snuck up on her again.

Lela and I were content during Mom's absences. We were free to meander in and out through our dog door. Dad tinkered with it so it wouldn't slap us if we were slow moving through. Mom always left the TV on and hid treats and chew toys in the yard to keep us entertained. But Lela slowed down considerably during those winter months, and growths appeared on the top of her head and above her eye.

Dr. Kagan said the growths were benign, so unless they became uncomfortable, we should leave them alone for the time being. He also recommended that Lela not jog with us anymore. The stress of surgery and jogging could do more harm than good. Mom watched the growths for any subtle changes, and our morning jogs turned to easy strolls.

Lela didn't care about the growths on her body. They weren't painful or bothersome though they fluctuated in size. It was Mom who hated the visible reminders that Lela was growing old. She couldn't bear the way strangers looked at Lela or the way they commented on her age. She resented their pity and the way they shied away at the sight of the bumps that sometimes cracked and oozed.

Lela's beauty radiated from within, and she aged with dignity. Our brushings, ear and teeth cleanings, and nail trimmings became more frequent. Mom even bought lavender-infused conditioning spray to keep our coats shiny and fresh smelling. Still Mom and I felt Lela slipping slowly away.

I was glad when the cold winter months bowed to spring. The tender buds and spring's familiar sweet songs revived me. My soul and Lela's body welcomed the sun's warm kiss. It eased time's cold, heartless grasp despite Lela's thirteenth birthday. We cleared a trail behind our house to accommodate more frequent, shorter walks on flatter terrain. We later dubbed it the "haunted trail" as it became the setting for our annual Halloween scavenger hunt and party.

Spring ushered in relief and hope. Mom was ready to accept an offer with another firm. A consulting firm close to home. She'd work five days from their local office. It was an easy commute. The kids would go to their after-school program and then summer camp full-time. Mom was waiting for the offer letter when a dark shadow filled the room.

"Raj. Maybe I should pick the kids up from school. There's a severe weather warning in effect. Did you see the e-mail alert?" Mom talked while she typed. Her fingers moved effortlessly across the keyboard.

"You're probably right. I'm being overprotective. OK. OK. Let me go so I can finish before the bus comes. No. The eFax hasn't come in yet. They're just ironing out the details. Yup. See ya later."

She hung up the phone and walked to the window. The sky was dark and the air was heavy. Nothing moved. Only thunder rolled in the distance.

"What's wrong, Lela? Why are you shaking?" I asked.

"A bad storm's coming," she stammered. "This one's big and it's coming fast." She trembled and looked nervously at Mom. The two wore the same worried expression.

The sky grew steadily darker. Mom led us downstairs. She closed the playroom door, and the lock clicked into place. She headed out early for the bus stop not wanting to get caught in the rain.

The thunder cracked, and Lela dove under the futon. Panic filled her eyes and she panted uncontrollably. The lights flickered eerily, then another crack of thunder ripped through the sky. Much closer and much louder. The TV and lights shut off.

I felt the storm's escalating energy pulsing through my veins. My fur stood on end. I stood frozen before the window, looking up at the threatening sky and dark, voluminous clouds.

Another crack. Then deafening rain poured from the clouds. It fell in sheets as the wind howled. Branches whipped back and forth, clawing at the window, seeking a way in to escape the violent storm. I knew I should take cover, but my legs abandoned me, immobilized by terror.

Lightening hit. Its bright, twisted fingers shattered the dark sky.

A loud roar. A loud boom. The storm seethed like a wild, rabid creature.

Power lines danced in the wind. Sparks flew through the air. Trees and limbs crashed to the ground. Feral winds whipped across the yard.

BOOM! BOOM!

Close to the house. Too close. The windows shook, and the entire house shivered and moaned, urging me to seek shelter.

My body responded to the cries and pushed itself under the futon. The wooden frame banged loudly against the wall as my bulk nearly smothered Lela. Air whipped in and out of our lungs while the storm raged. The vociferous, frenzied tirade assaulted our ears. Our chests heaved up and down. Lela's tongue dropped from her mouth. *Would her aging heart stop?* I feared.

Another big crash and then…

Eerie silence.

The wind ceased its madness and the rain stopped.

Lela and I held our breaths for what seemed like eternity. We listened to the distant thunder. Its grumbling grew faint. We exhaled. Then the clouds parted, giving way to the sun.

The storm passed.

Water flowed.

I heard only water. Heavy water cascading down the embankment.

Lela boldly stepped outside first.

"It's over," she said coolly as we stood side by side surveying the damage.

Uprooted trees lay like fallen dominoes across the yard. Others had twisted in two. Two blocked our driveway. Broken branches and leaves littered our yard. Sparkling power lines skipped between the broken limbs.

Sirens blared. First one, then two, and then a symphony of sirens echoed through town.

"Mom should have been back by now with the kids." Lela's voice was surprisingly calm yet etched with concern.

We waited as the sirens wailed.

Time   disappeared   as   we   waited   for

Commander's familiar hum. I sighed with relief when I saw the big black truck approach the turn below. But it couldn't get around the fallen trees or power lines.

Mom rolled down her window and called up to us.

"We're here. We're OK," Lela and I barked.

We watched Mom walk our neighbor's driveway until she disappeared into the woods.

Where are the kids? I wondered.

"She's going up through the back. Come on," Lela ordered.

We waited at the top of the stairs until we heard Mom's footsteps running toward the playroom door.

"Thank God, you guys are all right." She knelt down and gathered us in her arms.

Mom ran around the house filling a backpack with flashlights and rain gear. She left candles and a lighter on the kitchen table. No power. The lights on the stove were still out.

"Raj. If you get this message, come home. Come home now. I think a tornado just passed through. Trees have been uprooted; power lines are down. It all happened so fast. I don't know where the kids are. I'm going out to find them. I can't get through to the school. Traffic's backed up. I'm going to retrace their bus route. Come home. Please." Mom choked on her last words. She fought to stay calm, but I smelled her fear. It gripped my insides.

Lela reassuringly rubbed her muzzle against Mom's leg.

"You have to stay here, OK? I have to find

Haley and Logan." She led us down the playroom stairs and offered us two biscuits. But our insides were still taut from the storm's powerful grasp. The biscuits laid untouched. "You'll be safe in the playroom." I ignored my desire to run after her as she bounded up the stairs. She needed me to be strong. She didn't need to worry about me too.

I raced outside and joined Lela. We waited for Mom to emerge from the woods. She carefully maneuvered her way around the fallen trees and branches. We watched as she hurried toward Commander, keeping a safe distance from the steaming power lines.

"Be careful," Lela barked.

Mom paused and looked up in our direction. "Be good!" She jumped into the truck and disappeared down the lane.

Waiting was agonizing. Outside the sirens continued their bellowing. A helicopter hovered overhead. It was getting late. The sun was about to set. The village below was fading.

Lela sat by the fence, peering down at the road. She sat motionless, like a statue, as she waited for our family to return. Together we kept a silent vigil. I secretly asked Grammy's God to bring them safely home.

Like the sun, the sirens eventually faded. One by one.

A train whistle in the distance signaled that the trains were moving again. Not as many and not as fast, but some traffic was getting through.

"It's getting dark. We should wait inside." Lela stretched her back to relieve a crick. Her joints creaked, angry that she made them sit for so long.

The house was unnervingly quiet. Dark and quiet. Lela laid on the futon, and I took the pillow on the floor. There was nothing to do but wait and wonder.

The frogs resumed their mating calls, and the melody eased my mind. The sincerity of the song was soothing. I gave in to the weariness, drifting in and out with the rise and fall of the chorus.

"They're back." Lela's voice woke me.

I shook the sleep from my head. I heard them approaching. I knew the sound of their elated voices. And they were indeed ecstatic as they fumbled through the dark woods. They were all there. Mom, Dad, Haley, and Logan. They had come home.

Lela and I raced up the dark stairway and pushed against the locked door.

"We're here. Come get us," I barked.

Happy, light feet. Haley and Logan's happy feet skipped towards the playroom door. Pizza. I smelled pizza. A light beam danced under the door and bounced off my paws.

The lock clicked, and my body weight fell through the doorway. I tripped over Logan, blinded by the beam of light.

"Where have you been?" Lela and I barked. "We've been so worried." We circled around them, relieved that they'd come home. Haley and Logan circled around us, happy to be home.

"Easy now," Dad said. "Let's get everyone

settled."

Mom guided us all to her room with the light. She lit the candles she had placed on the nightstand before she had left. And there on her bed lay the kids' pajamas. She had the foresight to lay them out ahead of time. She knew the power might not be on when she returned. She suspected it would be dark. "I'll go get some drinks while you two get changed. Come on, Lela. Come on, Shamus. Want some dinner?"

My stomach gurgled, and then I remembered the two biscuits. I snuck quietly downstairs and sniffed them out. They lay where Mom had left them. I quickly devoured the smaller one and buried the bigger one outside. The village below was dark and the surrounding stillness unnatural. I decided not to linger. I turned from my endeavors and headed indoors.

I heard Emi in the crawl space between the boiler room and playroom. She sought shelter on the bedding Haley kept there for her. It was well beyond my reach, a place where Emi felt safe. I left her in peace and hurried ahead.

My family had gathered on Mom and Dad's bed. Lela sat near the edge, muzzle high in the air, eagerly waiting for crumbs. *Lela sure loves pizza*, I thought, snickering to myself.

"Yeah, and the fourth graders in the back of the bus were crying," Logan said excitedly. "They saw the fire." His hands and arms danced passionately in front of him while he spoke.

"Were you scared?" Grammy's gentle voice drifted through the speakerphone.

"It was hard to see. We were in the middle. I mean the storm was scary, but I didn't know a tree fell in front of us until we got off," Haley answered first.

"The power lines were scary! They were moving all over and sparks were flying," Logan jumped in. He wiped the pizza sauce from his mouth with his pajama sleeve.

"Yeah, that was scary," Haley agreed. Her head bobbed up and down like the bobble-head on Logan's soccer trophy. "And seeing the car crushed by the tree."

Logan nodded his head and bit deep into his pizza slice. Cheese and sauce dribbled down his chin.

"Well, I sure was worried for you," Grammy said.

"Yeah, we got picked up last." Logan slid his eyes sideways toward Dad. They sparkled in the candlelight. His tongue swiped up the cheese and sauce that slid from his mouth.

"Now wait a minute. Your Mom and I went back and forth three different times before the police said it was safe to get you. We had to walk through the woods in the back of those houses," Dad explained lightheartedly.

"I was scared," Mom said in a serious tone. "I was really scared. That storm came in so fast. I tried driving your bus route and figured you were stuck somewhere between school and South Landing. It took me forever to get through to the school. Your principal finally answered the phone and told me where you were." She sighed and pulled the kids closer to her. "I just wanted you home."

Lela and I watched the four of them snuggle close together. They said good-bye to Grammy and huddled around the portable DVD player. There was just enough battery left to watch a movie.

"Is Emi OK, Mom?" Haley asked with concern. "She is honey," Mom answered. "I checked and her food bowl was empty. She must have come in."

"She is!" I barked, drawing a smile from them both.

"Can Lela and Shamus come up?" Haley's eyes pleaded. "Please?" she begged. Her yearning was genuine. She needed to feel safe, surrounded by those she loved. All our eyes turned toward Dad.

"Please?" I whined.

We were only allowed up when Dad wasn't home. We knew to jump off when we heard his Jeep pull into the driveway. But that night Dad made an exception. He called us up onto the bed.

I fell into the kids' opened arms. Warmed by their embraces. Glad the day was over. Grateful we were together.

~Thirty-two~

The storm had been swift. But it took countless hours to clear the debris and repair the damage. Local businesses and schools remained closed the next day as much of the town was without power. Many families went powerless for days. We were lucky though. Our power was restored the next afternoon.

I felt the swell of energy just before the lights flickered. We held our breath until they grew steadily brighter. The electricity buzzed around us. Light bulbs popped, and air sputtered through the fish tank pump. The refrigerator hummed and the dishwasher beeped. Voices drifted up the playroom stairs, while the clock on the stove blinked on and off waiting to be reset. Mom picked up the telephone receiver. A dial tone. She heard a dial tone and knew our modem was working. She hurried to the den and rebooted the computer.

There it was. The offer letter she'd been expecting was waiting in her in-box. She hastily printed it. Her hands shook as she grabbed it off the printer. She steadied herself against the desk as she read it, and then held the letter against her chest. Her face softened and her shoulders relaxed. An aura of excitement surrounded her. It was strange seeing her excited about work. Work hadn't excited her in a very long time.

"A big acquisition is brewing, and I don't wanna wait to give notice. I'm supposed to meet with the clients next week for a kickoff meeting," she told Dad through the speakerphone. "I'm gonna take the kids with me. They can wait in my office. That way the meeting will be short and sweet."

She moved around with nervous energy and quickly fired up the laundry and dishwasher. She wanted to get as much done as she could just in case the power went out again. Our power supply was, at that point, tenuous at best. We could tell from the lights because they glowed dimmer than usual.

Water dripped from the ends of Mom's hair. "Time to go," she hollered.

I knew it was a big day. Lela told me that Mom worked at the firm for many years. She enjoyed working there initially. It was a small office where everyone knew everyone. It had felt like family. But over time, things had changed. And, well . . . work began to feel too much like tiresome work.

"It's time I divorce my work husband," Mom told Dad jokingly one night. "It's either you or him." But it wasn't entirely a joke. The events over those past two years had taken a toll on their marriage. Mom and Dad struggled to balance work and family demands. But there was little time for each other. I watched them run through their daily routines. There was one for weekdays and one for weekends. Even their conversations had drifted into a pattern that revolved around the kids and work.

Lela and I watched Mom grow increasingly tired. Tired and dissatisfied.

"Caught in a rut," Mom told Grammy as she patiently waited for an opportunity to arise. Mom was about ready to sink when Grammy's God threw her a life vest.

A consulting firm was in need of an in-house attorney. The position was close to home. Her new boss said she could work from home if the kids were sick or school was closed. Flexible, close, rewarding, minimal billable hours. It felt like a good move. That's what she hoped anyway. But still she worried about the kids and me and Lela, and how the changes would affect us. It was a full-time position. Five days in the office. Yet the prospect gave her hope, and the offer changed her disposition instantly.

"You'll take care of her?" Mom held my muzzle and gazed deeply into my eyes. She already knew the answer, but still I swiped my tongue across her cheek.

"No worries," I barked earnestly.

"And you'll make sure he behaves?" she jested, turning toward Lela. A kiss landed like a whisper on Mom's nose.

Yes, we'd look out for each other. That Mom knew. But she wondered and worried about Lela and what time was left. She wouldn't speak the words that hovered around her heart. She pressed Lela tenderly against her chest. I felt like an intruder.

Mom gave a full month's notice but spent more and more time working from home. She woke early to exercise and took Lela and me on leisurely morning and afternoon walks. The stress left her body, and her gait was noticeably lighter. In the early evenings, we walked along the haunted trail. Sometimes the kids joined us. Sometimes they watched us from the porch. We could always see them from the trail, but this bit of freedom, the opportunity to choose whether to stay or join us, empowered them. They were growing up and looking forward to attending their after-school program every day.

Lela and I accompanied Mom to the office on her last day of work. We waited in Commander as she packed up the last of her personal belongings and said her good-byes. I was surprised by the tears that tumbled down her cheeks and into the box she carried. She placed the box next to her, glancing reflectively at its contents. A framed diploma, a name plate, a stained coffee mug, a small cappuccino machine, a handful of tea bags, a few files, and pictures. Pictures of the kids at various ages, Mom and Dad on horses, and a picture of Lela. A much younger Lela. Mom leaned forward against the steering wheel, her forehead grazed the windshield. She glanced up at the office building she had worked at for so long.

"You know, I never saw myself leaving," she told us. She wiped the moisture from her face and spent the next two weeks doing all the things she never got around to doing.

She painted the playroom, cleaned the garage, and put loose photos into albums. She rearranged the linen closets, the kids' closets, and then her own closet. She cleaned out the attic and dusted every wall hanging and light fixture. She went to the dentist and the doctors and then had Lasik eye surgery so her contact lenses would no longer bother her. She exercised more and bought new work clothes and bags.

She'd never been unemployed. It was the first time since law school that she didn't have to check e-mails or voice mails. Nothing hung over her head. She looked and felt fantastic, and Lela and I savored her companionship. It was June. The three of us enjoyed spring's gifts, and we celebrated my third birthday.

Mom was ready to begin her new adventure at the end of those two weeks. Rested and hopeful. And while Lela and I missed her during the days, we could tell the change was good for her.

At least initially.

"They don't give me any work. And when they do, it's usually shit work no one else wants to do, and then they're not available to answer any questions. They knew I didn't have this experience when I took the job. That's why I took it. I've offered to do research for them and told them they could bill the hours 'cause I won't learn if I'm not brought into the discussions. But nothing. They just nod their heads with blank looks on their faces. What the hell?" Mom griped.

Mom became more and more frustrated as weeks turned to months. "What have I done?" she complained. "The guys don't socialize or talk to me. We had a conference call with a client, and Brian and Tom took the call from Brian's office, which is right next to mine. They didn't ask me to join them. I sat in my office alone on the same call." Her voice turned angry. Her face darkened. I could feel its heat. "What was I? Their equal opportunity employee so they could say, 'We hired a middle-aged woman in our group'?" She stiffened when Dad tried to pull her close. The air around her cooled.

She couldn't go back to Phillip, and she didn't

want to hop around from job to job. To make matters worse, the economy was slumping. "That's probably why they're hoarding all the billable work. They're trying to cover their asses." Mom knew she was stuck and that other opportunities weren't out there.

Dad stopped listening to the droning. His attention was on the football game. Mom didn't notice.

"No, I'll stick it out. I can do anything for two years." She took a long drink from her glass. "Besides, I like being close to the kids." She settled back against her pillows. Staring at the TV but not watching it.

She resolved to make it work and learn as much as she could. She volunteered for the tedious assignments no one else wanted to do. When billable work was light, she'd find issues to research and write about. At home she scanned her e-mails for new developments or client inquiries while the kids finished their schoolwork. Sometimes she'd work after they'd gone to bed. She wasn't going to give her colleagues any reason to talk bad about her. "Make yourself indispensable." That's what Grammy had always told her.

Mom started taking lunch breaks to ease the monotony of the workday. Sometimes she shopped at a local grocery store or ran errands. Occasionally she'd surprise Lela and me with a quick stop home to put the groceries away.

Mom kept herself busy at work and maintained meticulous records of all the projects she worked on. Her six-month review went well, and she was rewarded with a raise. She accepted things for what they were, and this helped restore her inner balance. Her career became a job. A way to pass the time while the kids were in school. Although she continued working hard, her heart wasn't into it. She once loved being a lawyer. Loved working at the prestigious firms, counseling clients, and feeling important. But those feelings faded, and she began to question what she was doing.

"Maybe you don't have to work," Dad said one night. "We can go through our budget and see where we are if you don't work."

Mom's eyes narrowed, and the muscles around her jaw tightened. Her brow wrinkled just before she spoke. "I never said I didn't want to work. I just want to work less and be around for the kids more without always feeling so drained. I'm just not sure I want to be a lawyer anymore. Besides, we couldn't afford me not working. Even if we could, how would we save for college?"

"They can take out loans."

"You don't know what it's like to graduate from school with loans over your head. There's no freedom or flexibility. I had to take the best-paying job I could get to make enough to live on while still paying my student loans. And I was lucky. I didn't have huge loans because of my scholarships." Mom sunk deep into the sofa's cushions. "I want the kids to take a job because they feel passionate about it. Not because they need the money." Her voice trailed off, but the desperation hung around her.

Dad remained silent. Confused and somewhat frustrated. He didn't know how to help. He couldn't fix the problem because he wasn't sure what it was. Mom wasn't sure. He wanted her happy. Plain and simple. Work, don't work. It didn't matter. "A happy wife makes for a happy life," he often teased.

He watched Mom quietly. He studied her hair, her brow, and her face. He watched her hand absentmindedly caress Lela's fur. He leaned in as if wanting to touch Mom, to comfort her, or to be comforted. But Mom didn't notice. She was lost in thought. No doubt wondering how she had ended up in the predicament she was in.

Dad's hand fell to his side. He patted Mom's knee and glanced down at me sadly.

He too was sometimes jealous of their relationship.

Mom and Lela.

~Thirty-three~

Summer was hot and there was little rain. The days melted together, and before I knew it, there were only two weeks left until the kids went back to school. Third and fourth grade that year. "Where did the time go?" Mom would say.

Lela was fourteen and I had turned four.

Where does it go? I too wondered.

I've always loved summer. The long, lazy days and the warm summer breeze. But it's the sounds and hubbub of summer I miss most when the cool autumn air settles in.

Lela and I appreciated the cool playroom. Not too hot and not too cold. The temperature was just right, and it was easy for Lela to move indoors and outdoors. Her hearing was just about nil, and she relied on my telling her when I heard Commander. Each afternoon, when the sun moved to the side of the yard, I'd bask outdoors and wait for the familiar hum while she slept. She slept a lot, mustering the strength to march up the stairs. Mom's embrace was her reward. One they both looked forward to everyday.

The kids' camp bus would rumble up the driveway shortly after Mom arrived home. It was a small bus that dropped them off at our door. Lela and I'd watch the kids hop off. Flushed faces. Exuberant yet exhausted. They loved summer camp, and I liked hearing about their day. The pool was too cold and the hockey field too hot. Haley earned an MVP award in tennis, and Logan held the ropes' course record for his age group. They were proud of their accomplishments, and Mom always had cold drinks and a special snack waiting for them.

It was a good summer, and we ended it with a family vacation. A trip to Lake Champlain. A trip Dad planned weeks ahead.

"What do you think of this lake house?" Dad asked. "It says pets allowed. I'll ask. Just to make sure we can bring two." Mom and Dad huddled around his computer screen. She didn't want to leave Lela and me behind. She knew it might be our last summer with Lela.

"I just don't get to spend as much time with them since I've taken this job. I miss them," Mom said of us.

Lela and I missed her too. We missed them all during the day, and we were excited to learn we'd be going with them.

As luck would have it, the mass on Lela's head erupted the morning before our trip. It oozed like a foul pimple, and Mom gagged when she first saw it. The mass had split into quarters.

"What did you do, Miss Lela?" Mom asked softly as she dabbed at the wound with a washcloth. Lela had ripped the top off the mass when she rubbed her head against the bed. Her blood and puss stuck to the bedsheets. Lela looked at Mom apologetically.

Dr. Kagan removed what was left of the mass. The procedure didn't require surgery or anesthesia. He was able to burn it off. Mom was instructed to keep the scab dry. Lela's face sported a grin when she trotted out of his office. "Now how are we going to keep her head dry, Shamus? We're going to a lake house," Mom chuckled. She was relieved the ugly mass was gone.

"Fat chance," I barked, and the three of us laughed together.

Nothing could keep Lela from the water. She was a Labrador. It was in her blood. She smelled the water's freshness and let her senses lead her to it. She used her paw and muzzle to open the screen door. She sauntered past the four Adirondack chairs and deep fire pit. When she was sure no one was coming for her, she turned and trotted quickly toward the water's edge.

Lake Champlain was large, and I couldn't see the other shore. The gusty wind whistled through the large pines trees. Waves danced against a dock and across the pebbled beach that belonged to the house.

Lela splashed into the clear, cool water. Stumbling on loose rocks until she felt herself floating. I followed her in, and we swam side by side. The water revived her. Years rolled off her fur as she paddled farther from shore. Water sprayed from her lips when she exhaled. She was completely soaked. Her bandage bobbed on the water behind her. No more than thirty minutes had passed since we first arrived at the lake house.

Mom fretted at first and tried wrapping gauze around Lela's head to cover the wound. But it was no use. Mom couldn't keep Lela from the lake or keep the wound dry. Lela looked ridiculous wearing the soggy white bow.

"Let her be a dog," Dad said. "She knows her

own limits."

Mom sighed and nodded. She knew the cool water soothed Lela's aching limbs, and swimming was easier than walking. Mom clutched the dripping gauze and backed hesitantly away. She didn't run to Lela's side when her paws slipped on the damp stones. The veins in Mom's knuckles bulged, and the color faded from her clenched fist. Mom watched, chewing her lower lip, until Lela swam effortlessly through the water. Mom knew it was time to stop protecting her. She looked reflectively upon her beloved Lela, and a faint smile emerged. I charged into the water, spraying cold water on them both. Mom and Lela beamed.

It was a perfect week. The days were sunny and warm. The nights breezy and cool. We spent most of the week on or in the water.

Lela and I swam after the kids in their kayaks. They spent hours paddling close to shore, back and forth along the embankment. They had never kayaked before, and they enjoyed the freedom of being on the open water by themselves as Mom and Dad watched from the beach. In the afternoons we took family rides in a small motor boat Dad rented for the week.

The kids learned to fish that summer too. Dad showed them how to bait a hook and cast their fishing lines. I think he spent most of his time untangling string. Lela and I weren't allowed near the fishing poles. We rested in the cool grass while Mom read her books.

Dad and I took his canoe out into deep waters each morning. He liked early morning best, when the water was smooth and the air cool. The only noises outdoors were the canoe and paddle slicing through the water and the geese honking overhead. Fish would occasionally pop out of the water searching for food. The early rays glistened off their wet scales.

Mom and Lela would wait for us at the dock. I could smell the coffee long before I could see the two steaming cups perched on the chair's arm. Mom's hair and Lela's ears swayed in the breeze. Some mornings the kids would be up. But mostly they still slept. It was early, and the days were long and languid.

That last morning, when the canoe glided close to the dock, Lela swam out to greet us. Her face was content and peaceful. Her eyes gazed first upon us but then rested on Mom. Lela's eyes, always full of love and longing. But that day sadness tainted the eyes that had grown cloudy with age.

I think Lela knew it was her last summer with us.

~Thirty-four~

Haley's scream rumbled down the stairs ahead of her feet.

"It's a bat!" she yelled at the top of her lungs. She flung herself across Mom.

"There's a bat in the bathroom." Haley's voice quavered. "A bat!"

"What?" Mom tried catching her breath. She reached over and turned on the light.

"It's a bat! In my bathroom." Haley awoke with a full bladder. The bathroom's light startled the bat that then startled Haley.

"Raj! Get up. There's a bat in the house." Mom prodded the immobile lump with her hand. It shifted and Dad's head rose slowly from his pillow. He turned to face the girls, who were staring wide-eyed at him. They both sat up straight, waiting for him to respond.

"What's happening?" Lela asked sleepily. She squinted, trying to focus her gaze.

"A bat's in the house," I told her.

She let out a yawn and lay her head back down. "Oh," slid from her lips.

"Raj! Get up!" Mom demanded. "If we don't catch that bat, we'll have to have rabies shots. That's what happened to the Vardens."

Dad groaned and tossed the covers to the side. He stood up groggily. Swayed slightly. Still partially asleep. The clock said it was 4:23.

"Can't I just open the window and shoo it out?" he asked.

"No!" Haley and Mom hollered in unison. The Vardens had to have rabies shots after a bat invaded their home. It escaped into the darkness. We listened to the story for days as the family underwent precautionary treatment in case the bat had bitten them while they slept. Haley was petrified of the shots her friend complained of.

"Trap it with a sheet. I'll check with the department of health and see what they want us to do." Mom headed toward the den to consult with Google. Google knew something about everything.

Mom's high-pitched shriek sent us running into the hall. She clutched one hand against her heaving chest. The other firmly grasped the den's doorknob.

"It's in the den. It must have followed Haley down." I heard the pounding of her heart and the bat's distressed squeaking. It flew frantically about the brightly lit room. Its fluttering wings cast eerie shadows beneath the door.

We drew in our breaths and waited for the ruckus to subside.

"OK," Dad said, armed with garden gloves and a sheet. "I'll go get him." He looked comical in his boxer shorts and socked feet despite the serious face he donned. Mom shoved him through the doorway and slammed the door shut behind him. We listened intently.

A sudden flutter and piercing squeal, Dad's squeal, resonated from behind the door.

Heavy footsteps followed beating wings.

A bump. A bang. A fearful eek.

The door rattled and the walls shook. Mom and

Haley snickered.

A bump and a groan.

A whack. A batter.

Flapping sheet and muffled screech.

Silence followed.

The door creaked open, and Dad emerged, perspiring and triumphant. He held the gathered sheet tightly with one hand. The fabric trembled. The felonious bat was trapped among the soft folds.

Haley held a plastic bin in her hands. "Put him in here," she instructed. Dad obliged, and Haley quickly sealed the container and carefully punched tiny holes in the top.

The sheet shifted slightly and the folds parted. The tip of a tiny wing appeared. The bat freed itself from the cloth and warily watched its captors.

"He's so cute!" Haley gazed at the bat affectionately.

I inspected the creature that peered back with tiny, beady eyes. Its face and wings were dark, and it had big, hairy feet. Cute was not the word that came to my mind.

Dad pressed his face close to the container. He peered inquisitively at the unmoving bat. The stillness was unnerving.

The bat hissed unexpectedly.

We gasped at the frightening vampire-like incisors.

Haley took pity on the imprisoned creature. She carried it to the mudroom, where it waited in the cool, quiet dark for its fate.

A woman from the department of health came a few hours later and took the bat away. It tested negative for rabies. We all sighed with relief.

How Logan slept through all the uproar remained a mystery.

~Thirty-five~

The familiar smell of cinnamon and cloves filled the house as the mulling spices simmered on the stove. An occasional spit and hiss erupted when the spices bubbled over and hit the flames. A sure sign that summer was over. We drifted into another autumn.

Halloween was approaching. The haunted trail was decorated for the party. The large transparent ghosts swayed in the breeze. The wind circled around and under and through the tattered and sliced drop cloths making an eerie swishing sound. Ten ghosts watched over the trail. It took Mom, Grammy, and Aunt Abbey three hours to hang them. It took another four to finish decorating the trail.

Every year our family threw a Halloween scavenger hunt, but that year we unveiled the haunted trail. "You need scarier stuff," the kids told Mom and Dad. They'd grown too old for the cute decorations, and so the two hundred yards of wooded trail were filled with flashing lights, glowing pumpkins, ghosts, spiders and webs, skeletons, rats, bats and vampires, tombstones, bloody corpses, pirates, witches, and a large bubbling cauldron. Spine-chilling music and sounds echoed through the barren limbs.

Mom, Grammy, and Aunt Abbey were putting the finishing touches on the trail. Guests would arrive within a couple of hours. That's when Mom told Grammy and Aunt Abbey we might be moving to Chicago. It was the first time the possibility began to feel more certain. Before then Mom and Dad's conversations had been speculative. But mentioning the possibility to Grammy and Aunt Abbey made it real. *We might actually be moving*, I contemplated.

"They're buying a business in Chicago, and they want Raj out there to run it. If everything goes according to plan, they want us out there by July." Mom positioned a giant rat with beady red eyes on top of my old crate as she spoke. She wrapped its spiny tail around the bars.

Aunt Abbey paused. The news took her by surprise. She was close to her older sister, and her facial expression told me that she didn't want us to move. She silently stretched a spider web across my crate, while Grammy propped a bloody head inside. My old crate was transformed into a gory prop. A shiver ran down my spine. The rat looked real, and its squinty eyes followed me. *It's a good thing I never have to sleep in that crate again,* I thought.

"What do the kids think?" Aunt Abbey straightened up and moved toward the next prop.

"We gave them a head's-up. They're tired of Raj being gone so much. They like the idea of us being a family again, but they're not happy about leaving their friends."

They worked as they talked, moving along the trail, hanging up last-minute props and scattering spiderwebs. The trio worked quickly together as the afternoon wore on.

Lela and I tagged along.

"If we're going to move, we have to do it before the kids get into middle school. And I'm not very happy with my job. You know that. This is a good way for me to get out without burning any bridges. I'll take a few months off, get everyone settled, and then start looking out there." Mom paused to reposition a large vampire inside a coffin. "I'm not thrilled about Chicago. I hate the cold. But it's a big opportunity for Raj."

I jumped when the head Grammy held came to life. It let out a gruesome moan, and its eyes started flashing. No one else seemed to mind.

Lela's face remained expressionless. Neither the props nor the news we might be moving bothered her, though I wasn't sure how much she had actually heard. Her hearing was weak and her eyesight failing. She kept to the trail. She was enjoying the break in the weather and sniffing around the fallen leaves.

Late that night, after the guests were gone and everyone was asleep, I asked Lela about moving.

"We've moved half a dozen times. Don't get worked up yet. It's still early," she assured me. She readied herself for bed, circling around her pillow and pulling the loose folds under her. She urged me to go to sleep.

She was tired. The day had been long, and she needed to rest. I would not keep her from the deep sleep her body craved. *What about Lela?* I asked myself.

Mom said it was cold in Chicago. That the winters there were long and frigid. I didn't mind the cold, but its bitterness was unkind to Lela.

I knew she'd go wherever Mom went. Her spirit was still strong, and I couldn't imagine moving to Chicago without her. Yet she was slowing down. She depended on me more and more to tell her pieces of conversations she missed. I knew her body was breaking down. I could sense something inside her. Something that shouldn't be there. But we didn't talk about it.

I laid awake fretting about the future. I thought yearningly back to the days when I worried only about my next meal.

It seemed the more I aged, the more I worried.

How human of me.

~Thirty-six~

Mid-January. Twenty-five degrees. It was a bright, sunny day. The pond was frozen. Dad cleared the snow so the kids could skate. Santa had brought them new ice skates.

They were clumsy on the ice and not yet used to skating. I couldn't help laugh at Logan as he sputtered across the ice, arms flailing, falling forward, and then sliding several more feet before coming to a stop. Haley doubled over laughing. She was much more cautious than her younger brother.

"Not so fast, Logan. You could hurt yourself," Mom warned. Her warm breath circled around her.

Dad said there'd be ice-skating in Chicago. We found out two weeks earlier that we'd be moving in the spring. The paperwork had started. Though the kids weren't eager to move, they did want to learn how to skate. Logan even expressed an interest in ice hockey.

Mom huddled next to Dad in the big, down-filled hooded coat Santa had brought for her. It went down to her calves. She looked like she did on cold Sunday mornings, all rolled up in a big feather comforter. Only she was standing not lying down. "It isn't so chilly out here in this thing," she remarked. She was getting used to the idea of moving. We all were. But she hadn't told her boss. Many details had to be worked out. She'd wait until after bonuses were paid, and then she'd go to Chicago with Dad and the kids to look at houses and schools during the kids' spring break.

Mom and Dad joined the kids, gliding across the ice in their snow boots, spinning and jumping like a pair of professional ice dancers. Mom nestled up against Dad, just under his arm and against his chest. They fit perfectly together.

Lela gingerly chased down ice chips Logan tossed across the frozen pond. Once she trapped them between her paws, she chewed until there was nothing left. The frozen wood I chewed made my gums bleed.

"How about some football?" Dad pulled a small football from his jacket pocket. The kids cheered and Mom laughed. Lela and I scampered to our paws. We were ready.

"OK, Logan and Mom against me and Haley. Ready? Seventeen. Forty-four. Three. Hike. Hike. Hike." I interfered and the first pass went wide. Lela intercepted and trotted circles around Haley and Dad. Our hoots and howls rang through the frosty air.

We'd been happy that day. Not a care in the world. But it all changed so quickly.

We were chilled to the bone and half frozen when we began the journey home. The kids were anxious for some of Mom's hot chocolate, and I was anxious for my pillow near the warm radiator. My paw pads were cold and my gums ached.

The kids and I raced ahead. Then I heard Mom's faint holler. "Oh my God, Raj. Look." Her voice was filled with fear. She fought hard to control her panic. She didn't want to frighten the kids, but she herself was scared.

I herded the kids up the driveway, so that Mom

could compose herself. Lela had left a clump of blood in the snow where she urinated. She hadn't felt well for a few days. But there had been no visible signs of illness. Not until that day.

Lela and I looked on as Mom sought answers from Google. It could be a urinary tract infection or a sign of kidney failure. Given Lela's age, Mom was convinced it was the latter. I didn't know if the blood was somehow connected to the thing growing inside Lela.

I listened that night to Mom's sniffles. She hunched over Lela, caressing her side, whispering in her ear. Lela remained quiet and still. What could she do? She knew she was dying, that her body was failing. She felt the thing take root. My heart grew heavy and sleep evaded me.

It didn't matter that Lela was diagnosed with a urinary tract infection treatable with antibiotics. There was relief, yes. But death grew impatient waiting for Lela. Their meeting was overdue. Lela would be fifteen in April.

~Thirty-seven~

Late March. The snow had melted. Yet it was a raw beginning to spring. Cold rain fell and dampened my mood. I sought relief in the pond's frigid water. The iciness cleared my head and dulled the despair that had settled in me.

"He stopped lifting and wagging his tail," Mom told Dr. Kagan. "He decided to take a dip in the pond." Her voice cracked and her hands shook.

"It's nothing serious. Labs are prone to a condition called 'cold tail.' Rest and anti-inflammatory drugs will help," Dr. Kagan told her. Relief flooded Mom's eyes.

"You can try this for a day or two and see how he's doing." Dr. Kagan handed her a bottle. The captive pills rattled against the plastic as Mom stuffed the vial into her jacket. "This type of thing usually heals on its own in a few days. Keep him out of the water though." He patted my side. "How's Lela?"

"She's doing as well as can be expected." Mom swallowed hard and looked away from him, but in the privacy of Commander she wept.

"Don't get sick on me," she pleaded. She held my muzzle firmly and then wrapped her arms around my neck. The weight of her caring and concern settled in my chest. I felt sorry for causing her more anguish.

"I won't," I whined. I had to be strong. *But how can I be brave when I'm so afraid?*

There was so much to do in the days that followed. Our home was going on the market the next week. Mom agreed to work part-time through the end of May. June always kept Mom busy, and she'd need time before the movers came in July.

Mom planted ivy, violets, and pansies in the flowerbeds around the patio. Newly planted rhododendrons were ready to bloom in the Japanese garden.

"What's this, Shamus?" Mom waved a decomposing, half-eaten bone in front of my nose. She held it loosely between her thumb and pointer finger. She looked on with disdain as I sniffed the remains. "Ugh," gurgled from her throat when I carried it away.

Mom rearranged closets, cabinets, and drawers. Curtains, bedding, and rugs were washed, and every window and mirror sparkled. Light fixtures were polished, and baseboards, windowsills, and doors repainted. Painted walls were touched up, and the wooden floors waxed. Mom looked peaceful patrolling the house with her vacuum.

"Nothing personal should be left lying around. Prospective buyers should be able to visualize themselves living in your home," our real estate agent advised as she moved from room to room snapping pictures for a listing brochure. Lela threw up her breakfast in the dining room. "Do you want that in the picture, or should I clean it up?" Mom joked half-heartedly. The other half silently worried and kept watch over Lela.

I too silently worried and watched, and I grew anxious waiting. Lela wouldn't speak about the thing that grew inside her.

The thought of strangers living in our home bothered me despite knowing that Mom and Dad had already found a house for us in Chicago. It was on two acres with enough room for a pool. A pool that dogs could swim in.

I kept close to Mom's heels while she decluttered our home. Anything that wasn't absolutely needed before our move was boxed up and put in the garage, out of sight. Family pictures and photo albums were wrapped and stored. Board games were moved to the downstairs playroom, hidden neatly in a cabinet. We'd taken at least a dozen boxes filled with books, clothes, house wares, linens, and toys to Goodwill. Our home looked barren. It was staged to sell and began feeling less like home.

Knowing that we'd all be in Chicago before summer's end eased Mom's burdens. It made Dad's commuting every week more bearable. She hated the separation and focused on the future to get through each day. She was looking forward to a new beginning. She talked about taking time off to be with us and to get the kids settled, meet neighbors, and maybe volunteer at the kids' new school.

"I figure I'll start looking at career options in the new year," she told Jenn.

Jenn and Mom had been friends for years. They worked together right out of law school and stayed friends ever since. They rarely saw each other, but Mom valued the friendship and stood by Jenn when she struggled with her own career path, divorce, and her father's tragic passing. "Mom tries not to lean on her because Jenn already carries a heavy load," Lela whispered so they wouldn't hear.

"I'm tired of juggling work and family. I'm not doing either one well," Mom confided.

"You've been burned out for a long time. Taking a break will be good for you. If you decide to return to the law, you have a legitimate explanation for leaving. Your family relocated, and you wanted time off to make sure the kids adjusted to the change. And it's a big change, Gwen." Jenn's voice was warm and reassuring.

"I just want us to be a family again. I miss Raj. Lately I feel like a single parent. I feel like I'm drowning. I don't know how you do it."

The smell of passion fruit filled the living room. Jenn smiled over her herbal tea. She was glad she had taken the day off, but the afternoon whizzed by. It was time for her to leave. Her daughter would be home from school soon as would Haley and Logan. She embraced Mom sincerely before leaving.

Mom looked contemplatively out the window while rinsing the teacups. The spray of the water splattered against the glass. Some rested on my nose. She was, no doubt, wondering what Chicago had in store for us. Where we'd be this time next year.

"Time to get the kids. Ready?" Mom asked. The cups rattled when the dishwasher's door closed. Mom grabbed her keys off the counter. Lela and I followed at her heels. We enjoyed the short ride down to the bus stop. A coveted ritual.

Mom opened Commander's tailgate and

carefully placed Lela into the back. One of Lela's many pillows waited to cradle her. I licked her muzzle and then took my place in the middle row. I didn't know that was to be our last trip in Commander. Dad brought Shelly home the next morning.

I growled and barked when I first heard the fit, strong engine winding up the lane. It was an unfamiliar sound. *Another unwelcome looker*, I assumed. There'd been several uninvited visitors since our house went up for sale. Mom hated when they drove up unannounced. They were supposed to make appointments. "It's an invasion of our privacy," Mom complained.

I was all fired up when the shiny SUV stopped in front of the house. I charged past Logan. My nails dug deep into the wood floors. My hackles were stiff and my canines exposed. I pushed past Mom and barreled through Haley. I was determined to teach the intruder a lesson.

My body weight shoved the door open wide. The storm door rattled. I was about to hurl myself at the glistening vehicle when a familiar face caught my eye. It was Dad who sat behind the wheel.

The new truck they talked about, I realized. *This is it.*

A tingle of excitement ran up my spine. I circled around the SUV and sniffed the tires. The truck smelled new. Unspoiled. I left my urine on one of the rims.

"Don't pee on Shelly!" Haley hollered. Logan laughed in the background.

They called her Shelly because she was an oyster shell color.

~Thirty-eight~

I smelled the acrid urine before Mom awoke.

Lela began leaking while she slept. It started that winter. Just a few drops Mom hadn't noticed. But Lela could no longer contain it, and her urine seeped deep into the pillow and rug during the early morning hours.

Lela was humiliated by the sudden incontinence. Her body was deteriorating, and the thing inside her grew. She knew and accepted her fate, yet she fought to remain strong because Mom still needed her.

Fear grabbed my heart and squeezed. *I still need you*, I silently wept.

My mother's words then came to me. *Don't be afraid. Have faith,* she whispered in my ear.

But I was afraid. Afraid of losing them both and I didn't know where to turn for faith. I'd always relied on Lela. Yet she stood in front of me with head and tail hung low. Urine clinging to her fur. Mom's eyes swelled.

What can I do to ease their suffering?

My heart wretched and my body lurched forward. I moved toward Lela and raised her chin with my muzzle. Gratitude gleamed in her cloudy eyes.

"It's OK, Lela. We'll get this cleaned up." Mom knelt down and wrapped her arms tightly around Lela's neck. She buried her face deep within Lela's coat. Lela accepted the embrace, while Mom's tears rolled silently off her fur. "Don't you worry. I'll take care of you." Mom sniffled and sat up. She swatted at her eyes and kissed Lela's muzzle.

"We'll take care of her," I whimpered. Mom stroked my muzzle tenderly. *I'll watch over you both*, I silently vowed.

Mom lovingly wiped Lela down with a warm cloth and stripped the soiled cover from the pillow. She mopped at the rug with a sponge and vinegar. The pungent smell lingered for hours. Thankfully there were no scheduled showings that morning, and Dr. Kagan prescribed some meds that alleviated the symptoms of Lela's aging bladder.

Mom called Grammy later that day. The leather squealed when she dropped into the swivel chair. More tears spilled over her bottom lids as she spoke. They flowed down her cheeks and splattered on the desk's top. Mom mindlessly smeared them with her finger. She took a few deep and deliberate breaths to calm herself.

Lela's burdened eyes followed Mom's every movement. She knew Mom had to go through this final stage of their journey without her. Death's day of reckoning was steadily approaching, and Lela could not ease Mom's pain.

"We have to go to Chicago in two weeks to meet with some contractors. Can I leave the dogs with you?"

The sadness receded from Lela's eyes. They softened when she thought about the grassy field behind Grammy's house and the deserted fair grounds Lela loved to roam. Grammy enjoyed her time with us, and Lela wanted one last chance to say good-bye. I held the pain of this realization inside.

"Thanks, mom. I really appreciate it. We'll come back Saturday, so we'll be at your house for Easter. I'll have to let the Easter bunny know where to find us." A fleeting smile brushed across Mom's face.

She hung up the phone and swiveled slowly around in the chair. Her head hung slightly over the back and her eyes were closed. She opened them when the chair stopped spinning. She stared at the ceiling, motionless, until her phone buzzed.

She read the message and let out an exasperated sigh. "Shit," she uttered.

She scurried around to tidy the house. A prospective buyer was coming in less than an hour.

~Thirty-nine~

Lela's appetite waned as the thing inside her grew. She lost a fair amount of weight those last few months. Mom added gravy and various moist foods to her diet, but Lela began looking frail. I regretted the times I pushed past her as she defiantly trudged up the playroom stairs to greet Mom. I was glad Mom was home, and I no longer had to hear Lela's burdened paws climbing those stairs.

The thing inside Lela grew angry, and Lela started vomiting some time before Easter. Around the same time Logan's odd, repetitive behavior started. Touching a door four times before walking through, stutter-stepping four times before getting into Shelly, touching the bed four times before getting in. He'd have to see a doctor if the behavior worsened.

Lela's episodes were infrequent at first, and she showed no signs of discomfort. Mom thought that perhaps Lela ate her food too fast or ate something she shouldn't have. We all knew Lela had a sensitive stomach, and Mom told the story of a young Lela running wild with a homeless man's dirty underwear in her mouth. Lela was amused and touched that Mom remembered.

The kids roared with laughter as Mom reenacted the tale. Ears and underwear flapping in the wind while Lela ran zoomies around the park. Lela was fast and Mom couldn't catch her. She had to wait for Lela to exhaust herself. Mom wiped Lela's mouth out and gave her a good shower. She didn't know what Lela ingested, but Mom spent the next hour cleaning diarrhea stains and vomit from the carpet. It was a funny tale, and it left me wishing that I'd known Lela as a pup.

The vomiting became more regular as the days passed. Most often at night after midnight. Mom would wake when Lela started the panting and pacing ritual that preceded the retching. She'd let us outdoors while she cleaned up the mess. She didn't care about the soiled rugs 'cause in those wee hours of early morning Mom knew, really knew, Lela wouldn't be with us much longer. She started preparing herself and the kids.

"Lela hasn't been feeling good. Make sure you give her some extra lovin'." Mom tried to sound composed, but Haley and Logan were perceptive and they ached too. They'd become sullen as the household stress bore down on them. Logan busied himself with his inventions, and Haley searched for Emi. But Emi was seldom to be found, and I wondered if she realized how sick Lela was. I knew Lela spoke to Emi on the nights she did come in. I never knew what they spoke about as I had learned to keep my distance. But Lela's nightly trips to the playroom became farther and fewer in between.

Mom lay next to Lela each night, stroking her fur and telling her over and over again how much she was loved. "When you're ready to leave us, it's all right," she'd sigh. Mom didn't want Lela to suffer. "Just let me know when you're ready," she'd sob. Lela and I knew Mom wasn't ready despite the display of courage. I wasn't ready either.

Mom took Lela off all medicines and put her on

a rice and chicken diet per Dr. Kagan's orders. Lela ate fervently and Mom's hope was renewed. But Lela and I knew it wasn't the incontinence medicine making her sick. Nor was it the many other meds that treated her other ailments. It was the tumor that'd been growing inside her. It started to bleed and Lela's vomiting worsened.

Lela had a follow-up appointment with Dr. Kagan. More tests and X-rays.

Mom brushed Lela's fur and cleaned her ears and teeth. Dad called to say good night around 8:00 p.m. Mom kept the nighttime routine intact. She read aloud another chapter from their favorite bedtime book and then tucked the kids into bed. Haley slept on a mattress placed next to Mom's bed, and Logan slept next to Mom. The three of them found comfort in each other's presence when Dad was out of town. Mom looked on with a worried grin as Logan smoothed out his pillowcase four times before laying his head down.

The lilac candle's gentle smell filled the room. The soothing fragrance was one of Mom's favorites, and it mingled with spring's other smells. Fresh mulch, newly cut grass, dogwood. It was a damp, rainy night. The only sounds outside were the rustling leaves and spatter of rain. More rain.

Mom's tears shimmered in the candle's warm glow. They sparkled against the deep, dark circles nestled under her lower lids. She'd been robbed of her vitality. The kids, work, the move, and Lela. Each one drained her emotionally and physically; ounce by ounce her strength seeped from her body. She stifled the sobs she held deep inside her chest so as to not awaken the kids. She sat in the dark trying to extract from the night whatever strength and courage she could. Her fingers moved gently up and down Lela's spine and around Lela's hind end as she whispered to Grammy's God.

Lela's body was weak without her pain meds. She laid quietly on the edge of Haley's mattress enjoying the massage. Mom's fingers assuaged the angry tumor and arthritic joints. Lela's eyes were closed, but she was not yet sleeping. Close to sleep, I could tell from the gentle rise and fall of her chest. I wondered what she thought about. *A trip to Vermont? A winter's walk in the snow? A tumble in the surf or camping at the lake? The smell of spring's moist dirt?* I would never know because I didn't ask. She shared with me what she chose to share, and I was content with that.

Mom looked up to find me watching her. "I'm sorry, Shamus." I wagged my tail softly. I understood. Lela needed her. They all needed her, but there wasn't much left of her to share.

Mom rubbed my belly before climbing into bed. She knew that 2:00 a.m. would come early, and she'd need to be up for Lela. She blew out the candle, pulled the cover up around her, and sunk into sleep.

"How are you feeling, Lela?"

"Tired, Shamus. Very tired." Her voice was weak, and merciful sleep came quickly for her. Her breathing was steady. An occasional grunt escaped her lips. Then a whimper. Her body ached and her stomach turned. It was good that she slept.

Sleep, however, left me behind.

Mom would find out the awful truth come morning.

Lela had a tumor. She may not be going to Chicago.

~Forty~

The morning sun bounced off Lela's white face as she looked at me through the rear window. She looked neither sad nor happy, just a bit distressed, as they drove away. I knew her stomach was upset. She'd told me soon before leaving. I threw her an encouraging smile and buoyant bark. She acknowledged the gestures with a light bob of her head. Then Shelly disappeared from my sight.

I waited, listening as the truck made its way down our winding road. Shelly usually beeped good-bye. But not that morning. All thoughts were preoccupied with Lela's condition.

Shelly's humming disappeared, and the loneliness set in. I wasn't used to being alone. The emptiness closed in around me. I yearned for an embrace. But no one was home. Dad was in Chicago, and the kids were with Mom and Lela. They had wanted to go, especially Haley who dreamed of being a veterinarian.

It was another raw morning, cold and unforgiving. Too cold and damp to wait outdoors, so I waited on the futon. My nose picked up the traces of dry urine. *It will be me one day*, I thought, and my own mortality bit me in the hind end. The reality of death stung.

The aching coursed through my limbs and settled in my chest. I might not, in this life, see Haley's dreams fulfilled. I might never know if Logan grows up to design race cars or rocket ships. *What about middle school, high school, first loves, broken hearts? What about college? Would I be here to help Mom and Dad adjust to life without the kids underfoot?*

My mind raced in circles. *Would I just slip away into the cold darkness?* I wondered. *Could I come back?*

The weight of my uncertainties squeezed the air out of my lungs. I couldn't breathe. I felt woozy.

Lela accepted her fate. She wasn't afraid of dying. She fought to stay with our family because she was their protector, their champion. That left me the jester. Lela should have died years ago, but she didn't. The kids were still young and Mom needed her.

There were so many changes to come.

Lela was fifteen. Her body was failing despite her will to live. Yet her dying wasn't about her. She wouldn't let it be. It was about our family. Lela was waiting. Waiting for those she loved to accept her fate.

I couldn't ignore the gnawing in my bowels. Deep inside I knew Lela was waiting for me too. She'd been preparing me. Teaching me to watch and listen, showing me how to protect and comfort, coaching me on staying out of trouble. More and more she leaned on me. Out of physical necessity? Yes. But she was cunning and calculated. I saw it then.

Lela was waiting for me.

This realization burdened my soul. So much responsibility. *How can I possibly manage on my own when I'd never been alone*?

But I loved Lela. I didn't want her suffering needlessly.

Shame on you, I scolded myself.

Lela never complained. Not even when she was forced to fast. No food or water during the night. She'd been so thirsty that last month. She'd wake several times during the night to drink. And that night I heard the smacking of her parched lips. Yet there wasn't any water to quench her thirst or ease the turmoil in her stomach.

I sought solace outdoors. But neither light nor warmth greeted me. The birds were quiet, and the squirrels and chipmunks remained in their nests. The sun stayed buried behind the gray clouds, and it smelled like rain. More rain was coming. I felt it in my bones.

I laid in my dirt bed outside, alone, sulking. *How will I comfort them should Lela pass before we move?*

I extended my legs hoping to relieve the knot in my stomach. But it remained there. Hard and uncomfortable. Unforgiving.

I thought about everything Lela did and didn't do. How her life revolved around our family. Then I thought about my role and what I'd done. Chewed rugs and phones, ran off after deer, slept instead of checking on the kids, basked in the sun rather than being attentive.

I knew I had matured over the years under Lela's firm paws. *But had I changed enough? Will I ever be ready to assume Lela's responsibilities?*

My selfishness shamed me. Lela needed me to be the strong one. She needed to know I was ready to accept my responsibilities. Perhaps then she could find peace and let go of the burdens that plagued her mind and body.

Lela deserved peace so she could pass on her own terms. I knew then that I would do whatever was necessary to prove to Lela that I was ready.

I was relieved when Mom and Lela returned.

Mom carried her into the den and placed her softly on a pillow. Mom's eyes were teary and swollen when she greeted me. I tasted her salty cheek and then nuzzled Lela gently. She was groggy from the sedatives.

I listened as Mom talked into the phone. She left a message for Dad explaining what she had learned.

Lela's X-rays confirmed the presence of a tumor on her spleen. The tumor had bled out slightly, and Lela was very anemic. This information explained her vomiting and lethargy.

Dr. Kagan gave Mom two options. Do nothing, in which case the tumor would most likely rupture within the month and Lela would surely die. Or remove the tumor. The doctor said Lela's type of tumor was usually cancerous, but he couldn't say with certainty unless it was removed and biopsied. Removing the tumor could give Lela a few more months depending on how much the cancer had spread. If Mom opted for surgery, Lela would need a blood transfusion the day before.

"I don't know what to do," Mom sobbed quietly into the receiver, slumped in the chair. She turned toward Lela for answers, but Lela remained quiet and still. She looked peaceful resting her head on her front paws.

What does Lela want to do? I wondered.

Mom hung up the phone and wept uncontrollably. Her shoulders shook as she cried. I placed my paw on her lap to steady her.

"It's OK," I whimpered. "The tumor's benign." Lela and I knew it wasn't cancerous, but we hadn't known it could be removed.

I dared to hope and my heart swelled with the possibility that Lela might be with us in Chicago.

"It isn't cancer!" I yipped, but Mom couldn't understand my words. There was no way of sparing her the agonizing choice she had to make. For I was sure she'd opt for surgery if she knew the tumor was benign.

Mom placed her forehead on mine and we wept together. *She'll know*, I told myself. *She'll know what to do. Have faith.*

We sat like that for an eternity, and my butt started to ache. I ignored the throbbing. I sat there, still and unwilling to shift my weight. It wasn't until Lela stirred that Mom moved. She looked beyond me towards Lela.

Lela's eyes were still closed, yet I was sure she'd been observing us. Listening to Mom cry. Watching my response.

Mom gently rubbed my muzzle, wiped her eyes, and grabbed a tissue. She blew her nose and deeply inhaled and exhaled. When her crying stopped, she turned to Google and read aloud everything she could find on canine splenectomies. In most cases, the tumor was cancerous and the prognosis wasn't good. But if the tumor was benign, removing the spleen often cured the problem. None of the cases involved a fifteen-year-old

Lab.

Mom studied the statistics and then called Dad. She was grateful he picked up the phone. I was grateful too.

"If I do nothing, she'll die. I'm not sure I can pull that trigger. You should have seen her on our walk yesterday. She was slow, but she was eager to go. She still tussles with Ronan and Shamus. She can still go up and down stairs. Her meds were controlling the incontinence, and Dr. Kagan said the surgical risks are low. And what if it's not cancer? She's had a lot of fatty tumors. None of them cancer. Not since her chemo." Mom wanted Dad to tell her what to do, but she knew he wouldn't. It was her decision to make. One she'd have to live with.

She hung up the phone and grabbed her keys. She left me to watch Lela while she picked up the kids. "Thanks, Shamus," she said as she closed the front door behind her.

When I returned to the den, Lela was lying on her side.

"It's OK, Shamus. I'm awake."

"How are you feeling?" I asked.

"Tired. I'm getting too old for all this drama." A chuckle escaped through her lips.

"Sounds like Mom may opt for surgery." I tried hiding my optimism.

"Yes. Sounded that way."

"What do you want?" I asked, though I wasn't sure I wanted to hear her answer.

"I want Mom to have peace when I pass. If that

means having the surgery, then I'll have the surgery. If Dr. Kagan says I'll survive it, I'm sure I will. Whether I live one more month or six more months is irrelevant to me. I've had a full life, and I myself have no regrets."

Typical Lela, I thought. "If you had a choice?" I pressed.

Sadness filled her cloudy eyes. "This is my home. I've had my fill of adventure." She stretched out her paws. Her vertebrae harshly realigned themselves. "They're starting a new chapter in their lives." Her milky eyes fixed on mine. "You must see them through the next phase," she said bluntly.

I nodded. The lump in my throat prevented me from speaking. I exhaled loudly to mask the low wail pressing against my lungs. I moved closer and licked her muzzle.

"Mom made chicken and rice for you," I blurted. What else could I say?

The sparkle returned to her eyes.

"Good, I love chicken and rice," she laughed.

~Forty-one~

Two families came to see our home while Lela was having her blood transfusion. While I didn't like the intrusions, the cleaning kept Mom's worries at bay. She worried about the pending surgery. Worried Lela might not survive. Lela's condition was fragile.

"Don't worry, Mom. Dr. Kagan said she'll be fine," the kids said with their youthful optimism. Logan stroked Mom's arm affectionately four times after hugging her.

Mom tried to hide her worries, but the deep lines etched across her forehead and her dark, sunken eyes gave her away. The smile she wore that morning was just an illusion, and it looked out of place.

Mom spent the morning dusting and vacuuming, mopping floors, making beds, and wiping down the kitchen appliances. Towels were aligned perfectly, and fresh flowers adorned the dining room and kitchen tables. Our home looked warm and inviting and, indeed, it was a joyful homecoming that evening.

Dad had taken an earlier flight to be with us. Gratitude filled Mom's eyes when he drove up the driveway that afternoon. She was drained and needed his emotional and physical support. It was a Thursday. Dad always came home from Chicago on Thursdays. He went with Mom and the kids to fetch Lela. I waited anxiously outdoors.

There was no smell of rain that day. Though the sky was cloudy, the sun's rays pushed hard against the gray clouds as I awaited Lela's arrival. The clouds eventually yielded with the help of a brisk breeze. They parted and the yard flooded with sunshine. I lifted my muzzle high into the air and let the sun pour over me. The warm rays embraced my burdened spirit. The stirring within quieted. *Perhaps spring is finally here*, I thought peacefully.

A distant sparkle caught my eye. A sunbeam danced across a mirrored ornament. The birds played a new sonata. The frogs sang harmony, and the butterflies flittered effortlessly about. Shelly's hum joined in; her purr's intensity increased until Dad silenced the crescendo. Logan came to get me.

Lela was happy to be home. She trotted around, tossing her head from side to side. She playfully slapped my neck with her paw, inviting me to tussle. I was surprised at how lively she was. She wasn't the weary dog she'd been when she left hours earlier. She was full of vigor and life. We ran gleeful circles around the yard.

"Look at her, Raj. She's not ready to die. Look at how she's acting. She hasn't had this much energy in weeks," Mom said. Mom was, for the time being, satisfied that surgery was the right option.

"Let's wait and see." Dad's response was practical, but Mom didn't want him to be practical. She needed him to be optimistic. She said nothing else as she stood there watching us.

We spent the early evening outdoors. The sun kindled everyone's spirit. Dad and the kids swung on the hammock, while Lela and I loitered close by. But as the early evening wore on, Lela's energy level began to fade.

"Dinner's just about ready. Come in and wash your hands," Mom called from the porch. "Where's Lela?" Her eyes scanned the yard.

I ran toward the hammock where Lela lay sleeping soundly in the grass. Mom quietly walked to her and gently enveloped the delicate body in her arms. She walked slowly and steadily toward the house. Careful not to disturb the treasure she carried. Lela would need all her strength to recover from surgery.

Lela stirred. She lifted her heavy head and grinned to reassure Mom that all was good. Her groggy body sunk deeper into Mom. Her muzzle rested against Mom's chest.

Mom brushed her forehead lightly against Lela's muzzle.

Lela's whiskers twitched.

I stepped to the side so they could pass through the doorway.

Doubt flashed once again in Mom's eyes.

~Forty-two~

"You OK, Lela?" I asked quietly. I didn't want to wake her if she was asleep.

She shifted on to her side. I noticed the fur on her stomach had been shaved. I could easily see her large incision and sutures. The area looked raw. Tender.

Dr. Kagan removed a softball-sized tumor from Lela's spleen. The thought of a tumor that size attached to Lela's insides made me retch.

"Tired, Shamus. Tired and sore." Her next breath carried her deep into a drug-induced sleep.

She woke hours later that night. She stood up uneasily and her legs quivered. I knew her pain meds were wearing off. I was afraid her legs might give way.

"I'll check on the kids. You rest," I told her.

The night couldn't hide her pain as she stood there wincing. She was embarrassed that I had seen. But she trusted me. She knew I would never betray her.

"OK," she answered, nodding her head. I felt her eyes and heard her labored breathing as I walked away.

Brave and stoic, I admired, heading upstairs.

Lela's surgery went well, but her recovery was slow and painful. She slept a lot and lost her appetite. When she wasn't sleeping, she paced around. It was hard for her to rest comfortably. Her incision was sore, and the anesthesia made her nauseous, very nauseous. For three days Mom tempted Lela with boiled chicken and fresh deli meats. But Lela rejected the food despite the rumbling in her stomach.

"Here, Lela. Want some of this?" Haley held a fresh piece of turkey between her fingers. Lela inhaled the juicy aroma. She smacked her lips and accepted the meat. She cradled it with her tongue. Then the panting started. The meat fell to floor and she left the kitchen. Her stomach was still too upset to eat. "It's OK, Mom," Haley said. "The vet said not to worry." Mom simply nodded. Logan touched the wall four times when Lela passed by.

"I'm sorry, Lela," Mom said each time she forced the pain and anti-nausea medicines into Lela. Mom hid the pills in a rice and peanut butter mixture that she pushed to the back of Lela's throat. It was painful for both of them. I too gagged each time it had to be done. "What have I done?" Mom asked herself tearfully.

The house showings continued while Lela recovered. Thirty minutes before each showing, Mom loaded us up in Shelly. She placed extra cushioning in the back for Lela. The thick, white spongy foam was supposed to absorb the bumps, but Lela still felt them.

"I like car rides. I'm just a bit stiff," Lela said bravely.

Mom resented the intrusions. She wanted Lela resting at home. But what could she do? The showings were necessary. We had to show the house to sell it, and Mom knew that, but for the move, she wouldn't be home to nurse Lela. She was grateful for that.

I could always tell when strangers had come. Their various smells drove me crazy. Some left more pungent odors than others. I'd follow the scents from room to room. I could tell whose prying hands had opened which drawers and doors. I'd lower my hackles only after I was satisfied that no intruders remained. *What would I do if I came upon an intruder in the house?* I often wondered.

Mom got the call on the first sunny day after Lela's surgery. The sun was bright and inviting that day. It took a moment for our eyes to adjust when we stepped off the patio.

Lela moved nimbly along the trail. The warmth eased her stiffness. Mom let the rays melt the weariness that contaminated her once joyful demeanor. She looked for strength in the light, while I urinated on a nearby sapling. She took notice of the young tree and its fresh, new leaves. She let one rest softly on her palm, tracing its veins with her finger. The limb to which it was attached was thin. But it was strong and flexible. It didn't snap when she bent it.

Lela leaned into me and whispered, "Mom looks forward to spring."

We both knew Mom's hope was fragile. At times she looked more frail and vulnerable than Lela. Mom looked lost, and this concerned us. She was our leader. Yet it was she who now needed to be led.

"If only I could speak to her so she'd understand," Lela said. I nodded supportively. Lela was recovering. It was a slow recovery, but each day there were signs of improvement. Lela was regaining her strength gradually, and the knot in her stomach was easing. Although I'd accepted that her time with us was limited, I knew she wasn't dying of cancer. I held on to the hope that she'd be with us in Chicago. Mom wanted to believe, but she was too scared to hope.

Lela instinctively moved to Mom's side.

Mom sniffled, and a weak smile appeared on her face. "I want one more spring and summer," she said, lowering herself to the damp earth. She buried her head in Lela's neck. "Just let me know when you've had enough. Please give me a sign," Mom pleaded. She wiped her eyes and nose on her sleeve.

The answering machine blinked on and off when we returned from our walk. A message from Dr. Kagan. He needed to speak to Mom, and she reluctantly dialed the phoned. She stood there, motionless, as he spoke on the other end. I could hear the excitement in his muffled voice. But Mom's face remained expressionless. It wasn't until after she hung up the receiver that the news sunk in.

Lela's tumor was benign.

Mom dropped to her knees and hugged us both. Happy tears flowed down her cheeks. She offered words of thanks to Grammy's God and basked in hope's luxury.

"It's not cancer. The doctor said your tumor was benign." Mom couldn't catch her breath. "We better start researching Winnebago rentals." We'd drive to Chicago because Lela wasn't fit to fly. Mom turned toward me, grinning from ear to ear. "What do you think, Shamus?"

I didn't know what to think. I knew Lela didn't want to go to Chicago, but she'd fight to give Mom one more spring and summer. *It would be nice to have Lela with us*, I selfishly thought. I turned toward Lela. She was smiling, lost too in Mom's joy.

That night we all slept peacefully, and Lela's appetite returned the next morning.

Mom was able to relax for the first time in weeks. Her steps were light as she moved around the house and tended to work. She was thankful for the part-time work. The extra money helped pay for Lela's escalating medical expenses. Mom allowed herself to run frivolous errands and pick out furnishings for the house in Chicago. It was safe for her to focus on things other than Lela.

But hope's visit was brief. It's joy fleeting.

~Forty-three~

Mom sat up and peered over the bed's edge. It was her morning ritual. She didn't move until she saw Lela's chest rise and fall. If it was dark, she placed a hand on Lela's side to feel the life underneath her palm. Only then did she exhale.

Lela was already awake that morning. She stood next to her pillow, panting, eyes cast down, embarrassed by her incontinence. Her panting did little to ease the gas pains or relieve the swelling in her bowels that started the day before. "Gas. Not uncommon after surgery or once eating resumes," Dr. Kagan assured us.

"It's OK, Lela," Mom said sweetly as she removed Lela's pillow cover. "You'll be OK, and we'll get this cleaned up." She patted Lela's forehead and then reached for the soft, fuzzy robe lying on the bench. It was the robe Logan gave her for Christmas a few months before. The thought that Lela might not be here for another Christmas saddened me. But I shook the sadness off. *Lela is here with us now, and the gas pains will subside,* I told myself.

But the gas pains didn't subside. For two more days, we watched Lela's stomach expand though Dr. Kagan's X-rays assured us that she was suffering from gas pains. Lela would wake each night, panting and pacing to relieve the pressure. Mom and I looked on helplessly as we waited for the gas medicine to kick in.

"Lela has bad gas. She's having a hard time farting," the kids told Dad over the speakerphone. They rolled around on Mom's bed, laughing as they said it.

"Her belly was filled with all these gas bubbles. We saw them on the X-rays," Haley informed. Dad laughed with them.

But neither Mom nor I laughed as Lela lay panting on the floor. Lela hadn't acted right since she came home from the vet a few hours before. She was wobbly on her feet, and she stumbled down the driveway when Mom let us out to pee.

"Don't overreact," Dad said unsympathetically to Mom. His insensitivity surprised me. "Dr. Kagan said she's doing fine. She's had every possible test and now X-rays. Nothing showed up. You're tired. You haven't slept well in weeks. Get some sleep. I'll be home in the morning."

Dad flew in from Chicago earlier that day but was spending the night in the city. His friends were throwing him a "bon voyage" party, and Mom wouldn't ask him to come home. Dr. Kagan, the tests, the X-rays, all signs indicated Lela wasn't in any danger. Still Mom's inner voice suspected it was more than gas.

I knew Mom wasn't overreacting.

"Sharp, sudden pains in my head," Lela told me. They started shortly before she left the vet that day. The pressure in her gut and in her head was increasing, and the pain was taking its toll.

Mom dragged a twin-sized mattress into the kitchen and laid Lela's pillow next to the water bowl. She gated off the kitchen's entrances to keep Lela from wandering. She didn't want Lela stumbling during the night on any rugs or stairs, and Mom needed to sleep. One night of sleep without waking up to panting and pacing and late-night potty trips.

"Come on, Lela. Let's get you up on the mattress. You'll be more comfortable." Mom scooped Lela up and positioned her on the makeshift bed. Classical music played on the radio, and Mom's hands glided over Lela's body, tenderly kneading the soft tissue. Her fingertips paused on Lela's white paws and tail tip. They'd once been glossy black like my own.

Lela finally farted and her labored breathing quieted. The pain in her gut and the pounding in her head eased. She succumbed to the weariness and fell into sleep. Mom hoped the worst was over. She laid a soft kiss on Lela's forehead before gating the entrance.

Mom couldn't smell the stench. Only I sensed death was near. Its presence scared me, and I decided to watch over Lela. I laid by the gate listening to the sounds of the night. I didn't know how close death was until Lela awoke a few hours later. Her shrill yelp curdled my blood.

"Lela. Lela, are you OK?"

Lela stumbled blindly into her water bowl, and it crashed to the ground. Water flowed around her feet.

"My head. It's my head. The pressure hurts," she whimpered through clenched teeth. The pain flashed in her eyes. Her breaths were short and hollow.

I turned to get Mom, but she was already at my side.

"Lela. What happened? You OK?" Mom saw Lela standing in the spilled water. "It's OK, Lela. Come on. Let's get you out."

We stepped out into the night, and Lela's legs

betrayed her. They sent her stumbling uncontrollably down the sloped yard. I froze on the gravel, unable to speak or move. Too stunned by what I saw.

"Lela. What are you doing?" Mom shouted, running after her. She caught up to her and cradled Lela's shaking body.

Lela was unresponsive. She couldn't hear beyond the pounding between her ears.

"Oh, Lela. What have I done? I'm sorry. I'm sorry. I'm sorry," Mom kept crying out as she carried Lela inside. I wanted to run from the misery, but I knew they needed me.

I followed them in and felt death retreat from the light. It brushed against my tail, and a cold shiver ran up my spine. It ran deep into the darkness, cackling.

Mom returned Lela to the mattress and slowly stroked her head and sides. "It's OK, Lela. Just rest," Mom implored. The pain in Lela's head moved into Mom's chest. I heard the crack of her heart as it parted. She leaned over our Lela and wept.

Lela's breathing relaxed when the pounding subsided. She lay still and quiet. Mom moved to clean up the spilled water. "My Lela," I whimpered, lowering myself next to her. My tongue softly grazed the white muzzle. I resisted the urge to throw myself upon her and wail.

"Come on, Shamus," Mom whispered. "Let her rest." Mom gently pulled me from Lela's side and gated the entrance.

I couldn't sleep. Death loomed nearby. The foul odor seeped in through the windows. I heard its long cold fingers scraping against the glass. It wanted to come in. It wanted Lela. But I wouldn't let it take her. I patrolled the gated entrances.

"Not yet," I howled mournfully. "Please," I begged, "not yet."

"Shamus." Lela's weak voice. I hadn't meant to wake her.

"I'm here, Lela. Next to the gate."

"Shamus. I need you to be strong. Can you do that for me?"

A lump formed in my throat. Hot tears stung my eyes. I held them back with all my might. I wouldn't cry. Not in front of her. "Of course," I whispered. "But if they give you more meds?"

"Not this time, Shamus." Her voice was barely audible. "Promise me you'll comfort Mom and protect them."

Fear and sadness ripped open my chest. I secretly begged for a miracle.

"I promise," I choked on the words. "Just rest now. Save your strength." The pain was unbearable. "I'm here," I cried. "I'm here."

~Forty-four~

Lela slept for a couple of hours, but then the pounding in her head started again. She began panting heavily.

"Lela, Lela," I yelled, peering over the gate. Pain glazed her eyes, but I knew she heard me. She struggled to stand, stumbling towards the gate. She tripped, wedging herself between the mattress and the refrigerator.

Mom rushed toward her, pulling the gate down. "What are you doing down there, Lela? Come on. Let's get you up. Come on. Let's go out." Mom tried keeping her voice low and calm, but panic set in when she realized Lela couldn't get up. She carefully lifted Lela and carried her outside. She gently placed Lela on the moist grass, but Lela stumbled and fell over. She was too weak to stand.

"Oh God," escaped from Mom's lips. She held Lela in her arms, rocking back and forth. "Oh God, no. What have I done?" Mom's body trembled, and she walked briskly into the kitchen and laid Lela down. "Rest, Lela. Just rest. We'll go see Dr. Kagan first thing. Just rest," she said, stroking Lela from head to hind end.

She picked up the phone. "Raj, you've got to come home. Something's wrong. Lela can't stand." She choked on her next words. "I think this is it."

I braced myself and pushed aside the panic that crept into my gut. I stood firmly in place to keep my paws from fleeing. I promised Lela I'd be strong.

Mom held the receiver in her hand. She couldn't

control the tears. She was tired, angry, and scared; and her small voice told her the miracles had run out. She hit the redial button. "Please pick up your phone. Pick up the fucking phone," she yelled into it. But Dad didn't answer. He didn't pick up his phone or respond to her text messages.

Mom swallowed hard and sat upright. She wiped her eyes with the back of her hands and composed herself. She inhaled and exhaled deeply, again and again. Lela rested quietly at her side.

It was Friday. There were usually afternoon showings on Fridays. Mom moved around the kitchen putting dirty dishes in the dishwasher. She organized the clutter on the counter and picked wilted flower buds off the floral arrangements. Her coffee mug sat on the counter. She stared into it and then emptied it in the sink. She looked out the window and wept.

Death hovered in the doorway, mocking her feeble attempts to stay in control.

The clock on the stove read 7:00 when Haley and Logan stirred. One more hour until the vet's office opened.

Mom splashed water on her face and ran her fingers through her hair. She grabbed a rubber band from a drawer and tied her hair back.

I scampered to the bedroom to greet them. "Shamus!" The kids greeted me in unison, and I jumped up next to them and smothered their warm, smiling faces with kisses. They were oblivious to what was happening. I was glad they didn't yet know. It would be a difficult day for them. They would lose their Lela, who'd been with them from their births.

"Shamus, what are you doing up there?" Mom tried to keep her voice light, but the kids sensed right away that something was wrong. Logan caressed my ear four times before Mom responded to their questioning eyes. "It's OK, guys. We've got to get Lela to the vet first thing. She can't stand. Can you come eat your breakfast?" She patted my head as she stretched across the bed, catching both of them in her arms. She kissed their faces. "Come on now," Mom said.

Lela hadn't moved from the spot where Mom carefully placed her. Haley squatted next to the mattress. "What's a matter, Lela? Don't you feel good?" She patted Lela's head and kissed her nose. Logan looked on from his seat at the counter. There was concern in his eyes and on his brow. He wasn't sure how to act. His tender age made him both brave and vulnerable. He touched his plate four times.

The minutes passed excruciatingly slow.

Mom hurriedly made her way to the den to answer the phone. "Where have you been? I've been trying to reach you for the last couple of hours. I need you here. I think this is it. She can't stand. She isn't moving. Why didn't you pick up the phone? I can't wait for you. She needs to go to the vet, and I have to get the kids to school." Her low, angry voice drifted into the kitchen. The kids exchanged worried glances.

Logan climbed up onto the counter and grabbed Mom's camera from the shelf. He experimented with the video feature. "Say hi, Lela. Come on." She didn't respond when he snapped a photo, and he didn't realize how serious her condition was. She looked like she was sleeping. Muscles relaxed. Eyes closed. Breathing regular.

"Look, Mom. Look at the picture I took of Lela." Logan held the camera up to Mom's face. It was much too close to her eyes, and she backed away from it.

"Let her rest, Logan," Mom said, running her hand down Lela's back.

"If you're done with breakfast, get dressed and start your reading, OK?" she half-asked, half-ordered. She went through the motions, counting down the minutes. She headed upstairs to tidy the rooms and wipe down the bathrooms. It's what she did every morning since our house went up for sale. She'd dust and vacuum after taking the kids to school.

I waited with the kids in the TV room. I laid at their feet while they read their books on the cozy sofa. The carpet smelled like Lela, the old Lela. The Lela before the blood transfusion, surgery, and office visits. The Lela who didn't smell like the dog perfume Dr. Kagan's assistants used. "I can't get the smell out of my nose. It reminds me of funeral home," Mom told Grammy.

I inhaled Lela's smell from the wool. An earthy smell tinged with the scent of Lela's urine. It was the faintest of smells, a smell unnoticeable to humans. It comforted me.

A timer went off. Reading time was over. I followed the kids to the kitchen and watched as they brushed their teeth and packed their school bags.

I sat next to Lela and whispered, "I'm here, Lela. Rest. Just rest."

Her eyes opened ever so slightly, and the faintest smile appeared on her beautiful face. I knew death stood behind her as the white foam slipped slowly from her lips.

Mom's breath stuck in her throat. She raised her hands to her mouth, and her breath escaped in ragged gasps.

"Lela, Lela!" Mom cried out in a panicked voice. "Haley. Logan. Get in the car. Get in the car!" she yelled. She struggled to lift Lela's limp body. "Haley, Logan, please. Someone open the door. Open the back of the truck," she pleaded. Lela's head rolled back over Mom's shoulder. "No, no, no," Mom cried out.

Haley looked on in dismay. "Get the door, honey." Mom said, trying to control her voice. "Logan, get Shamus in the car."

"Oh God," Mom whispered as she placed Lela's body in Shelly. Mom took a half step back to look at Lela. She bent over her and swallowed the anguish. She clutched Lela's fur and held back her grief.

I sniffed the air and listened intently. No sign of Dad.

Mom held Lela's muzzle between her hands and kissed her cold, wet nose ever so lightly. She paused to study the light butterfly freckle on the tip of Lela's nose. A scar Lela obtained years before after digging her way out from under a fence. She'd been spooked by distant fireworks.

Mom grudgingly closed the door.

There was no parking in front of the vet's office when we arrived, so Shelly blocked the driveway. Mom raced into the office and returned seconds later with Lauren.

"We'll get her stabilized. Dr. Kagan's on his way. We'll call you as soon as we know something." Lauren carefully lifted Lela, and I knew I'd never see her again. She couldn't fight the thing beating in her head.

"Lela," I whimpered as Lauren carried her away. Death's shadow followed them indoors.

The aching in my chest was unbearable. I wanted to escape the intense pain. Run until my legs collapsed and my lungs screamed for air. But I'd made a promise.

I dropped my butt between the kids.

Haley's eyes filled with tears. Her body felt heavy against my shoulder. Logan sat quiet and still, looking out his window. He clenched my fur in his hand. Their anguish sapped my strength, and I had to lay to mask my trembling limbs. They needed the courage that was failing me.

Mom watched us through the rearview mirror. "I'll let you know as soon as I hear something, OK?" Neither child moved. "If the doctor says it's time for Lela to go to heaven, would you like me to come get you so you can say good-bye?" They nodded. "OK, let's just wait and see. Lela is our miracle dog after all, right?" Mom tried sounding optimistic, but neither of them answered her. The ride to school felt unusually long.

I missed Lela already.

Mom put Shelly in park when we arrived at school. "If you start feeling really sad, you call me and I'll come get you. OK? But right now I think you'll feel better being with your friends. Yeah?"

Logan reached for Mom first. He wrapped his arms around her neck. "It's OK, Mom," he said. He grabbed his backpack and exited the car. He's always been her little man. "Bye, Shamus," he added. My tail wagged a "bye" back. He touched the door four times before closing it.

Haley hugged Mom, her eyes still brimmed with tears. Mom cupped Haley's face with her hands. "You OK?" Mom asked. Haley nodded, and Mom stared deep into her eyes. "I love you, Haley," Mom told her. "Love you too, Mom," Haley murmured before pulling away. She patted my head and then shut the door.

They headed reluctantly into school. Shelly beeped and Mom waved good-bye. The kids looked back and waved as Mom blew them kisses. They all made the "I love you" sign with their hands.

Mom's phone beeped just as we pulled onto the main road. She read aloud Dad's latest text. "On Saw Mill. Home in fifteen minutes." She tossed the phone into the cup holder without otherwise acknowledging his message. She was angry, and she didn't want to see him. She retreated to the wooded trails Lela loved so much. But the woods provided little comfort. She leaned against a moss-covered boulder and wept.

Surely her heart is about to break, I thought.

Mine is. I laid at her feet and cried too.

Dad was waiting for us when we returned. "I'm sorry," he said. "I had my phone off. I tried to get here sooner, but there was traffic getting out of the city. How is she? How are the kids?" His expression was grim.

"They'll call when they know something. I told the kids we'd let them know too."

She moved past him to finish cleaning the kitchen. She stripped the sheet off the mattress and moved Lela's pillow to the bedroom.

"What happened?" Dad pressed.

Her grief-stricken face looked up at him. She clung to Lela's pillow, which she'd only partially tucked under the bed. She always stored our pillows under the bed when Realtors brought their clients.

"I shouldn't have left her in the kitchen. But I was so tired. I needed to sleep. Deep down I knew something was wrong. But I was so tired. I laid with her and massaged her until she quieted down. But last night . . ." She paused to wipe her face against Lela's pillow. "I thought maybe the gas felt like labor pains. And she hasn't had any of her medicine in days. She's got to be sore. She's been at the vet's so much. I kept telling myself it can't be anything serious. She was just at the vet's and had X-rays and more tests." She started crying again. "I shouldn't have left her alone. She was all alone last night." Guilt shoved its ugly head into her chest. She winced from the impact.

Dad took a small step toward her, but she raised her hand signaling him to stay. Nothing would appease Mom's grief and anger.

The deep shadows under Dad's eyes accentuated his forlorn look.

"I need to clean up. There are showings this weekend and maybe one this afternoon," she told him. Her voice was unfeeling.

He retreated from the room. The gurgling washing machine told us he started the laundry.

Mom grabbed her dust rag. Heavy tears fell to the floor.

"Don't do this. Don't be sad. Lela wasn't alone," I whined. But Mom couldn't hear me as she ran the rag over the end tables. I lunged at the cloth. "Down, Shamus. Not now." Her voice was flat, numb.

I have to get through to her. I have to tell her Lela wasn't alone, I thought frantically, running around her legs. I nipped at her fleece top and she tripped. Her shin knocked against the wooden bed, and she let out a painful groan. She rubbed the sore spot and turned toward me. Her puffy eyes looked deep into mine.

Lela wasn't alone. I concentrated on the words coursing through my mind.

Lela wasn't alone! *Lela wasn't alone*! *Lela wasn't alone*, I screamed silently. Mom had to hear the words. She had to know the truth.

Then something stirred behind Mom's eyes.

"You knew," she stammered. "You stayed with her."

"Yes," I cried softly, grazing her leg with a gentle wag of my tail.

"You knew," she whispered, leaning into me.

Yes, I knew.

~Forty-five~

That morning passed slowly. Minutes felt like days. No word from the doctor's office. All we knew was that Lela had been stabilized.

"Stabilized is good." Dad tried to sound reassuring. "You know Lela. She's always full of surprises."

I watched from the gate as they walked down the driveway to the corral. Dad had left his Jeep at the county airport. They had to pick it up. Mom clutched the travel mug in her hand. The color drained from her knuckles. Chai. She was drinking Chai tea that morning. I knew the smell. She drank the dark tea when she was tired. She'd been drinking a lot of Chai.

As they approached Mom's truck, our neighbor David, Bridgette's human, drove up. He spoke briefly to Mom and Dad. A client wanted to see the house. Mom and Dad nodded. They drove away, and a middle-aged woman stepped out of David's truck. I'd never seen her before. She was wearing dark pants and a dark blazer. David wore a tie instead of his usual playclothes. He was dressed like Dad.

I eyed them suspiciously as they strolled up our driveway. They stopped to admire Mom's Japanese garden and the pansies adorning the patio. I lost sight of them but then heard the front door open and close.

I was suddenly enraged by the intrusion. Didn't they know? Didn't they know what was happening?

I ran inside and hurled myself against the playroom door. I dug my nails deep into the wood. "Get out. Get out," I snarled. "Show some respect."

But they didn't listen. I could hear them. Her heels clicked loudly on the wooden floors. The noise drove me wild. *Don't they know? Don't they know? How dare they,* I thought as I madly scratched at the door.

When my lungs were empty of air and when the anger fled my heart, it occurred to me. They couldn't possibly know our Lela was dying. Angst and shame ripped open my soul.

I looked at the mess I made. Pieces of wood and paint littered the top two stairs. Mom would have to mend and repaint the door.

My heavy paws trudged down the stairs.

Lela was everywhere. Her fur, her urine stains, her discarded chew toys. This was our room. This was where we stayed when Mom and Dad couldn't take us with them. This was our sanctuary when no one else was home.

I could barely stand. I needed fresh air.

The bed I had dug for myself was soft and cool. It cradled my body. The earth pressed around me, and I felt safe. I waited for the sound of Mom's truck. I laid there gathering my strength for what was to come.

The front door opened and closed again. David and the woman talked about our house. "It's charming," she told David. "Yeah. They've done a lot of work on it. Nice family too. We're sad to see them go." Although she loved our house and our property, she couldn't make an offer to buy it until she sold her house. I stopped listening. I didn't care what they had to say. I was glad they were leaving. I wanted to wait alone.

I didn't have to wait long. Soon after David left, I heard the hum of Mom's truck. I leaped to all fours and headed to the gate. I sensed immediately that something was wrong the moment she stepped from Shelly. Her body convulsed with heavy sobs, and she leaned against the truck.

"Not like this. Not like this," she kept saying. She shook her head from side to side. She paced around the corral, back and forth, like a wounded animal, clutching her chest as if somehow it might ease her pain. I heard her, but she didn't come to me.

Something was terribly wrong. "I'm here," I barked. But she couldn't hear me. "Let me help," I cried. I couldn't help her from where I stood behind the gate. I jumped, but my legs failed me. They wouldn't propel me up over the fence so that I could go to her.

She inhaled, trying to breathe. She picked up her cell phone. She spoke to Grammy as she paced. The vet called. Lela had a seizure. It was time. She had to get the kids so they could say good-bye. She couldn't breathe. The oxygen had been sucked out of the universe. She couldn't stop crying. I knew Lela was very near to death.

I felt useless. I promised to protect Mom, but I couldn't shield her from the pain.

I too began to wail.

Dad pulled up in his Jeep. Mom looked confused. She started coming toward me, but Dad touched her arm and said it was time to go. She fell into his opened arms. "Oh God. I knew this day would come." Her tears strangled her words, and I couldn't make out what else she said.

Dad held her close. His body trembled against the weight of her sobs. Her sobs turned to whimpers. She pulled away first. She wiped her eyes and nose on her fleece. Her breaths were rough and ragged. Dad helped her into Shelly. Neither looked at me. I cried but no one heard. "Mom. Lela. What can I do?" I asked aloud as they drove away.

I pressed my muzzle hard into the metal gate. I couldn't feel the pinch. I couldn't feel anything but my anguish.

Time stopped.

At the lowest depths of my despair, she came to me. I sensed the familiar presence.

"Lela, is that you?" I asked.

"Yes. It's me, Shamus."

"Lela, what's happening? Mom and Dad left. Mom was so upset. I knew something was wrong. I couldn't do anything. I felt so useless," I rambled on.

"It's OK, Shamus. I've passed on. I'm glad Dad's home."

"Me too," I mumbled.

"Be strong for them, Shamus. They need you, especially Mom. These last few weeks have been hard. She's very tired and feels that she needs to be strong for the kids."

I nodded, understandingly.

"She feels responsible for my passing, but she's not. She loved me so well for so long. Be strong for her, Shamus." Her voice was calm and clear. "I felt the depth of her pain as she stroked my muzzle, telling me how blessed she was to have me in her life. I hope she knows that I too feel blessed to have been a part of this family."

"She knows, Lela."

"The kids will need you too, Shamus. Haley and Logan were so brave. They all came to see me at the hospital. I knew they were there, as hard as it was, because they loved me. Dad broke down crying and left the room with Logan. Haley stayed with Mom until the end. She has such an old soul for a nine-year-old. My spirit ached as I watched them embrace my lifeless body, and I wished then that I didn't have to leave. But it was my time, Shamus. So be brave and comfort them as best you can. Healing is a process. It takes time. Be patient. They love you, Shamus. You know that."

Yes. I knew they loved me. But I also knew I could never fill the void her passing created.

"What's it like, Lela? What's dying like?"

"It's just another transition, Shamus. It's painless and it's peaceful. The hardest part is saying good-bye to those who love you."

"Will I see you again? Will you be back?"

"Yes, I'll be back. Our paths will cross again. But I have to go now. Our family will be back soon. Take care of them, Shamus. Take care of yourself."

"I'll miss you, Lela. I'll miss you so very much." I refused to cry. I missed her already.

"I know. But you'll be fine. You're ready, Shamus."

A wave of peace washed over me.

A light breeze tickled my nose.
She was gone.

~Forty-six~

I recognized the engine's sound. They were home. I ran to the fence and braced myself for what was to come.

Mom, Dad, Haley, and Logan emerged from Shelly. But the air was void of their laughter and usual bantering. They silently made their way up the driveway, shoulders slumped, heads bent. Mom carried Lela's collar in her hand. The only sound I heard was the jingling of Lela's tags.

It was Dad who came for me. His eyes were puffy and moist, and I remembered what Lela had said. I had never seen Dad cry, and I knew I didn't want to. His tears would make my teetering courage collapse, and I needed to be strong. He knelt down and stroked my back. We drew strength from each other. Only after he stood did I race to the kitchen.

Mom had begun placing Lela's things in a box. She rummaged through the drawers fingering Lela's collars before packing them. There was her Halloween collar, her ladybug collar, her Christmas lights collar, and her flowered, tapestry collar. "Some other dog may be able to use these. I don't think they'll look good on you, Shamus," she said to me as the tears slid off her cheeks.

Dad embraced her from behind, but she was numb and didn't feel his touch. She said nothing as she reached for Lela's medicines. His arms fell to his sides as he watched her. He didn't know what to do or say. Neither did I.

"This is a new bottle. And this." She held three different vials against her breasts. "Do you think the shelter can use these?" she asked him glumly.

"I'm sure they can." His tone was equally sullen.

Mom's footsteps were heavy as they trudged along to her bedroom. She knelt down and steadied herself against the bed frame. She pulled Lela's plaid pillow out from under the bed where it had been neatly stored should Realtors come.

The pillow was old and tattered. The plaid fabric hung from the back. The dogs embroidered on the front were barely recognizable. They'd been washed and worn away. But Mom wouldn't replace that pillow. She was superstitious about it. After all, Snuggles and Nikko both died soon after Grammy and Aunt Abbey replaced their dog pillows. So Mom kept Lela's plaid pillow and simply bought new ones. No less than six dog pillows littered the house. But it was that old pillow that Lela loved most. It was the pillow Mom cradled in her arms as she rocked back and forth. She buried her head in its fabric, inhaling deeply, trying to smell Lela. But Mom washed the pillow's cover earlier that morning because Lela had leaked on it. Mom smelled only the dryer sheet's lavender and vanilla scent, perhaps making it easier for her to let the pillow go.

She sensed my presence. "You don't need this pillow now, do ya, Shamus," she said. My tail wagged gently, and the pillow dropped to her lap. I inched my way forward, and she gathered me in her arms. She sobbed. "I'm gonna miss her, Shamus."

I brushed my tongue along her moistened cheek. I licked it repeatedly hoping to wipe the grief away.

Mom didn't recoil from the roughness. My slobbering tongue had always been rough. Not delicate like Lela's.

I rubbed Mom's cheek nearly raw before she felt the salty sting and rose to her feet. "Come on. I need to finish before the shelter closes." We walked side by side to the kitchen. Her one hand rested on my neck while the other hand clutched Lela's pillow. She placed the pillow on the kitchen table next to Lela's plaid collar. The one that matched my own. I sniffed the collar and inhaled. Lela's scent still lingered on the dirty fabric. It was hard not to cry.

Mom rummaged through a drawer and pulled out the pliers. She removed Lela's tags and placed the collar in the box. She held the tags, kissed them, and then placed them in her front pocket.

"Mom, can I keep Lela's flowered collar?" Haley asked with swollen eyes. My brave Haley who stayed with Mom until Lela passed. Haley held the flowered collar to her chest along with a picture of Lela. It was a picture she took at her ninth birthday party. "Of course you can." Mom knelt next to her. "Of course you can." They wept silently together.

"I have just the perfect frame for that picture." Mom jumped up, wiping her face with her hands. She returned carrying a beautiful, jeweled picture frame. Haley smiled approvingly. Together they put Lela's picture in it, and Haley tenderly arranged Lela's collar over the frame's edge. She placed the memorial next to her hamster's memorial.

Snuggles was Haley's teddy bear hamster who had died the year before. Haley named her after Grammy's beloved Maltese. A car hit Grammy's Snuggles a couple of years earlier. Haley and Mom cried with Grammy over the phone, and they placed a picture of Grammy with her Snuggles in a pearl-adorned picture frame. That picture still sits in Grammy's living room.

Haley's Snuggles was cute and furry, and Haley loved her dearly. Haley instinctively knew Snuggles wasn't feeling well and saw that Snuggles had diarrhea. Google told us that Snuggles probably had wet tail, a curable illness when diagnosed and treated quickly. So Dad and Logan went to buy the medicine, and Haley and Mom stayed with Snuggles. Lela and I watched from the hall as Snuggles's condition deteriorated swiftly. Snuggles took her last breath before Dad and Logan returned. Snuggles's lifeless body was wrapped gingerly in an embroidered washcloth. We buried her in the Japanese garden.

Haley mourned Snuggles's passing for days. I wondered how long she'd mourn Lela's passing.

Logan waited in the TV room watching a Sponge Bob rerun. He seemed outwardly indifferent, but I knew he was silently hurting. I could feel the heaviness he carried.

"Logan, it's time to go," Dad said. "We're taking some of Lela's things to the animal shelter. But we need to go before they close."

Logan silently picked up the remote, pushed a

button, and the television shut off. He compliantly got off the sofa and headed out doors. He took eight tiny stutter steps before crossing the door's threshold. He touched Shelly's door eight times before jumping in. Eight times instead of four. *Always an even number*, I thought. *Why eight?* I wondered.

No one spoke as we made the trip to the shelter. Dad focused on the road ahead, and Mom hid behind her thick, dark sunglasses. Haley and Logan looked absently out the windows. Haley sobbed silently while Logan's grief lay dormant. I placed my head in his lap and wondered how his sorrow would manifest itself. *Would eight stutter steps turn to ten?*

I could hear the mournful howls of the shelter's inhabitants well before we pulled into the parking lot. I knew instantly it was not a place I wanted to be. Dogs of various shapes and sizes paced back and forth in outdoor cages. Some were anxious. Some were frightened. Most were despondent. Many more wails emanated from inside the main building. Some canine. Some feline.

"Wait here, Shamus," Mom's voice sliced through the agony in my ears. I curled deeper into my seat, not wanting to get out or be left behind.

The pitiful howls continued while I waited. I wished I could stop the noise. The yearning and pleading was too much to bear. There was no happiness inside. *No animal should ever be caged like this*, I thought. *How do they survive? How do they manage from day to day without grass under their paws or a family to cuddle up against?* I would surely lose my mind.

And then I remembered.

It was the shelter where Emi had lived before Mom and Dad adopted her. "She had a hard life," Lela told me. What a sad place to be. I better understood why Emi acted so detached and distant, and why Lela felt compelled to protect the strange cat. She wasn't strange, not really. She was guarded, wary. I wondered if she knew Lela had passed. Her one true friend was gone. *How would she react to the news?*

"How about going to the river and taking Shamus for a walk?" Dad asked once they all buckled in. "It might make us all feel better." But it was obvious that none of us wanted to go, except maybe Dad.

Surprisingly Logan broke the silence that followed. "I don't wanna go for a walk. I wanna go home." Tears flowed freely down his face. "I wanna go home," he stammered.

Haley nodded in agreement. Her face streaked with new tears.

"OK. It's OK, Logan. We'll go home." Mom reached back and grabbed his hand, trying to comfort him. "It's OK to cry, Logan. Let it out. It's OK. It's normal to feel sad and to cry. You loved her."

"She was my sister," he cried out. He choked on his tears, swallowing hard, trying to make them stop. But they didn't stop. They gushed madly from his eyes. He swiped at them with his T-shirt.

Their grief was palpable. Shelly's engine whined from the weight of it as we made our way home.

~Forty-seven~

The events of that morning had begun settling in. While Lela's passing seemed like a distant dream, her absence from our presence was real.

Haley and Logan rested in Mom's bed. They were tired but couldn't sleep. It was too early for sleep.

They snuggled deep under the goose down comforter. Their red, swollen eyes gazed mindlessly at the television. I was sure their tear ducts were empty. How many tears could a child shed? Surely, there was a limit.

"Every day will get easier. I pinky swear. It's supposed to hurt. You loved her. But in time we'll be able to think of her without crying. We'll be able to share stories and laugh and remember how wonderful she was," Mom told the kids as she pulled the comforter up under their chins. I, like Mom, clung to those words. We needed reassurance that the pain would lessen with time.

"Molly called again, Haley. Do you want to call her back or have her come over? She's worried about you," Mom stated softly. Haley slowly shook her head and stared blankly ahead. Molly hadn't been over for a visit in quite a while, and it felt like Haley was avoiding her calls. I could feel her pulling back. "OK, honey. I'll call her," Mom murmured. Haley sluggishly nodded.

I perched myself on the hard, cold rocks overlooking the corral. A chill seeped into my body, keeping me alert despite my weariness. I sat watching and waiting for nothing in particular. Dad had canceled all showings until Monday. There'd be no Realtors or their clients. But there I sat, out of habit, expecting Lela to creep around the corner. *What would I give for one more chance to catch her sneaking back from Ronan's?* I thought.

I could picture Lela perfectly, her face, her eyes, her swaggering gate as she'd come around the bend. But I knew she wasn't down there. It was only a memory. A vivid, painful memory. I had to turn away before my heart and mind deceived me.

Mom sat still on the glider, looking longingly down the driveway. She too was waiting for Lela. I saw it in her eyes as I approached her.

"I keep looking for a sign. Something to tell me she's OK. I want to believe she's in a better place." Mom's sorrowful voice drifted toward the clouds. "But I feel nothing."

"Maybe it's too soon," Dad offered. He sat next to her. His arm wrapped tightly around her shoulder.

"And where's her body? Why does it take two weeks to get her remains? What if she's cold?" Her sobbing started again.

"Don't think like that. It's just a shell. It isn't Lela. Her spirit isn't there anymore." He brushed the matted strands of hair from her wet cheek.

"He's right, Mom," I howled as I ran to her. "He's right. She came to me." I placed my paws on her lap. "She's all right," I barked, throwing my full weight onto her.

"Down, Shamus. Not now." She pushed me from her lap.

A familiar hum stirred up the driveway. I knew it was Lara even before she stepped out of the car.

"You didn't have to come. I know how busy you are." Mom accepted Lara's embrace, but she wouldn't cry in front of her. To cry over a dog, especially one who lived a long, full life, might somehow trivialize the loss Lara had recently suffered.

Lara understood love and loss. Canine or human, it didn't matter. She knew we lost a beloved family member. "How could I not come?" She smiled warmly at us, and her tender fingers grazed my neck and back sympathetically. "You know," she said cheerfully, "if it weren't for Lela, Teo would still be afraid of dogs." Her upbeat disposition fed those who knew her. "We all loved her, Gwen."

Mom found solace in Lara's words.

Dad retreated to the house to make them tea and check on the kids. He knew Mom needed someone to talk to. Someone to listen without trying to fix everything. He wished it could be him, but he felt the resentment she still harbored. He'd turn back time if he could to be there for her. But he couldn't. What he could do was get her some tea. Chai tea. Her favorite.

"Gwen. What happened? I thought she was in the clear, and it wasn't cancer." Lara radiated kindness and caring, despite the tragic death of her brother earlier that year. He was twenty-four when he succumbed to cancer. The pain of his passing clung to Lara and her family. Sometimes the smell was sharp, sometimes more subtle. Yet Lara stayed optimistic and looked for joy in little things. "I'm convinced that a butterfly carried his spirit on its wings," Lara shared with Mom days after his funeral. She had felt her brother's presence and knew he'd moved on.

Mom held back the tears and told Lara all that had happened those last few days.

"You did everything you could for her, and you did it out of love." Lara's voice was comforting.

"Yeah. But it makes me wonder if I did the right thing. All that just to have her die a few days later of a blood clot. I don't know, Lara." Mom stopped to regain her composure. "I wasn't with her. Last night I left her in the kitchen. I was so tired. I needed to sleep." Mom's voice cracked. I placed my paw on her lap to steady her.

"You can't think like that. She knew you loved her," Lara said compassionately.

Mom nodded and looked away. Anger overcame the grief. I felt its bubbling heat emanating from her. "And I'm mad. I'm mad that Raj wasn't here. I'm mad that I've had to go through this alone. The kids. The move."

Lara said nothing as Mom collected herself. She knew Mom needed to release the pent up hurt and anger. The tirade was winding down.

"Well, her passing certainly makes leaving this place easier." Mom's chest heaved in and out as she looked around the yard. "It just doesn't feel like home now. But then . . . I can't image going to Chicago without her." The tears she fought to contain pushed against her lower lids. The slightest stir would send them gushing down her face. She breathed deeply, deliberately, blinking them back. "You know, today's our anniversary. Raj and I've been married for fifteen years."

Dad appeared as if on cue. "Here you go. Two cups of hot Chai." He handed each of them a mug of the steaming, fragrant tea.

I shook my head wondering if he'd been listening through the opened windows. His timing was too perfect.

He nodded and winked.

Lara cupped her mug between her hands. "This smells sooooo good!"

Mom smiled at the friend she cherished. Grateful Lara had come. Thankful she reminded us that Lela had touched lives other than our own.

There was peace in knowing that.

The thought comforted me.

~Forty-eight~

I was drowsy the next morning. Fatigued. Worn-out. I'd spent the night thinking about Lela and how I would fill the void her death created. The endless commands circled around in my head. *Stay close to the kids outside. Check on the kids while they sleep. Don't jump on people. Stay close to Mom during walks. Don't chase Emi. Keep my nose out of crotches. Bark when strangers get too close.* My new responsibilities weighed heavy on my mind.

Five times I climbed the stairs that night. Five trips to check on the kids. Neither had slept well. Their mattresses squealed under each toss and turn, competing with Logan's soft cries and whimpers. The audible pain jabbed my insides. I resisted the urge to lay next to them and lick their faces. They needed to sleep.

Mom woke before the others. Her bloodshot eyes peered over the bed's edge. But neither Lela nor her pillow were there.

Mom remembered.

She rolled onto her back, resting her arm on her forehead. Her chest rose and fell in intermittent flutters. An occasional snivel escaped her lips. I didn't pounce on her, pull her pajamas, or tug at the comforter as I normally would. I patiently waited for her grief to subside. I patiently waited until her arm flopped over the side of the bed, and her long fingers beckoned me to come.

I rested my weary head on the mattress and let her fingers caress my muzzle and ears. Her touch was soothing, but her thoughts were somewhere else. Her eyes rested on a loose abandoned strand of cobweb that gently swayed above her head. I supposed she was collecting her strength.

She sat up cautiously, waiting to see if there'd be any repercussions. Her movements were slow and sluggish. *She probably shouldn't have finished that last bottle of wine last night*, I thought. But Owen, Nadine, and Ronan had stopped by sometime after Lara had left. It was easy for Mom to talk to Nadine. Mom's words flowed freely like the wine.

Nadine's voice was sincere when she said she'd miss Lela's morning visits.

"I'll miss Lela too," Ronan whispered somberly. I knew he would. He and Lela had been good friends. They shared the lane for more than five years. "I'll let the other dogs know," he added. His paw patted my shoulder gently, understandingly, just as a large flock of crows noisily ascended into the sky.

Nadine leaned in toward Mom before speaking. "Some believe the crows carry the souls of the dead to heaven."

"I don't believe that crock about crows," Ronan snorted. I nodded in agreement. Lela's spirit had left hours before. That I knew.

Mom silently watched the disappearing flock. Her eyes reflected the skepticism she'd been feeling.

Why did Lela come to me? I thought. *Why not Mom?* The question plagued me throughout the night. It plagued me during the days and weeks that followed.

The house was unusually quiet when Mom and I

made our way to the kitchen. Only one set of clicking nails and only one set of tags jingled next to her. There were no visible signs of Lela. No tangible reminders. A stranger passing by would never know that Lela had roamed our halls the day before.

Mom pressed the cappuccino machine's top button. It wailed as it spit out its thick, dark fluid. She grabbed two mugs from the shelf. The plaid mugs they'd brought back from Scotland. Grammy had stayed with Lela and me during that trip. Two years earlier. So much had changed since then.

A familiar twinge rippled through my chest.

The mugs clanked as they hit the hard, black granite counter.

Mom crossed the kitchen and grabbed the milk, whipped cream, and caramel sauce from the fridge. Her hand then reached for the cheese but stopped abruptly. She caught the offending hand in the other and drew them both close to her breasts. Mom didn't need to hide Lela's meds in the cheese.

"You OK?" Mom and I jumped at the sound of Dad's voice. His eyes were also sunken and bloodshot. I nuzzled up next to him.

"Yeah. I just wasn't sure what I should do. It's like my mom said when she told me Snuggles had died. 'It's easier but not better.' I thought I understood what she meant, but now I know. It is easier. I don't have to give her all those meds. I don't have to take her for a walk before feeding her. I don't have to wash her bedding because she leaked again. I don't have to make another trip to the vet or wake up at two in the morning." She choked and her knuckles whitened around the mug's handle.

Dad moved toward her and wrapped his arms around her waist. His chin rested on her shoulder. His lips grazed her neck, but her body stiffened.

"Yeah. It's easier, but it's not better. Now I know what she meant." She turned and held a mug out to him.

His arms dropped from her waist, and his shoulders sagged. He looked sad. Dejected.

"We should probably get the kids up. Haley has riding in an hour, and Logan has a soccer game, right?" she asked. "We should try and keep things as normal as possible."

"Yeah. But why don't we finish our coffee first," Dad suggested.

Mom and Dad settled under the covers, but they didn't cuddle. They sat on separate sides of the bed drinking their coffee. The morning news played in the background. The distance between them felt wide. I wanted to lie near them, in between them if I could. Dad frowned upon my being on the bed. Still I took a chance and nestled near Mom's feet. No one seemed to mind.

"What about Asha's party?" Dad asked. Asha was one of five cousins on Dad's side of the family. She was turning thirteen.

Mom didn't notice the white foam clinging to Dad's scruffy facial hair. It would have been funny under different circumstances.

"We should go. Seeing their cousins may help keep their minds off Lela. Maybe it will help them fall asleep tonight." She paused to ingest her morning caffeine. "It'd be good for the kids to get out of the house. Haley hasn't wanted a playdate in weeks, and Logan has gone through a case of duct tape."

I'd never been alone for any extended period of time. My heartbeat quickened at the thought of staying in the playroom without Lela. I could feel the heavy palpitations. I tried being courageous despite my feelings of dread, but a telltale whine leaked from my lips.

Mom took notice of me and understood. "We can bring Shamus. He can wait in the car." Her eyes were full of sympathy. "I'm worried about leaving him alone." She knew I too was grieving.

Dad nodded and relief filled me. My tail bumped happily against the footboard nearly drowning out the kids' footsteps descending the stairs.

Haley and Logan shuffled in to their parents' room. They wore matching dark circles under their puffy eyes. They crawled over Mom's legs and planted themselves between their parents. Their legs and feet burrowed deep under the comforter. Haley leaned into Dad, and Logan huddled under Mom's arm. My heart cringed when neither one noticed me, but I knew not to take it personally. They were grieving.

Mom and Dad told them the plans for the day. "Do we have to go?" they complained. Neither felt like moving from beneath the covers that sheltered them.

"We have to keep going. It'll get easier," Mom reassured them.

"One day at a time," she reassured us all.

~Forty-nine~

"Do you have your poems?" Mom hollered from the kitchen. She wore her old, faded Black Dog sweatshirt and cropped jeans.

It'd been two weeks since Lela's death. It was time to scatter her ashes. The kids woke up early to make final edits to their eulogies. They'd started them the night before, after we'd retrieved Lela's remains from Dr. Kagan.

"Got 'em," they yelled, racing from the den and falling up the stairs that led to the dining room. They held their poems behind their backs. "No peeking," they giggled. Their flushed faces beamed in the early morning sun that spilled through the kitchen window. It was good to see them smile. The gloom that hovered around the house since Lela's passing had begun to lift. It was as Mom predicted. Each day the loss became more bearable. Pockets of laughter filled the air once more. *How resilient children are*, I thought.

Mom's heart was harder to mend. She was alone during the day at home, surrounded by memories. Lela was everywhere but nowhere.

Mom sought refuge in life's daily routines. Get the kids off to school, clean the house for prospective buyers, work, lunch, walk, pick the kids up at the bus stop, review homework, fix dinner, bath time, read, bed. These rituals kept her moving forward. They kept her from drifting too far into despair. For it lurked around every corner, on every wooded trail, even on the comfy sofa, waiting to snatch the faith she held on to. I stayed by her side, always on guard, ready to help her shrug off the heaviness.

Though I missed Lela, I knew I'd see her again. Her words bolstered my courage, and I embraced my responsibilities. Mom talked to me and took me everywhere she went. For the first time in my life, I was someone's companion. I became Mom's confidant as Lela foretold.

Mom would never forget Lela. None of us would. Lela's memory was tucked safely in our hearts and in the memory book Mom made. Mom sorted through hundreds of pictures. Some I'd seen before. Most I hadn't. I watched Mom piece together Lela's life. Sometimes she shared the story behind a photo. Sometimes she didn't. The photos and stories comforted us both. But it was time to accept the loss and honor the life that meant so much to us all.

A small tin box, decorated with flowers and tiny strawberry prints, housed Lela's remains. It wasn't what I'd expected to see. Then again, I hadn't known what to expect at all.

"It's heavier than it looks," Logan commented. "How can she fit in here?" He thumbed the lid eight times but didn't open it. Not that he didn't want to. I sensed he did. But he was scared. Scared at what he might see.

"They use a very hot fire and all that remains are her ashes. Like the ashes in the fireplace," Mom explained.

"Are her teeth in there?" Logan wanted to know. Mom sensed that his curiosity was about to get the better of him.

"I don't know, Logan," Mom said quietly, taking the tin from his hands. She wasn't prepared for all his questions. A tear splashed onto the lid.

"Are you crying, Mom?" Haley asked.

"I'm trying not to. I know this isn't Lela. Her spirit's already gone." Mom placed the tin next to Lela's memorial stone. Her hand brushed over the memory book that laid next to it. Lela's aged face and cloudy eyes watched her. It was a beautiful picture, and it captured Lela's smile.

"I think I saw her, Mom. I saw something in the woods, and it felt like Lela," Haley said earnestly. Mom smiled affectionately at her daughter. Not surprised that Lela would show herself to Haley. Still we both wondered why Lela hadn't shown herself to Mom.

It wasn't until after the kids were asleep that Mom opened the tin. She found courage in the merlot she sipped. She fingered the contents, carefully, slowly, allowing the ashes to seep between her fingers. "They're gritty, Shamus. Coarse, like sand, rough sand."

A small dust plume settled on my nose. I was afraid to breathe. Afraid I might inhale particles of Lela. I vehemently shook my body to free the ashes. Mom chuckled sadly. "You'll break my heart too," she said to me. She replaced the lid and quietly made her way to the bedroom. She fell asleep not long before Dad came home.

His workbag and overnight bag dangled from his arm as he pushed his way through the front door. They bumped into my chest when I jumped up to greet him. The dark circles under his lower lids accentuated his tired eyes. It was late and he'd missed his earlier flight.

"Hey, Shamus," he said drowsily. His coarse facial hair tickled my tongue. He dropped his bags and kicked off his shoes, pushing them slightly under the table. His fingers kneaded my neck and side. Then he saw Lela's memory book. He saw her face in the dim light. He slowly traced the lettering on the cover, sounding out each letter. "L-E-L-A." He sighed deeply. "I never realized how much I'd miss her," his voice filled with remorse.

Lela's memorial service took place in the Japanese garden. We convened around her memorial stone. It rested at the garden's center, just to the front of Snuggle's grave marker. The garden's rhododendrons that Mom planted a few weeks earlier were in full bloom. It was a tranquil place and one Lela often meandered through.

Mom spoke first. The words poured from her heart. There was no need for a rehearsal. She had lived the words, sometimes dreaded them. She spoke of love and treasured companionship, devotion, and caring. She thanked Lela for the long, joy-filled journey they shared, and for loving us so selflessly. She hoped that Lela was in a better place, free from pain and suffering. She reassured Lela that we would always carry her memory with us. Then she cried for forgiveness, hoping Lela knew that every decision was made out of love. Guilt strangled her words.

Dad leaned in and kissed the side of her head.

Her body shivered. She didn't want to be sad. She wanted to honor Lela. "I just want to put the last couple of weeks behind me and forget how much she may have suffered. I want to be able to look back on our journey and smile."

If only I could have told her that there was nothing to forgive. Lela knew the depths of their love. That even in death she had felt it.

"Logan, you wanna go next?" Dad asked.

Logan moved closer toward the stone. He read the poem he held between his hands. He spoke the words softly, yet courageously. "It's different now you're no longer here. We all loved you. We always expect to find you in your bed or on the couch. We love you Lela."

Mom wrapped her arms around him and kissed his cheek. "That's beautiful, Logan. She'd like it a lot."

Haley's eulogy captured Lela's inner and outer splendor. She described Lela as being wise like an owl and strong like a lion, courageous and brave like the mightiest warrior. Haley praised the kind eyes and favored butterfly kisses, and she thanked Lela for the courage she bestowed on us. Haley spoke of heaven and Lela's face looking down on us with warming love, love that would guide us through life. It was an impressive tribute, and it left us speechless. Hard to believe Haley was only in the fourth grade.

The kids were rightfully proud of their memorials and delighted when Mom asked if she could put them in Lela's memory book.

Dad finished the ceremony with a brief

accolade. His words were simple and pure. "Lela," he said, "thank you for being such a good dog. We love you and we'll miss you."

Less is sometimes more, I thought.

Their words were moving, and I hoped that Lela, wherever she was, had heard them.

Mom opened the tin box and reached in. She slowly sprinkled dust on and around Lela's stone. I stepped to the side to avoid stepping on the scattered remains. "Good boy," Mom said, patting my side.

I checked to make sure Lela dust wasn't on my fur. Her ashes belonged to the earth, to the places she loved most. They didn't belong on my coat, to fall off in random places.

The kids hesitantly held out their hands, studying the texture and color of Lela's ashes. "Don't forget to keep your hand low when you sprinkle. Otherwise you might end up with Lela dust in your nose or on your clothes," Mom teased. A look of concern flashed across their faces.

That was the beginning of our memorial procession.

Mom, Dad, and the kids sprinkled Lela's remains sparingly through the woods Lela loved, trying to cover as much earth as possible. The haunted trail and sanctuary welcomed our gift and lovingly embraced the ashes. The moist earth drew them in while the birds sang their dirge.

We spread Lela's remaining ashes near Grammy's. It was a quiet ride there. I spent the first part of it thinking about the last trip Lela and I had taken together. We had spent the week with Grammy while Mom and the kids flew out to Chicago. We celebrated Lela's fifteenth birthday when they got back. The kids made Lela a biscuit and peanut butter birthday tower. Mom thoughtfully watched Lela devour the cake. Her eyes reflected gratitude. Then the knowledge that it might be Lela's last birthday crept in and covered her eyes in a fine mist.

We picked up Darren on the way. He too wanted to say good-bye. I hadn't seen him since he came down a few weeks earlier to catch a baseball game. That was the last time he'd seen Lela. He knew she was sick, and he made it a point to sit with her before he left. "Darren's soul has always been gentle and kind. I'm blessed to have been able to watch him grow from young boy to man," Lela had said fondly as we watched him drive away.

Mom asked Dad to make a second stop that day. It was a small house I'd seen before. We passed it whenever we went to Grammy's. It was Lela's birthplace. She always gazed upon the yard when we passed. Sometimes trying to recall the faces of her birth mother and siblings. But she had no concrete memories of them. Only faint images that she couldn't wrap her paws around.

"I remember this place," Darren said with a smile when Shelly came to a stop. "There was a dog house in the back over there and a fenced-in area." His eyes looked beyond the vacant spot in the back yard as the memories flowed. "I remember all the puppies and Lela. She was about to climb up and over the fence. Her teeth were sharp. I remember that." Darren laughed, remembering the sting.

Mom wanted to know if the people who gave Lela to us still lived there. She wanted to thank them for their precious gift.

"You OK?" Dad asked when she returned.

"Yeah. I needed the closure. She seemed happy to know that Lela lived a full, happy life." Mom stared out her window. The faintest smell of salt hung in the air. She didn't look at him again until we reached our final stop. It was a pond. A large, picturesque pond.

"I remember this place. Isn't there a big swan?" Haley asked.

"Sometimes. Come on. This way." Mom directed us to a trail that wound along the water's edge. She kept the tin box close to her side. We looked for the swan, but there was no sign of her. A few ducks floated on the water's surface. Occasionally one would plunge its beak into the water. Searching for food. Leaving tail feathers bobbing high in the air. The sun kissed the earth, and weeping willows danced with the breeze. Intermittent "plops" preceded our steps as frogs dashed out of our way.

It didn't take long to reach our last destination. A small, natural beach made of dirt and pebbles graced the pond's edge. The other bank was just a stone's throw away. Logan picked up the flattest stone he could find and skipped it across the water. Lily pads danced among the ripples.

"Three skips. Not bad." Dad picked up a stone, but his toss was blunt. The stone skipped only once before dying in the water. Logan stifled his laugh.

Mom stood at the water's edge and breathed. A gentle wind tussled her hair and carried her back in time. Back before the kids. Back before me. Back to when she and Lela would run this trail and stop here to rest. She looked mournfully up toward the sky.

It was time.

Mom poured a tiny amount of Lela's ashes into Haley and Logan's opened palms. Darren shied away. "It's OK," Mom told him. I nuzzled up next to him. He would find peace in his own way.

Logan stepped out above the water on a fallen tree limb. He hurled the dust as far as he could, careful to throw it with the breeze. Haley squatted near the water's edge, holding her hand high above the water. She let the dust trickle slowly through her clenched fist.

Mom crouched next to Haley. Her head hung toward her chest. I couldn't tell if she was praying to Grammy's God or talking to Lela as she emptied the remaining ashes into the water. Mom watched as the gentle current washed over the little mound of dust. Mom watched until the little mound was no more.

All that remained of Lela's physical body became a part of that place for eternity.

Mom discarded the tin in a nearby trash can.

~*Fifty*~

"My first official day of unemployment," Mom joked with Dad earlier that morning as he scurried around packing his things. It was the last Monday in May, and Mom wanted to clean out the den. Realtors rarely called for appointments on Mondays. Still Mom knew she needed to work fast just in case they rang.

"Why don't you just throw it all away," Dad suggested. "You won't need it. And most of those treatises are old and outdated." He pecked her cheek before leaving.

Mom thought about Dad's words as she sat there in the den surrounded by the stacks of papers and treatises and reference books she'd collected over the years. Her eyes glanced around the room, surveying the materials that represented her life's work for more than a decade. She was hesitant to throw it away, but she knew Dad was right. She wasn't planning to go back to work until January at the earliest. Even then she wasn't sure she wanted to practice law any more. All the hours and pressure. Always having to be right. Always on call. She'd wait and see how she felt in the new year. She'd wait until we were settled.

Mom shook her head and shrugged her shoulders. Her eyes passed over Lela's memory book that rested on the shelf near us. She picked it up and placed it safely on the desk. "All right. Let's do this," she said to me. I was her moral support.

She took a deep breath, pushed up her sleeves, and began the purging process. She started sorting through folders, files, and binders. Paper piles soon littered the floor. She carefully plucked certain documents from the rubble and placed them neatly in a storage box.

"There," she said, shoving the box toward the desk and out of the way. The rest of the papers and books she stuffed in large, black plastic bags.

"This will definitely make dusting easier. Don't you think?" she asked me.

"Yes," I yelped.

Mom dusted and vacuumed daily. Our house had been on the market for two months. There'd been a lot of traffic but no offers. The economy and housing market had grinded to a near halt. Buyers loitered around like vultures, coming back two sometimes three times to see our house. They nitpicked while they waited to see how desperate we were. They waited to see which homes would go into foreclosure and if interest rates would fall again. Their criticism infuriated Mom. "I can't move the master bedroom upstairs, and I can't change the incline of the driveway," she'd complain. She resented cleaning for them and buying fresh flowers and air fresheners.

So, yes. Making dusting easier was a good thing. I thumped my tail in support.

It took five contractor bags and two large rubber trash cans to hold all the discarded materials. The den that had served as Mom's home office was empty. All that remained were the rug, a desk and computer, a chair, and the baby grand. The shelves were void of papers, books, and pictures. All personal things that weren't disposed of had been securely packed.

"It's not our home anymore," Mom said as her eyes inspected the room. Mom didn't want to stay. "Lela's passing makes it easier to let go of this place," she told Aunt Abbey.

My heart tightened as I looked at the empty room. So many hours Lela and I lay on the rug as Mom worked. We'd nap despite the clicking keys, humming printer, and conference calls. Sometimes I sought shelter under the desk. I always felt safe nestled between the wall and Mom's feet. I loved the feel of her toes kneading into my skin. I envisioned my crate, sitting in the corner as it used to, protecting me when I went inside. The den had always been my private sanctuary.

So much had changed. I wasn't the same pup I'd been when I'd first come to the lane. I couldn't afford to be since Lela's passing.

"Hard to believe that all I have to show for my work fits in one file box." Mom's voice carried a tinge of sadness. She kicked the side of the box lightly with her sneaker. Her fingers scratched behind my ear. Her insecurity seeped into my flesh.

The day was bittersweet. She was looking forward to time alone with Lela and me. "Like it used to be," she had whispered to Lela.

But fate had other plans.

She's left with only me, I thought regretfully.

"Come on, Shamus. Let's finish up and grab some lunch." She picked up the box and we left the room.

I missed my crate at times.

~Fifty-one~

"Mom! Tell him to stop touching me!" Haley screamed. Her nostrils flared and her body stiffened. She kept her clenched fists coiled by her side. Mom had asked her to be patient with Logan. But Haley's patience was wearing thin. She was about to unload.

I quickly positioned myself in front of Haley, using my body as a physical barrier to prevent her from attacking her brother. Their fights had become more vocal and physical over the years. I knew what would follow if Mom and I didn't intervene.

"I don't want to do it. But I can't stop," Logan said sincerely. His eyes misted over, and he rubbed his hands together. It was true. He couldn't help touching Haley eight times if she brushed up against him.

Mom's heart fell to the floor. I felt the small thud when it hit the cool slate. She saw his behavior worsening as our move to Chicago drew closer. She tried working with him at home. "Touch me instead," she had told him. But she wasn't always nearby, and he couldn't control the urge. She had, more than once, regretfully lost her patience with him.

"Logan, do you think you want to talk to someone about this?" Concern filled Mom's voice. He nodded slowly, and the tears rolled down his cheeks. She drew him into her arms. "It'll be OK, Logan. I pinky swear."

The doctor said Logan had a brain bully. A bully in his head, taunting him, telling him that if he didn't do what the bully said, something bad would happen. But it was just a bully, like a playground bully at school. The bully was powerless unless Logan gave it control. The doctor assured Logan nothing bad would happen if he stood up to the brain bully. Lots of people have brain bullies. If they could stand up to their bullies, Logan could stand up to his. Together the doctor and Logan drew a picture of the ugly beast that haunted him. Logan had to learn to tell him "no."

"She wasn't surprised, given everything that's been going on, that his stress is manifesting itself like this." Mom stifled a yawn as she explained to Dad what the doctor had told her.

I knew the kids were nervous about leaving. I could feel their anxiety when Mom asked them what they thought about the move, the new house, their new school. They didn't want to disappoint her, so they kept their fears to themselves. Mom, like me, sensed their insecurities and did what she could to ease their unspoken worries. Still Logan had his brain bully, and Haley had become distant, somewhat of a recluse. She didn't call her friends or invite them over. Though her suffering was less apparent, she nonetheless was suffering.

Mom told Dad only what he needed to know. She didn't want him to worry. She worried enough for the both of them. "If we recognize the brain bully's around, we have to tell him to leave. Tell Logan to make him go away." She patted the cushion inviting me up, carefully holding her glass above her head while I made myself comfortable.

I circled around and fell gently into a worn spot.

Lela's odor lingered. No human would pick up the faint scent trapped within the foam and feathers. But I smelled her. This was her favorite spot. I dug my muzzle deeper into the fabric and let the cushion wrap itself around me.

"We also have to encourage him not to get into routines. So tonight I made him get in and out of bed three times, each time a different way. To prove to him that nothing bad would happen if he didn't stutter-step. He was nervous at first but settled down by the third time. We made a game of it."

I pushed him through the bathroom door so he couldn't stutter-step, I wanted to tell them. But I knew they wouldn't understand, and that was all right. Logan knew. He patted my side and appreciatively kissed my head.

"It gets so frustrating, Raj. But I like that the doctor personified it. I like yelling at the brain bully because God knows I want to yell at someone."

She told him about the Realtor who called earlier that day. The one who wanted to show the house but had given Mom only an hour's notice. Mom scrambled to clean up the dusty tile samples spread across the dining room floor. She'd spent the morning arranging them into particular patterns. They were samples for the new house. "We never have showings on Tuesdays. I couldn't believe it," Mom protested. "At least I cleaned the house this morning."

She cleans the house every morning, I thought.

"I don't know what I'm paying the designer for. I'm doing all the design work. You should have seen the samples he sent. Nothing like what I had described and he charged me for them. I had to go out and get my own samples and send them to him with pictures of how they're to be laid." Her pulse was racing, and she paused to catch her breath.

I placed my head on her lap to soothe her. Her fingers found the soft spot under my chin. The tension in them relaxed as she listened to Dad. She pressed the receiver against her ear. I couldn't make out his muffled words.

"Did the relo company approve the price reduction? Our Realtor said she can make it happen for the weekend, but she needs to know by Friday morning." Mom wanted the selling process to be over. As long as Dad's company made us whole on the buyout, she didn't care what it sold for. But there were uncertainties as to how the buyout would work if we didn't have an offer or if the house sold for less than the agreed buyout price. We were supposed to move in four weeks. The contractors she'd lined up were pestering her for more specific start dates.

"Anything else we need to talk about?" she asked. "I'm getting tired."

She nodded her head. Their meeting adjourned.

"Love you too. Talk to you in the morning." Her voice was flat and devoid of feeling. It was hard to tell if her weariness had caught up to her or if something Dad said annoyed her. The commuting had grown tiresome and put more than just miles between them.

I lifted my head, and she uncurled her legs. We stretched our backs, and she rolled her head from side to side. She straightened the table runner on the coffee table and plucked the dead flowers from the arrangement.

She folded the laundry that sat in the basket next to the kitchen counter. She arranged the folded clothes into neat piles. One for each of them.

I watched as she methodically put the kids' clothing away, laying their shirts and pants in evenly spaced rows. She straightened the tops of their dressers and arranged their pictures and whatnots. She moved to her room and did the same. She stepped quietly, careful not to awaken the kids. They'd been asleep for over an hour. Dad missed their bedtime again, forgetting which time zone he was in.

Mom couldn't resist straightening up the linen closet before putting the clean towels away. She stacked the towels neatly, one on top of the other. Their edges perfectly aligned. She wiped down her bathroom, despite wiping it down earlier that morning. Then she rearranged the toothbrushes and adjusted the bath mat so it lay evenly between the tiles.

Only then was she satisfied.

Cleaning became her obsession. The one thing that calmed her. The one thing she could control.

Mom wasn't strong enough to defend herself.

She befriended her own brain bully.

~Fifty-two~

Lela's death touched Emi deeply. I didn't know how she found out, but she was there the day we spread Lela's ashes on the haunted trail and throughout the sanctuary. Her light steps followed us that day. She mourned in isolation, keeping to herself, hidden among the young fern.

For days I watched her from the window. She huddled close to Lela's memorial stone each night. She'd lay there, still like a statue, camouflaged by the rocks and earth and early evening shadows. She'd stay well after the sun sank behind the ridge. I'd lose sight of her when the darkness swept in.

Lela and Emi. They'd been friends for many years. They'd shared stories I'd never know. Lela protected Emi and made her feel safe.

Lela told me to leave her alone. But I couldn't resist chasing her. So cute and small and furry. I'd been young, stupid. I had no idea what the consequences would be.

I scared her away. It was me, my doing. My thoughtless actions kept Emi from the family that loved her. They kept her from Haley, the one who needed her most of all. *Did Emi know how much Haley yearned for her?* I wondered.

The remorse in my gut made me ill.

"Emi, Emi. Come here kitty, kitty," Haley called. But I knew that if Emi came in, it wouldn't be until well after dark. She'd sneak in through her cat door and find refuge in the crawl space between the boiler room and playroom. She'd then slink away in dawn's early hours. An empty food bowl meant the coyotes hadn't snatched her.

If only I could apologize, make things right. Emi would have her family, and Haley would have her cat.

"Don't worry, Haley. I'll find her. I have to take her and Shamus to Dr. Kagan's tomorrow. She'll come in. Don't worry. I bought some special treats for her." Mom smiled at her daughter, but her eyes said something different. "I hope she comes in," they said.

Mom and I knew Emi came in during inclement weather, but the skies were clear that night. Emi also had a way of disappearing just before her scheduled vet visits. It was unlikely she'd come home.

I became more anxious as the hours passed. *This could be my chance to make amends*, I thought. *If only she'd come in.* And I looked to the sky as Mom often did. "Please?" I asked.

Someone heard my plea. I knew Grammy's God or Lela spoke to Emi that night when I heard the light swing of the cat door. I didn't race to the playroom like I normally would. I waited patiently for Mom to find Emi snuggled in her bed. Mom coaxed her from the crawl space. She spoke softly as she stroked Emi's back. Emi purred. The trust between them restored.

Mom gently scooped Emi into her arms and carried her upstairs where extra food, bedding, and a litter box waited for her in the guest room. Emi caught my scent, and her nervous eyes searched for me over Mom's shoulder. I quickly turned and headed down stairs. I wanted Emi to feel safe. I'd talk to her in the morning.

Hope returned to my guarded heart.

All night I rehearsed what I'd say 'cause I knew I'd only have a few minutes to convince her. It was a short ride to Dr. Kagan's office. *Would a few minutes be enough time to show her I'd changed?*

Now or never, I thought when Mom placed Emi's small crate next to me. Emi was crouched in the crate's tiny corner. I almost didn't see her in the shadow.

"Don't be afraid," I said in my most comforting voice.

She looked warily at me through the crate's slits. Her tail curled tightly around her legs, only the tip of it moved, flipping around as she burrowed her eyes deep into mine. I sensed she was scared and a wee bit annoyed.

"I won't hurt you, Emi. I would never hurt you," I whispered. The silence bore down on me. My pulse quickened, and that sick feeling in my gut returned.

"I never meant to scare you away." Precious time passed too quickly. My rehearsed lines faded from my memory.

"Please," I whined. "They need you. Haley needs you!" I implored.

Her twitching tail stopped, and the black, hard eyes softened. Something I said struck a chord inside her. She knew Haley often called for her.

She shifted and her crate rocked against the seat when she took a step toward me. She was about to speak. I could feel it. I edged closer to her, slowly, very slowly. I didn't want to frighten her or interrupt her thoughts. I held my breath as I waited. Just as she opened her mouth to speak, Shelly stopped abruptly. Emi's mouth shut tight and her eyes went wide. She backed herself into the corner.

We were at the vet's.

"Wait," I yelped. But Mom had already attached my leash and had Emi's crate in her hand. She closed the door with her foot and escorted us to our appointments. Emi remained silent. She was taken to room two and I to room one.

Had I missed my opportunity? I wondered as they carried her away.

The appointment dragged on. Dr. Kagan drew my blood and checked my stool. He took my temperature and poked around my soft tissue. He peered into my eyes and ears and checked my teeth and gums. He said I'd lost a few pounds, but was otherwise in good health. We both were. Emi and I.

Mom walked out with Emi's crate in one hand and my leash in the other. A vet bill and two certificates of health were tucked in her back pocket. Emi and I needed the certifications to land in Chicago. We were healthy and fit. We'd be flying. There was no need to rent a Winnebago.

"Emi. Please, Emi. Talk to me?" I pleaded when Mom placed the crate next to me. Emi remained crouched in the corner with her tail wrapped tightly around her frame. I felt my opportunity slipping away. Desperation wrapped its claws around my chest. "Will you never forgive me?" I choked.

Her silence was deafening.

It's useless, I thought. *She'll never see me for who I've become.* I'd carry my guilt in my heart. I'd take it to my grave. I turned my head from her and plopped down into the seat. It felt hard and cool as I lay there sulking. Lela would be so disappointed.

Just when I thought the quiet would suffocate me, the faintest voice called out.

"There's nothing to forgive," Emi purred ever so softly. "I'm old and foolish. I've let too many years slip by."

That was all she said that day. But her words liberated me. They liberated us both.

Emi began spending more time indoors. At first she'd come in only at night. But as she grew more comfortable around us, she extended her stays. Mom still kept her food bowl in the mudroom, so I wouldn't get into it. But Emi's bedding and litter box were kept upstairs. That's where Emi felt safest. Upstairs. In Haley's room. Nestled among the comforters that adorned Haley's bed.

Together they found peace and comfort in the days and weeks that followed. Emi embraced Haley's love, and her presence eased Haley's insecurities.

Haley had a new best friend.

One that'd be with her in Chicago.

~Fifty-three~

Darren and Dad loaded the comfy sofa and other pieces of furniture into a rented truck late one Sunday afternoon. We had to make space. The new furniture would arrive the next morning. Mom shopped till Dad and the kids dropped at local retailers. Lela and I had waited with Shelly. Three different stores. Three different deliveries. Yet Mom managed to schedule the deliveries for the same day. Monday. The most unlikely day to have a showing. The last full day of school for that year.

Darren was moving into an apartment, his first apartment. He was so excited. Mom was happy to give him the furniture. Each piece carried with it a set of memories. She wanted to keep them in the family. She told Darren she'd help him decorate.

Dad scoffed at the idea. "It's his first bachelor pad!"

Darren appreciated the sofa and fine wood furniture and said he'd take the velvet and chenille throw pillows too. Mom welcomed the thoughtful gesture.

Lela would've been happy to know that Darren was taking the sofa. But it was sad for me to watch it go. Mom felt an attachment as well. I knew by the way she caressed the gently worn chenille fabric that it wasn't an ordinary couch. It was Lela's favorite nesting place. It still carried her smell. Another piece of Lela was leaving us.

Would Mom have ordered a new couch had she

known? I wondered. She ordered the new furniture weeks before Lela died. When we thought Lela would be with us. Although Mom never said so, I suspected she would have kept the sofa and found a place for it in Chicago had she known. Yet Darren needed the sofa, and the new furniture was on its way. She had to let it go.

Mom tried staying positive, focusing on the future, but there were so many uncertainties. Mom and Dad didn't know what would happen if they didn't get an offer before we moved. Two weeks had passed since the relo company dropped the price and still no offer. Our Realtor said nothing was moving, and there were over a dozen foreclosures in town competing with our house. And if things weren't complicated enough, the bank refused to underwrite the mortgage for the Chicago house due to some minor water damage that the sellers wouldn't fix.

The uncertainties turned to added stress as our anticipated moving date drew near.

Dad's company started waffling on the buyout price and the gross-up necessary for Mom and Dad to recoup their investment in our house. The company wasn't doing well, and it would cost twice the amount they had initially projected to make good on their promises. They began to question the renovation costs Mom and Dad incurred over the years. "Unbelievable" was Mom's response.

I didn't understand most of what Mom and Dad argued about that night, but I knew it had something to do with our family's security.

"I told you to get it all in writing before you agreed to anything," Mom yelled. "But you didn't listen. You never listen." Her fingers raked through her hair, and she shook her head back and forth. Angry tears streaked her weary face.

Dad sat quietly on the edge of the bed. He too was frustrated and drained. He would never do anything to hurt our family. He was lost. I saw it in his eyes. Mom was his confidant, the one person he turned to for advice. He needed her, but he felt her growing distant. The air around him was heavy with sadness.

"I'm meeting with Ned tomorrow. What should I tell him?" Ned was the head of human resources. He and Dad's boss, Stan, would make the final decisions about the relocation. They wanted to know if Dad would be willing to commute to Chicago for another year and revisit the relocation the following spring.

"They wanted us out there by July," Mom sighed. "And here we are. Two weeks before we're supposed to move. We've done everything they asked." She took a swig of wine. It didn't rest on her tongue as it normally would. She gulped it down, eager to feel the wine's lulling effects.

Dad said nothing as he waited for her to answer. She was processing the facts. I could almost see them swirling around in her head as her mental scale weighed each pro and con.

"How could we afford to live here? I quit my job. I can't go back and no one's hiring. I can't even collect unemployment. But if we move now, there's no guarantee they'll move us back East if it doesn't work out for you. All we have are e-mails about the buyout price and their commitment to make us whole. What would we do? Sue them? I don't have a job, and they can fire you anytime they want, for any reason or no reason at all." She paused to catch her breath. "Do you still trust them?"

"No, I don't trust Ned. But delaying the move would buy us some time. Hopefully the economy and housing market will be stronger next spring," Dad rationalized. "I can ask for a salary bump. I've gone through our budget, and we should be all right if they agree to a small increase, just until they make a final decision about the relocation. And you wouldn't have to work. Not right away. You said you wanted to be home with the kids and explore other career options."

Mom looked at him inquisitively and cocked her head to the side. She drew in her breath before speaking. "I said that when I thought we were moving to Chicago. When we wouldn't be under any financial pressure." Her voice was low, the tone condescending. Dad recoiled from the sting.

Mom shook her head. "None of it feels right. Nothing's falling into place." Her anger turned to despair. "Shouldn't things be easier if this move was meant to be?" She turned toward Dad. Her eyes searched for an answer. But she knew there wasn't any.

She yawned and took another swig from her glass. "We can't make any decisions until you meet with Ned tomorrow," she added bitterly.

Dad nodded. He knew the conversation was over. Mom had shut down. She was unwilling to talk and speculate about the things she couldn't change. Her resentment festered, and her iciness filled the room. Dad shuddered from the chill.

I worried for Mom. Always have and always will. But her disdain toward Dad annoyed me. *How could she begrudge the man who loved her unconditionally?* I nuzzled up against him.

"She'll come around," I whimpered. His spirit was battered, but his hands filled with gratitude as they stroked my head. He sought refuge in the den behind his laptop's screen.

My thoughts turned next to the kids. I hoped they were asleep, lost in pleasant dreams, far away from the loud, angry voices that had bellowed below them. They too were coping with the stress, and they'd been unusually quiet at dinner. I was relieved to find them sleeping.

Logan lay still. His brain bully was quiet though his sheet and cover lay crumpled on the floor. He squirmed when my cool wet nose grazed his forehead. He was neither too hot nor too cold. I pushed his door wide open when I left. He liked when the hallway's night-light filled his room.

Haley's door had already been propped open. She and Emi looked snug and content curled alongside each other. I couldn't help smiling warmly at the sight. I watched from the door as their chests moved in unison. I was careful not to breach the boundary I'd set for myself. Haley's room was Emi's safe haven. I respected that and watched them from the threshold.

Emi sensed my presence. "Good night,

Shamus," she purred. She stretched out her legs and arched her back. She blended into the shadows.

Mom was in the kitchen when I returned. She dumped the last of her wine down the drain and then turned off the lights. The full moon illuminated the room, and she stopped in front of the big picture window. She looked out into the distance and placed her hands against the glass. A worried look settled on her face.

I stood next to her, peering out into the night.

Nothing moved outdoors but spring's sweet song as it drifted in through the opened windows. Mom closed her eyes and listened. Drawn to the night's symphony. Her body swayed ever so slightly from side to side. She waited for the music to soothe her soul.

"You know God does things for a reason," Grammy told Mom earlier that day. Grammy trusted her God completely, drawing strength from her faith. Mom wished she had Grammy's faith.

What was God's reason? I pondered. I looked to the stars for an answer. None came to me that night.

At last Mom said, "Come on, Shamus. Let's go to bed."

I nodded and yawned.

I too had grown tired.

~Fifty-four~

The buzzing under my butt startled me.

I'd been dreaming, lulled to sleep by the warm sunlight beaming through Shelly's windshield. I'd been chasing Logan and Haley as they sped down the driveway on their scooters. It wasn't really a dream. It was a sleep-induced memory of what transpired just two hours before. Right before Mom and I took the kids to school.

"Haley, come on," Logan hollered.

Haley snatched her helmet from the fence post where she had left it the night before. Her eyes glared at her brother as she snapped it in place. She grabbed her scooter and marched to the starting line where Logan was waiting. She looked to the finish line and then back to Logan. She gave him the nod.

"Go!" Logan yelled.

The race was on.

I chased after them, keeping a safe distance, as they maneuvered the driveway with skill and care. Their scooters weaved in and out of the obstacle course they had designed. It was a close race. Too close to call before Haley made a tactical error. She brushed away the hair whistling madly about her face. As she did she lost her balance ever so slightly. The bobble was just enough to give Logan the advantage.

He was about to cross the finish line a breath ahead of her when Mom's phone buzzed beneath me. It was wedged between my left buttocks and the passenger's seat. It fell off the center console where

Mom had left it.

Mom wouldn't be long. Just a quick stop at the grocery store before the kids came home. They'd be home at noon. Only two half-days left to the school year.

I was circling around in my seat when Shelly's locks shot up. I saw Mom in the distance. She carried a bag of groceries in one hand and Shelly's keys in the other. Her strides were long as she hurried toward me.

She placed the bag in the backseat and shut the door. "Hey, Shamus," she said, scooting into the driver's seat. She tugged playfully at my cheeks and kissed my muzzle. Shelly's engine giggled when Mom turned the key. "Mom. Connected," Shelly's speakers sang.

Mom had Shelly in reverse when her phone rang. The familiar song played around us. It was Dad. I knew from the melody.

"Did you see the Realtor's e-mail?" Dad's voice circled around us.

Mom hadn't seen it. Her phone was still wedged between my butt and the seat.

"We got an offer on the house," he told her just as she pulled the phone out from under me.

She scanned the screen and put Shelly in park.

"I can't believe it," she said aloud. She rested her head on her thumb and finger, her arm propped up against the window. She sat rigid, momentarily lost in her thoughts. "I can't believe this." She shook her head back and forth. "Now what?"

"I'm gonna call Ned and see what they want us

to do. This offer might make them change their position about the relo."

"It's a shitty offer, Raj. The e-mail says they're trying to see how desperate we are."

"We're not desperate."

"Look, I'm on my way home. Call Ned. See what he says about the offer and the salary bump. We can talk more when I get home. I'm leaving now. I'll be home shortly." Her cheeks ballooned as she blew the breath from her lungs.

"Why is this happening now? We waited almost three months for an offer. Now we decide we should stay, and the next day we get an offer. Why are you doing this?" she yelled looking up toward the sky.

I followed her gaze and strained to hear a voice. But Grammy's God didn't answer.

How does he talk to Grammy? I wondered. *Why can't we hear him?*

Her breathing slowed and she stared ahead. Expressionless. The lines etched across her brow looked deeper, more visible. I felt her growing numb as we drove in silence.

I gently placed my paw on her forearm. The weight of it anchored her. "It's OK," I told her. My shoulder started to throb.

Shelly lunged unexpectedly.

I lurched forward as we made the sharp turn onto the lane. My nails scraped across Mom's skin, leaving three scratches on her forearm. I leaned back against the seat as we ascended upwards. Mom didn't notice the scratches that began to swell.

Dad was waiting for us. Outside. Still dressed in pajamas. He worked from home that day.

"What'd Ned say?" Mom asked with a terse tone. She didn't say "hello" as she brushed past him carrying the bag of groceries.

"He said to take the house off the market. They agreed to give me the salary bump, and we'll see what your job situation looks like in January. We'll revisit the relo next year, in the spring. That's how we left it. I already called our Realtor."

The kids were thrilled to learn we weren't moving. The stress they'd been carrying those last several months rolled from their bodies. Their smiles grew wide, and the bounce returned to their steps. They spent more than an hour calling their friends, spreading their good news. Haley invited Molly over for a playdate.

Their joy appeased Dad's anger.

He'd continue commuting to Chicago until his company made a final decision about the relo and his role. He hoped they'd make good on their promises, but a decision wouldn't be made until the new year. Until then he had to tread lightly and hide his disappointment. Mom was without a job, and unemployment had escalated to unparalleled numbers. Our family was, for the first time ever, financially vulnerable.

Mom didn't know how to feel. She was glad that there'd be no more showings. The process had drained her physically and emotionally. Yet she'd been ready to leave. She wanted time to breathe, to figure out what she wanted to do next. She had until January to sort it out. Six months until the company pulled the salary bump. Six months to find a job when no one was hiring.

She pushed her concerns aside that afternoon and allowed herself to celebrate with the kids.

We hooted and hollered as we marched down the driveway and ceremoniously yanked the "For Sale" sign from the ground. Logan threw it onto the bank, where it lay among the ferns. I peed on it for good luck and for good riddance. New York. Chicago. It didn't matter to me. What mattered was my family's happiness. And they were visibly happier than they had been in weeks.

Haley had the honor of dumping the listing brochures in the garbage. Dad tucked one in his pocket. "A souvenir," he said with a wink. Mom rolled her eyes. She wanted no memories of those past three months.

Mom retreated to the patio once the kids were tucked into bed. It was a warm, cloudless night, and the stars shone brightly.

Dad joined her on the glider. It squeaked as their weight shifted back and forth. It needed more oil. Dad hadn't yet oiled it as he did every spring. "You OK?" He rubbed her thigh and let his hand rest there.

"Just thinking about everything I have to undo. I have to call the school tomorrow and reregister the kids. And call the soccer club. But I don't think they'll let Logan try out now. They already posted the roster. I've got to give some thought to summer camps. We haven't signed them up for anything, and I know all the good programs are gonna be filled. Then I have to unpack all those boxes in the garage. And what if they ask us to move next year?"

"It will all work out," Dad offered optimistically.

Mom simply nodded. "I had to convince myself moving would be good. Remember? When you first told me about Chicago? God, I hate the cold. But now . . . now I have to convince myself staying will be better."

~Fifty-five~

That summer on the lane couldn't have been more perfect. For me anyway.

Mom decided not to look for a job until the fall, when the kids were back in school. She wanted time to unwind. Time to enjoy her children because the sad truth was there hadn't been a lot of joy those last couple of months. Besides, the economy's outlook was still very bleak. The national unemployment rate raced toward an unprecedented ten percent. "Why bother," she told Lara. "No one's hiring anyway."

"You should take the summer off. Relax and unpack. You'll be back to work before you know it and begging for time off," Lara warned in her pleasant way.

Mom nodded and laughed because she knew Lara was right. "I haven't lined anything up for the kids. I guess it's Camp Mom this year," she said jokingly, wiping down the counter and rearranging the dish towels. But behind the laughter I sensed the insecurity. She'd never been alone with them for an entire summer, and she knew they'd fight if they were together for too long.

"It'll be fine," Lara said reassuringly. Like me, she sensed Mom's concern.

"I know. They're burned out too, and they've made it very clear that they don't want to go to town camp. I'm just not sure what to do with them, and our budget's an issue now that I'm not working."

Mom consulted with Google. I laid at her feet while she researched her options. The popular nature camps, sports camps, hobby camps, and art camps were either full or too expensive. Most were full-day programs, and Mom couldn't justify spending the extra money when she was home and not working. Luckily the kids had no desire to spend their entire summer at camp. They were looking forward to some unstructured time at home. So Mom narrowed her search to half-day programs and joined a gym that had outdoor and indoor pools and tennis courts.

That was the beginning of Camp Mom.

The first couple of weeks were hectic. Mom spent her mornings chauffeuring the kids to their various summer activities. Tennis one week, gymnastics the next, even golf. They visited the pool most afternoons before lunch, and Mom snuck in an exercise class or tennis lesson when time allowed. Some days Mom would wake up stiff. She'd hobble about nursing her aching muscles. "I'm so out of shape," she'd complain.

I was glad to accompany Mom when I could and spent the little time I had to myself catching up on my sleep. They were never gone for more than a few hours though. They worried about me being alone. "He's always had Lela," Haley reminded Logan. Her thoughtfulness caressed my heart because I did miss Lela. I was glad Mom and the kids were home that summer. Their presence calmed the loss that still tugged at my insides.

They always came home for a late lunch, followed by a worksheet session, and then my favorite part of the day: our nature walks.

Every afternoon, about an hour or two before dinner, we'd walk through the sanctuary. The kids recorded in a journal all the things they observed. Like the size of the mushrooms, the blooming plants, the pond's water level, and the weather. They paid particular attention to the wild blueberry, blackberry, and raspberry bushes. They eagerly waited for the fruits to ripen and spent hours collecting the berries that stained their fingers. They recorded the number, color, and sizes of the frogs, snakes, birds, and turtles we spotted. They learned to distinguish between male and female bullfrogs, and they made note of the tracks we found in the mud.

"Do you think they're in there?" Haley never stopped searching for the ducklings that hatched beside our back porch earlier that spring. The mama duck had moved her babies. I could smell their presence deep in the sanctuary's swampy waters. I couldn't see or hear them. But they were there. Safe. Hidden among the reeds.

Mom was, at times, quiet. Seemingly lost in the sanctuary's tranquility. I suspected she thought often of Lela, but I had no way of knowing.

We slipped easily into our summer routines. Like my winter coat, my family was able to shed the anxiety they stored through the winter and spring. The warmth of the summer sun melted the tension and renewed their energy. But finances were still an issue.

"How are we doing with our budget?" Mom would inquire. Dad's response was always the same. "We just have to be careful."

Mom conserved our money as best she could. She shopped around for groceries and stopped ordering takeout. She spent more time planning and cooking meals.

"Are we poor?" Haley asked one afternoon. Mom gagged on the iced tea she'd been drinking.

"No, we're not poor. We just have to watch what we spend our money on." Haley's question surprised her, but she recovered nicely.

"Then why couldn't we get ice cream at the pool?" Logan wanted to know.

"Well, you picked out ten mini-melts for ten dollars at the grocery store yesterday. Same ones they sell at the pool. Right? And how much are they at the pool?"

"Three dollars," he answered.

"So how much money will we save if you eat one of the mini-melts we already have at home rather than buying one at the pool?"

"Two dollars." Logan was Mom's little calculator.

"That's right. So you save two dollars each by eating mini-melts at home. That's four dollars a day we're saving. At the end of the month, that'll pay for golf camp." The kids nodded their heads as they poked at the mini-melts with their spoons.

"If we were poor, you wouldn't be taking tennis and golf lessons, now would you?" The kids smiled and sucked in the ice cream pellets. They seemed satisfied with Mom's answer.

Mom's heart was burdened. She hated denying

them something as simple as ice cream at the pool. Yet she knew Dad's employer could pull the salary bump at any time.

"It doesn't mean it's going to be like this forever. Don't you think you're giving them something more valuable than ice cream?" Aunt Abbey asked.

Mom silently nodded. "You're right. I'm overreacting. They certainly aren't going without." She embraced her younger sister. Grateful for the time they had together.

Aunt Abbey hesitated before speaking. "You know, I thanked God that he let you stay," she confessed.

"So it was your doing then," Mom teased. "I'll send you our bills."

Mom was careful with whom she shared what information. Most of her friends worked. She knew the tension that existed between working and non-working mothers. Mom had become one of *them*. A mom who didn't have to juggle career and family. She reached out to her friends and made herself available to help. No one took her up on the offer, and I felt her retreating inwards.

The lane became her haven and she drew strength from the kids. They in turn found a deep sense of security and calm. Logan's brain bully seldom came to visit, and Haley returned to her preteen self, rekindling neglected friendships. The bond between the three of them grew stronger.

"I'm learning so much about them. Little things that make them tick," she shared with Dad.

He was content knowing they were being taken care. But still he felt himself growing more distant from them. He was only home three nights a week. "How about I take a long weekend and we go away?" he suggested.

~Fifty-six~

The water's white arms swept across the sand. The waves took turns rolling over each other. First one set of waves, then another, and another. Small pieces of sand danced on the light wind and stung my eyes. The salty air filled my nostrils and lungs.

A beach vacation.

My first trip to Cape May.

My family had been there before. Many years ago when the kids and Lela were young.

I ran ahead and threw myself into the chilly surf. The crashing waves were deafening. Laughter swirled around me. First vague. Then familiar. Haley and Logan's distinct squeals. They were somewhere behind me.

I turned to face the voices. The sun sparkling off the sand and water made it difficult to see. I squinted and moved toward the distant images. My paws began to feel the heat. *Best to stay along the water's edge where the sand is wet and cool,* I thought.

A young bulldog that looked like Winston meandered in the distance. No time for distractions. I had to reach my family.

The familiar laughter grew louder and their images grew clearer. Haley and Logan had their boogie boards. They were already in the water. I ran toward them as fast as I could. In and out of the waves. I gagged on the salt water.

Dad stood guard at the water's edge. He inched his way forward and shrieked at the chilly waves that slapped against his legs. He dug his toes into the sand when the waves retreated. He inhaled and charged straight ahead. He dove into the next round of waves with a boisterous cry.

Mom watched the scene from behind her sunglasses. She sat a safe distance from the surf. The kids called for her to join them. She waved them off with a smile. She'd already felt the water. It was too cold for her liking. She picked up a broken shell and mindlessly dug it into the sand.

I ran to her and begged her to play. My zoomies scattered water and wet sand everywhere. Her arms were her only defense against the assault. "Join us!" I barked playfully.

I tugged at the beach towel beneath her, and she tumbled backwards into the sand. "Shamus!" she hollered. She rose and brushed the sand from her backside.

I dropped the towel and approached her slowly.

Her cheeks were moist.

She'd been crying behind her shades. Remembering, I was sure, a time when it was Lela charging in and out of the waves.

Mom shook the towel and laid it out flat on the sand. She sat upon it, legs outstretched, propped up on her elbows. I lay next to her, hoping she could forget our loss for just an hour.

I wished I could make her laugh.

~Fifty-seven~

The smell of warm, sticky cinnamon buns and cranberry juice lingered in the kitchen. *Mom always serves cinnamon buns on Fridays when the weather cools*, I thought blissfully. I loitered around the dishwasher that morning, swabbing up the sweet icing that had begun to harden on the breakfast plates. Mom scurried about clearing dishes and wiping down the counters. She pushed the canisters into a straight line and rearranged the dish towels so that their ends were perfectly aligned.

"Come on, Haley. We can't be late again. Your school sent a letter saying you've been late seven days already this semester. We've got to be in the car by 7:30. Get your shoes on." It was easy to tell from the tone of Mom's voice that she was growing increasingly impatient with her daughter. "Come on," she repeated firmly. She lifted the dishwasher door with her sneaker and then closed it with her hip. The lock clicked and the swishing sounds drowned out the "humph" that Haley snorted.

Mom didn't see Haley roll her eyes or the way she lifted her chin defiantly. "I am," Haley snapped at her mother.

Oh no, I thought. *Here we go again.*

Logan kept his head down, pretending to read his book. He didn't want to become a victim of Haley's unpredictable wrath. He didn't understand the mood swings or sudden verbal attacks. He adored his sister and her unprovoked scorn hurt him.

Mom stared into the kitchen sink and drew in her breath. She held it while the anger inside subsided. She didn't want another confrontation. There'd been so many as we tried settling into the new school year. It was only mid-October.

Haley had started middle school. Family and friends warned Mom of the changes middle school would bring. Yet Mom hadn't been prepared for the changes to start so quickly. Overnight it seemed that Haley replaced her sweats and shorts with jeans and skirts. She took an interest in her hair and appearance. She began worrying about the dark hair above her lip and on her legs and the swollen pimples on her forehead. Mom could handle the clothes and make-up, but Haley's volatile temperament left her defenseless.

Our soft-spoken, thoughtful, and mostly cooperative Haley had changed. Her tirades began late that summer and escalated in the fall. I smelled the hormonal changes long before the rantings began. Lela had sensed them too. They were subtle smells at first. But as time passed, the smells became more pungent, and Haley's behavior became more erratic.

Haley was a tween. A blossoming adolescent longing for greater freedom and searching for her place in the world. She succumbed to the pressures and physiological changes Mom read about. Yet she was still vulnerable. A child surprised at times by the intensity of her feelings. Young and unable to restrain herself. Mom felt compelled to protect her. But in the blink of an eye, Haley could turn into a rabid creature. Demanding and self-centered, disrespectful, and spiteful. The friction bounced off the walls. "Patience," Mom would remind herself. "Patience."

Emi and I remained unscathed. Immune to Haley's rage. Perhaps because we spoke no human words that could irritate her. Haley turned to us when she felt no one else understood. "They treat me like a baby. I'm not a baby. I know what I'm doing," Haley would often cry.

Mom turned to face Logan. She watched as he feigned reading. "Come on, Logan. You too. In the car." Although her tone had softened, he felt the dangerous undercurrent and walked hurriedly outdoors. Elementary school started later. He'd finish reading when we got back home.

Haley's fingers expertly manipulated her phone's small screen.

"Haley, put your phone away. Let's go," Mom repeated as she walked toward the front door. She was determined not to start the day quarreling. "It's just a phase," she whispered to herself just loud enough for me to hear. The muscles in her face relaxed slightly.

Haley hoisted her backpack up over her shoulder. She clutched her buzzing phone tightly. A message waited for her. She glanced at her mother.

Mom's face was neither angry nor glad while she held the door open for Haley. I sat by her side for moral support. "Please," Mom said softly, urging Haley forward with her eyes.

Haley's bubbling insolence now merely simmered.

"Come on, Shamus. Good boy," Haley said. She

kissed my muzzle and rubbed my chin on her way out the door. Normally I welcomed her affections. But that morning I resisted the urge to nip her butt as she brushed by Mom.

What would Lela do? I wondered. *She may very well have taken a nip.* The visual made me laugh.

"Have a good day, Haley. Don't forget to find out what's on your social studies test," Mom added just before Haley slammed Shelly's door. A concerned look crossed Mom's face as Haley disappeared into the school.

Haley's transition to middle school had been bumpy. She struggled to keep track of which classes she had on what days. She wasn't used to participating in class or asking teachers to clarify what was being tested or what the format would be. The more Mom tried to help, the more Haley resisted.

"Aren't you worried that she might fall through the cracks?" Mom asked Dad later that night.

"She's smart. Her interim report card isn't bad. This is a big adjustment for her. We just have to be patient."

"It isn't just about being patient. It's about keeping on top of what's going on. All I know is what she writes down in her assignment log." Mom grabbed Haley's notebook and pulled out a piece of paper. "Look at this." She shoved the paper in front of him. "She got a 78 on this math test. Not because she doesn't know the math but because she didn't ask the teacher what would be on it. I can't help her if I don't know when and what she's being tested on."

Dad looked at the test through weary eyes and shook his head. He was tired. His flight had been delayed again, and he hadn't gotten home until very late the night before.

"She says she feels like she has to get all A's. I told her that's not what I expect. I expect her to do her best. That means knowing what's due when and then adequately preparing. I told her that if she doesn't know then she needs to ask." Mom plopped down in the chair next to him sending his elbow and beer bottle into the air. A small amount of beer dribbled down the bottle's curvy side. I lapped up the bitter drops that fell to the floor.

"I don't want to alienate myself from her, Raj. I want to help. But I don't know how or even how much I should be helping, and I hate feeling like our kids' success depends on my parenting skills. I hate the pressure." Her brow crinkled in aggravation.

"I'll help when I can, but I'm not here like you." Dad shifted closer to her and rested his hand on her shoulder. "I think we should focus on teaching them how to prepare and study and then step back."

Mom didn't shy away from the weight of his hand. She stared straight ahead, lost in thought.

"I'm glad you're here for them. They're good kids, Gwen. Don't be so hard on yourself. They'll be fine." Dad's eyes filled with adoration as he spoke. "And so will you."

Mom leaned into his chest, and he pulled her close. He sniffed the lavender scent that remained in her hair. She used lavender shampoo and conditioner that morning. Lavender. One of her favorite essential oils.

Calm filled the house. I rested in the peaceful wake knowing it might not last.

Their relationship had become volatile, much like Haley's mood swings. While each was trying to be strong for the other, the uncertainty and financial stress made them anxious. They could do nothing but wait and see how life played out. As they waited their uneasiness grew, especially Mom's. She resented being at the mercy of Dad's employer. She usually snapped first from the pressure, and an argument would inevitably ensue.

But that night we relaxed in the cool, tranquil air while the kids slept.

"Can you imagine what it would be like if you were working?" Dad said quietly. He worried less about us and could focus more easily on work with Mom at home. The kids were less hurried and Mom less stressed at the end of each day. He heard it in their voices when he called at night, and he saw it in their faces when he was home. He was glad that Mom was taking better care of herself. She had started exercising more, and he had encouraged her to join a tennis league, to get out and meet people.

Mom sighed.

"Speaking of work, Phillip called again. He asked if I could work for a few weeks to cover for an associate going out on a medical leave. I told him I could. From home a few hours each day. He was fine with that."

Phillip called Mom every couple of months.

They had even met for lunch and talked about the possibility of her working for him again once we moved to Chicago. Mom wasn't convinced she wanted to practice law any more, particularly if it meant working with Valerie, but we needed the money and Mom couldn't afford to burn any bridges. The legal community was surprisingly small.

"That's good," Dad replied. "It shouldn't impact my salary bump, but I'll let Ned know. When will you start?"

"In a couple of weeks."

The thought of Mom eventually going back to work saddened me. I'd gotten used to her being around. *At least she'd be working from home through the fall*, I thought.

~Fifty-eight~

Lela's memory book rested on Mom's lap. Her feet were propped up against the small table where it was kept. In the den. In front of the small green and floral couch Lela used to curl up on when the big comfy sofa was occupied. The couch's fibers housed the dried urine drops Lela leaked while she slept. Only I could detect the faint, sour odor that grew weaker as time passed.

Mom moved the small couch to the den when the new furniture arrived. She placed it in the corner, near the piano, along with the table and memory book. The nook became a place of healing and remembrance. It was a place to honor Lela, and I memorized her pictures. We had looked at them countless times. Less frequently though as the year wore on.

"It's all I have left of her. These pictures. I don't want to forget," Mom told Dad, holding the memory book tight against her chest. I knew she'd never forget, and Lela's memory book would never collect dust on a bookshelf. I secretly wondered if she'd make a memory book of me and where it would go. The table wasn't big enough for two.

That night, nearly eight months after Lela's passing, I sat next to Mom as she gently turned the pages of Lela's memory book. Mom sipped her wine and studied each image, smiling as she reminisced. The holidays, the vacations, the birthdays, and every day in between.

It was the last picture, the one Logan took just

minutes before we rushed Lela to the vet, that stole Mom's smile. The picture captured Lela resting, eyes closed, as though she were sleeping. Lela looked peaceful. The fatal blood clot hadn't yet lodged itself in her brain.

I heard a faint splintering sound from somewhere deep within Mom's chest as she trapped the pages between the book's covers.

I sat quiet and still as Mom intently studied the familiar face that adorned the front cover. She gazed into the glossy eyes that shone almost white in the middle where deep, black puddles once lay. Her fingers swept along the bridge of Lela's muzzle towards the top of her head. It was the only dark fur left on the aged face. We had watched Lela age within the book's pages. From puppy to adolescent to the mature dog we both adored and missed.

"Where did the time go?" Mom spoke to Lela's picture.

She smiled weakly, raising her hand to her brow. She felt the creases on her forehead and the soft folds around her eyes. We had all aged, and Lela's book told more than her story. There was a story for each of us unfolding still against time's elusive backdrop.

It didn't surprise me that Mom turned to the memory book that night. She reached for it when she felt exposed, searching for solace among the pages. That night she felt vulnerable. I saw it in her eyes. "I'm officially unemployed," she told the kids over dinner. "I know God has a plan for me. I just wish he'd give me a sneak preview." The smile and half-hearted chuckle didn't hide her despair.

I'd been with her when she logged on to her work e-mail earlier that day. The words "invalid credentials" popped up on the screen. She tried logging in through different servers, but the same message appeared each time. Her contract work had ceased without Phillip telling her.

Mom wasn't surprised. Phillip hadn't sent her any billable work in seven weeks. Every morning Mom logged in and waited. Her early disappointment turned to resignation. She used her time and temporary employee status opportunistically. She read legal updates and downloaded legal seminars. I learned a lot about employment and immigration law that fall.

Mom was much too hurt to call Phillip that morning. She didn't trust what she might say. So she punched out a short e-mail. One that couldn't be misconstrued. The callousness of his curt response confirmed what she had known. Phillip cared about his practice. Mom was just an insurance policy in case work picked up. He wasn't trying to help her. He was looking out for himself.

Mom was annoyed at herself. Annoyed that she believed he might have changed. Her annoyance turned to anger. It festered throughout the day while she waited for Dad's nightly call.

He called shortly before the kids' bedtime. Mom and I retreated to the den so she could talk privately to him.

"Did you see his e-mail? I forwarded it to you. He didn't even have the decency to call. No one called or e-mailed. No one thanked me for wanting to help. Nothing." Rage coursed through her veins. "I feel so used."

She sniffled and shook back the angry, hot tears. "And he wants us to meet for lunch next month, when he's not so swamped. What is that? Like I want to have lunch or work with him again? Nothing's changed."

Haley and Logan argued in the background. Their yells escalated, and I knew it'd only be a matter of time before the shouting turned physical. Mom struggled to ignore them. Her hands shook as she sat at the desk. She fought to retain her composure. The vein at her temple pulsed.

Haley stormed into the den.

"Mom, didn't you hear me? Logan keeps turning off the Wii. He won't let me finish," Haley hollered. She stomped her foot while one hand rested firmly on her hip. Her lips were drawn tightly together and her nostrils flared as her chest heaved in and out. She brushed the hair from her face angrily. "Well?"

So much like her mother, I thought. *Passionate and expressive.*

Then came the snap. The eerie sound that emanated from somewhere deep inside Mom. I felt it more than I heard it. From the look on Haley's face, she felt it too.

"Haley, can't you see I'm on the phone?" Mom yelled. She was on her feet. The empty chair spun around behind her. The color of her face deepened.

Haley stood there frozen. Her mouth dropped open. She didn't dare say a word. She saw her mother's damp cheeks, and Haley's face softened. Her large, apologetic eyes gazed at Mom. Her sudden stillness quelled Mom's rage.

Mom instantly regretted the harshness in her tone. "I'm sorry. I didn't mean to snap at you."

Haley accepted her mother's embrace. The tender moment made me whine.

"It's OK," Haley said softly. Her hand felt light on my back.

"I'm talking to Daddy. I'll call for you in a few minutes. OK?"

"Hi, Daddy," Haley chimed. It wasn't the same, harsh tone that bellowed through the house moments before. Her youthful gentleness returned, and she threw Mom a smile as she left the room. Her long, dark hair flowed behind her. She didn't wait for Dad to reply.

The muscles in Mom's face relaxed as she sunk back in the chair.

"I'm trying to be positive, Raj. I haven't sat around complaining. I finished my CLE, and I even downloaded some employment and immigration law classes. But now what? We still don't know if we're moving in the spring."

Mom paused to chew on the end of a pencil she picked up. I stretched my back legs, and the crick in my spine faded. My body wasn't quite as young and nimble as it had once been.

"No, I haven't heard anything. There's a legal issue with my volunteering for them. He said he'd pass my resume on to their benefits department." The chair under her swayed from side to side.

"Raj, I can't even give my services away. Do you have any idea how that feels?" The chair stopped abruptly. Her shoulders slumped. "I feel like a loser," she said hopelessly.

Mom enjoyed being with the kids. I knew she did despite the frustrating, trying moments. "You're my favorite job," she told them. Yet we both knew that the more time she spent with them, the harder it would be for her to go back to work.

She was afraid. Afraid Dad's employer would arbitrarily pull the salary bump. Afraid of relying on Dad when she'd always been financially independent. Afraid of losing herself. I did what I could to comfort her.

Mom rubbed her forehead. "I *am* looking at this as a time of opportunity. I'm just hurt, Raj. Why are you always acting like a Martian? Can't I just be hurt right now?"

She couldn't shrug the sadness that enveloped her that night. The passion that she once wore outwardly was gone.

She kissed the kids good night and turned to her memories for comfort.

"This too will pass," she said aloud as she embraced Lela's memory book. She tenderly returned it to its resting place on the table.

She smiled at the cover.

Lela smiled back.

~Fifty-nine~

Logan wasn't himself when he got off the school bus. He wasn't lively and talkative, and he had no interest in playing with the tug toy I dropped at his feet. He ate his snack in silence and then worked slowly through his math worksheet. He kept inside whatever it was that bothered him. And whatever it was festered through the late afternoon into the early evening. It wasn't until after dinner that he opened up.

"She thinks I'm weird," Logan sniveled.

"Who?" Mom asked.

"Jules thinks I'm weird and creepy." He looked at Mom with pleading eyes, and a look of concern washed over her.

"Did she say that?" Mom's tone was defensive.

"Her friend told me today when we were on the playground." Logan scooted up on the couch next to his mother. The lamp's soft light illuminated the disappointment that he openly wore.

"Aw, honey," Mom said pulling him into her chest. "First of all, you don't know if Jules really said those things. Even if she did, you're the sweetest, kindest kid I know. She's just too young to realize it."

Jules had been Logan's love interest since the second grade. He'd spent hours making special holiday cards and gifts for her. His gestures were always thoughtful and heartwarming. But she hadn't shown signs of returning his sentiments. Mom was surprised that his infatuation had lasted so long.

"Maybe I should call and ask her?" he asked.

"No. You don't want to look like your stalking her because that would be weird and creepy." Mom smelled his hair and brushed her lips against the top of his head. "Just wait and see how she acts at school. You'll know by her actions if she said those things."

"Brian said I should comb my hair and ditch the sweatpants."

"Who's Brian?"

"Another fourth grader on the bus. He's cool." Logan's voice was filled with admiration.

"He is, is he? Hmmm. Is that what you think you should do?" Mom asked.

"No, but Brian said he has ten girls chasing after him. He wears jeans."

"Has anyone made fun of you, or is this about Jules and trying to impress her?"

"I just want her to like me," he slowly answered. His face was long.

"What's important is who you are on the inside. And you're fabulous! If she hasn't figured that out, then it's her loss. You shouldn't change for anyone. You're wonderful just as you are." Mom squeezed him and rubbed the tip of his nose with her own.

"I know kids can be mean. When I was about your age the girls used to make fun of my clothes. It really hurt my feelings," Mom shared. "Grammy and Poppy didn't have any money to buy us nice things." She ran her fingers through his hair.

Logan gazed up at her. His eyes filled with compassion. "I know Mom." He returned the squeeze. "I just want a pairs of jeans. I still like my sweatpants."

"Combing your hair would be good. And having a nice pair of jeans seems sensible. But wear them because they make you feel good." Mom hugged him tighter.

"OK, Mom!"

She planted an exaggerated kiss on his cheek and tickled his ribs until he screamed.

"How about we go shopping this weekend?" Mom asked when she caught her breath.

Logan smiled and pecked his mother's cheek. He popped off the couch, transformed. "Come on, Shamus! Wanna play catch?"

Of course I did!

~*Sixty*~

It was just after Thanksgiving when we learned we wouldn't be moving to Chicago. Not the following spring. Not ever. The business out there wouldn't report to Dad, so there was no need for us to move.

I celebrated with the kids when I first heard the news. *Dad would be home more, and we'd be a family again,* I naively thought. I didn't understand the implications. I couldn't appreciate the importance of one job over another despite knowing that Dad yearned for the opportunity to run a business. He wanted to implement the strategy he conceived. The experience would "pave the way for other opportunities," he exclaimed.

But Dad was needed in New York. The company was about to go through another reorganization. He was charged with overseeing the design of a new corporate strategy. He'd commute to Chicago only to finish integrating the acquired business and transitioning its leadership to a newly designated team.

Just like that, Dad's aspirations of running the Chicago business were abruptly snuffed out. He was in a foul mood when he got home. I was glad the kids were asleep.

Mom and I listened patiently as he vented his frustration. He found the business. He sold the strategy to senior management and then wooed the owners into selling it. He was instrumental in negotiating the deal and had spent endless weeks learning the business and building relationships. The business was to report to him when the owners formally stepped down. That's what he'd been promised. "We could have been stuck out there had we moved. And for what?" he growled.

The more I listened, the more I understood. It wasn't just the lost opportunity that left him discouraged. It was the betrayal. Dad never trusted Ned, but he had foolishly trusted his boss, and his boss offered no apologies or condolences when he dealt the blow. "It was a business decision. Nothing personal. That's what Stan said," Dad howled.

How could he not take it personally? I thought, looking sadly at him. *After everything our family has been through?*

Mom wasn't surprised. Disappointed? Yes. But not surprised. She'd seen their true colors months before, back when they started grumbling about the cost of the relo. "We are *all* expendable," Mom counseled Dad. "Don't think for one minute they care about you," she had warned. Profitability first. Phillip had taught her that. She spent the following few months hoping she was wrong. But Ned and Stan were no different than Phillip.

Mom sat silently while Dad ranted. I could see the irritation in her hardened eyes and stiff posture. She just sat there. Listening. Trying to act supportive. She was displeased but at whom I couldn't tell. *Ned and Stan for their callousness? Dad for his naivety? All of them?* I wondered.

She spoke only after she was sure Dad had finished. "Now you know," she said cautiously. "What are you gonna do about it?" Her voice was nonjudgmental.

Dad's eyes filled with insecurity and doubt. He shrugged his shoulders and spent the next several days licking his wounds, mending his bruised ego. He wasn't himself. He was despondent.

I dropped my tug toy at his feet and pawed at his leg while he scanned the Internet for job postings. "Come on," I barked. "Let's play." But he wasn't in a playful mood. He patted my head and turned back to his computer.

"You can be angry. But don't be stupid. Don't use your work e-mail to look for another job," Mom scolded. Dad pretended not to hear. "You have every right to be upset. But you need this job. We need it," she sneered down at him. I didn't like the brusque tone, and I too ignored her when she tossed my toy into the hall.

"Suit yourself," she said, frowning down at me. She didn't stop to scratch my side.

The resentment Mom harbored grew while Dad wallowed. "He can only blame himself," she told Lara in a harsh, cold voice. "This was his choice. At least he has a job."

Dad loitered around the house, avoiding the office. He didn't want to answer the questions he knew would come once word got out. And word did get out. It was easier to respond to an e-mail than to engage in a face-to-face conversation. His electronic voice more easily hid his disappointment.

Then the unavoidable call came. Stan and Ned were headed to Chicago where they'd evaluate the business and announce to employees the new leadership team. Dad had to be there. He couldn't hide any longer.

Haley noticed his unusually quiet, subdued mood that morning. "He's just tired and doesn't want to leave us. That's all." Mom chose her words carefully as we waited in the middle school's drop-off line. Haley raised her eyebrows questioningly, but she didn't press her mother.

Dad and Logan were huddled on the couch watching football highlights when we got back. Dad looked childish and vulnerable in his oversized flannel pajamas. His slippered feet rested on the coffee table next to his mug. Mom glared at him and the dirty dishes he had left lying about.

She silently filled the dishwasher, wiped down the counters, and started a load of laundry. She didn't come into the family room until it was time to go.

"Give Daddy a kiss now. Time for school." Logan wrapped himself tightly around his father. Dad returned the embrace and looked down lovingly at his son. "I'll only be gone for one night this time." He tussled the hair on Logan's head.

Mom let Dad brood at home while we dropped Logan off at school. We returned to find him showered and dressed. He looked handsome in his suit. He was clean-shaven, and his hair was slicked back with gel. I inhaled the soapy scent that mingled with his cologne. The combination made me sneeze.

Dad grumbled and threw his undershirt and boxers into an overnight bag. He collected his socks and slammed the armoire's drawer. He mumbled something about an injury and insult while forcefully tugging at his bag's zipper. The words he muttered became unintelligible.

Mom and I withdrew to the kitchen where her jasmine tea was steeping. The light, floral scent filled the air though there was nothing light about Mom's mood. I knew she'd had just about enough of Dad's unpleasant temperament. She had held her tongue that week while he moped and sulked. But the aggravation swelled inside her. I feared the balloon was about to burst.

I retreated under the kitchen table when I heard Dad's footsteps approaching. He dropped his bags near the front door. "This ought to be a pleasant trip," he said sarcastically.

The balloon expanded. The pressure pressed my body against the cool slate. I didn't dare interfere. I wouldn't take sides.

"God. Enough already!" Mom reeled toward him. The suddenness of her attack sent him stumbling backwards.

"Did you ever think that maybe you're not qualified to run the business? Maybe that's not what they see as your strength?" She didn't wait for him to respond. "I'm sorry you're embarrassed and tired of people asking you what happened. You have a right to be pissed off. But get over it already!"

"You have no idea what it's been like," Dad retorted.

"Maybe not. But we can't afford to lose your job. I don't have one, remember? So, until I find work or you find another job, just deal with it and leave your shit somewhere else because I'm tired of it," she fired back. "I'm tired of my life revolving around you." She drew in a deep breath. "This is your doing!"

The balloon didn't pop. It exploded and Mom's words flew out relentlessly.

"You wanted to run a business. You were willing to move us to do it." Mom thrust her rigid finger near his face. "I know. I bought into it. God knows I was ready to leave my job, and I wanted to spend more time with the kids. But I trusted you." Her finger jabbed at the air he inhaled through flaring nostrils. "I trusted you to take care of us. And you haven't. Look at us," she screamed, throwing both hands into the air. "You can't," she snapped. Her steel eyes cut deep into him. "You can't take care of us!"

I felt the force of Mom's words as they pounded against Dad's chest. He cringed from the weight of each compression. He hadn't expected her to turn so vehemently upon him. Disdain filled his dark eyes. He grabbed his bags and fled the onslaught.

She couldn't retract the hurtful words.

"Raj. Wait," Mom called after him. Her hands reached out for him, but he was already gone.

"Wait," she whispered.

Dad didn't look back and she knew he wouldn't. She waited for the familiar sound of gravel crunching underneath truck tires. Then she collapsed into the chair and cried uncontrollably.

I waited in the shadows for the tumultuous air to settle.

~Sixty-one~

"Nude or sheer black, Shamus?" Mom held up two pairs of pantyhose. I had no idea why it mattered. She chuckled at my inexperience and pressed her nose against mine.

"Nude it is," she said, tucking the black pair into her small handbag.

She hoisted the nude hosiery up over her legs before reaching for her black suit. The creamy silk neckline of her blouse peeked out from under the lapels. Her hair was pulled neatly back, clipped together just above her neck. The loose ends cascaded down her back, resting between her shoulder blades. The pearl jewelry Dad bought her a few years before graced her slim neck and adorned her ears. She applied her makeup sparingly and dabbed a subtle fragrance on her wrists.

The buckles on her new black shoes sparkled as she walked toward me. Flats. She bought sensible flats because she'd have to walk four blocks from Penn Station to the interview.

"Well?" Mom asked. I nodded my head and barked approvingly.

"Thanks, Shamus." She scratched under my chin and then pulled her trench coat tightly around her. It was a bleak winter morning, but she radiated with confidence.

A firm had posted the full-time, senior attorney position the month before. But Mom wasn't ready to work full-time. There'd be too many changes too soon for our family, and financially she didn't have to work full-time. We had learned to live on less, and being around for the kids was more important to her. The kids too had voiced their opinions. They hadn't liked Mom coming home tired and grumpy.

So Mom took a chance and asked if they'd consider a part-time arrangement. They were impressed with her credentials and experience and had wanted to meet her. She'd already gone through three rounds of interviews. That day was the last round. They had narrowed their search down to two candidates.

Mom returned that day feeling exhausted but confident. "Five interviews in four hours," she told Dad. No break. No beverages. But everything had gone well. She liked the people she met and found the offices appealing. The commute itself wouldn't be bad.

She optimistically waited for the offer.

She was stunned when she learned it would never come.

I secretly rejoiced.

~*Sixty-two*~

My nose was buried deep in the fresh, new snow when I sensed her presence sauntering slowly toward us. She was smaller than Lela, and her face was not quite as aged. But her demeanor and graceful steps were hauntingly similar. My chest tightened, and I could barely breathe as I watched the beautiful black Lab push her white muzzle into Mom's fuzzy mitten. Her name was Sophie.

Mom knelt in the snow and looked deep into the cloudy eyes. "We lost our girl this past spring," she said sadly, rubbing Sophie's side. "You remind me of her." Sophie pressed her face deeper into Mom's hand, keenly aware that a painful wound had opened. She pulled slowly away when her human called out. "You best go now," Mom whispered to her. Sophie tossed her head thoughtfully and walked briskly away. I couldn't shrug the heaviness even after she disappeared around the bend.

Where are you Lela? I wondered. I begged the cold, crisp air to numb my aching heart.

Mom didn't mention the incident to Dad or the kids. There were Christmas presents to wrap and cookies to bake. Christmas was just a few days away, and she knew the kids waited eagerly for her.

She bravely tucked her sorrow in some deep, safe place, took a yawning breath, and donned a smile when we walked through the door. Haley and Logan greeted us with laughter. Their gaiety was gratefully contagious, and Sophie's face was soon lost among the wrapping paper, ribbons, gift bags, bows, and tags. Mom and I found peace among the chaos.

For a short time anyway.

"Pinky swear no crosses count, it's not you and Dad?" Haley asked coolly. She remained huddled over the gift she was wrapping and plucked two pieces of tape from the dispenser. She held the paper firmly in place with one hand while securing it to the box with the other. She admired her work and then calmly looked toward Mom for an answer.

Mom's scissors sliced through paper. She pretended not to hear. But her pulse quickened when Logan's head shot up from the mounds of wrapping paper that surrounded him. The Christmas tree lights bounced off his inquisitive eyes when he exchanged glances with his sister. He'd obviously heard the question and was gauging Mom's reaction.

Mom suppressed the panic that had begun setting in and feigned a coughing fit. She thumped her fist against her chest and hurriedly shuffled out of the room.

It was the dreaded question. The question the kids asked every year. But this was the first time it'd been asked under the infamous pinky swear.

No one in our family would ever dare break a pinky swear. It was sacred. The supreme symbol of trust. Everyone knew that silence was the same as an affirmative admission of guilt. Mom's performance fooled no one.

"I knew it," I heard Haley declare as I trotted after Mom.

Mom gulped down a glass of water and then slipped into the den.

"Raj, I think we need to tell the kids the truth about Santa. Haley asked me to pinky swear. I pretended I didn't hear her and then left the room coughing. But they know the truth. I saw it in their eyes." Mom's voice quivered with emotion. Santa was about to become another ghost of Christmases past. "I don't want them to feel like we've lied to them all of these years."

Dad nodded in agreement. It was time. They couldn't avoid the inevitable.

I wedged myself between the kids while Mom and Dad told them the truth.

Mom explained how Saint Nicholas, a man of God, took care of those in need. He gave his own money and food selflessly. He didn't seek thanks or recognition. In most cases, he acted anonymously. What he did, he did out of love. Over time the stories of his kindness spread throughout the world.

The story of St. Nick captivated me. Lela never told me about the man who lived a long, long time ago in another country. *Maybe she didn't know?*

"So, yes. We are Santa Claus. Anyone who gives with love keeps Saint Nick's spirit alive," Mom clarified.

Santa isn't a farce, I found myself thinking. The stories and traditions were based on a man whose spirit I'd come to believe in.

Haley shared my sentiments. "I still believe in the spirit of Santa. It's not about getting presents anyway." *An old soul at the age of ten*, I marveled.

Logan's reaction, on the other hand, was quite different. "I knew it," he shouted. He hopped off the couch and marched around the room declaring, "Death to Santa. He's evil." His response was unexpected.

"Logan, don't say that." Mom's voice became firm. "You're not a baby anymore. You now know a very special secret. You can't tell anyone who still believes, especially your cousins and friends," she pleaded. "Do you understand?" Mom held her breath, wondering if he'd been ready for the truth.

"I won't tell," Logan said with a smirk. Mom stared into his mischievous eyes. "I pinky swear," he quickly added. Mom sighed with relief.

The kids were glad they'd been entrusted with the truth. It empowered them. They suddenly seemed older than they had the minute before.

It was Mom and Dad who mourned the truth. They spoke about it later that night.

"They're no longer our babies. They won't run down the stairs early Christmas morning wondering if Santa came," Mom said wearily. "Maybe we shouldn't have told them."

Dad dropped another log on the crackling fire. "No, it was time." He poked the log and waited for the fire to engulf it. The flames kicked up, and shadows danced across his somber face. "What a year it's been though," he sighed.

Mom nodded slowly. Her gaze fell upon Lela's illuminated face. It looked down at us from atop the Christmas tree where her ornament always rested. My ornament dangled next to it. It too shimmered in the light. "They're still together," Haley said when she placed them there. Her words tugged at my insides.

I rested my head on Mom's lap. Her hand moved lightly up and down my spine. "Yeah. It's certainly been a year of change." Her fingers dug deeper into my back.

"I wonder what next year will bring," she thought aloud.

~Sixty-three~

Mom's stomach had been sour all day. She managed to feed the kids their dinner without throwing up. But shortly after the table was cleared, she couldn't contain the bug that contaminated her insides. She spent the early evening trying to expunge the virus. And it was indeed a mean one that zapped more than her strength on its way out. She eventually left the confines of the bathroom and stumbled into bed.

"Come on, Logan. Let's say good night to Mommy," Haley instructed. She poured a cup of water for her mother and placed it carefully on the nightstand.

"Thanks, hon," Mom said weakly but without moving. Haley leaned in and kissed the warm, damp forehead. She didn't notice the acerbic smell that tainted Mom's breath. "Not too close, babe. I don't want you to get it," Mom's voice was frail.

Haley brushed the matted hair from Mom's forehead and wiped the pale face with a cool, damp cloth. It was something she learned from Mom the year before when Logan had a similar flu.

Mom smiled wearily at her children. "Bedtime, OK?"

A solemn Haley nodded in reply.

"How can I go to sleep if no one tucks me in?" Logan wanted to know.

Haley shot him a glaring look. Logan lifted his shoulders and hands. "What?" he silently mouthed at her.

"You can do it." Mom slowly shifted her gaze

toward him. "I know you can," she whispered without lifting her head. She carefully raised her fingers to caress his cheek.

"Well . . . can you come up in ten minutes and check on me?" He lightly pressed his mother's fingers into his skin. "Please?"

Tears gathered at the corners of Mom's eyes. "I can't. I'll throw up again if I move." Haley placed a comforting hand on her shoulder and the tears receded.

"Just tell me you will," he quietly pleaded. "It's psychological."

"OK," Mom faintly replied. "I will."

"Really?" he asked sanguinely.

"No." Mom's voice drifted off.

Logan bent over her. "It's OK, Mom." His puckered lips fell on her cheek.

"Come on, Logan. Let Mom rest." Haley led her brother upstairs and tucked him in. Then she climbed into her own bed where Emi waited for her.

Emi and I exchanged thoughtful glances.

I settled at Logan's feet as he slumbered.

The belly bug absconded during the night.

~Sixty-four~

It would have been Lela's sixteenth birthday. That was the morning the robin first came to Mom's bedroom window.

The drumming above my head startled me from sleep. I jumped to my paws; my breaths were ragged and my heart beat wildly. *What's happening?* I thought as I gathered my senses.

It was alarming to see a robin hovering so close to the windowpane. Its flapping wings and claws rapped persistently against the glass. It wasn't bothered by my sudden appearance. It continued to hover and flap. *How odd*, I thought, looking into its beady eyes.

I pressed my nose against the window trying to ascertain what was troubling the bird. But all seemed quiet outside, and I was sure Emi was still curled up next to Haley.

"What's that crazy bird doing? It's going to hurt itself," Mom said, flipping the covers off her. The gesture startled the bird, and it stopped its fluttering. The robin dug its claws into the windowsill. It sat silently still as if waiting. I knew it wasn't waiting for me because it had already dismissed my presence.

As Mom drew near, the bird resumed the ruckus. "You're gonna hurt yourself. Now go on," Mom ordered. She waved her hand, and the bird stopped to rest on the sill once more. It cocked its head to the side and followed her with its eyes. Mom shook her head disbelievingly.

I didn't know what to make of it. I'd never seen

a bird act so strangely. And when Mom turned her back to the bird, the commotion started again. That robin relentlessly beat its wings against the glass.

"OK, I see you. What?" Mom asked the bird. We stared at it suspiciously. Of course, it didn't answer.

Day after day that bird came to Mom's window. It began following her from room to room. The fluttering of wings against glass became a customary sound.

"Look. Do you see the outline of its wings on the glass?" Mom pointed to the dining room windows. The evening sun filtering through the dusty glass highlighted the bird's angelic silhouette. "And here. Look here." Mom led the kids to the family room and then the den. Each room contained nearly identical images of the two stunning, outstretched wings. Yet as beautiful as the images were, the robin's presence and behavior began to unnerve Mom.

"You don't think it's somehow connected to Lela, do you?" she asked Dad and the kids a week later. They raised their eyebrows. None of them seemed bothered by the bird's appearance.

"Maybe it's just looking for a safe place to lay its eggs," Logan suggested.

"Yeah. Open a window and let it in," Haley added.

"It could get hurt," Dad said. "What if it poops everywhere?" He smirked and looked sideways toward Mom. The kids giggled at his antics, and Mom played along. "Who'd clean it up?" she teased.

But later that morning, when Dad was at work

and the kids at school, Mom placed Lela's collar on the windowsill.

"Lela knew spring was my favorite season. And a robin certainly symbolizes the arrival of spring and new beginnings. What do you think, Shamus? Maybe there's a connection?" She stared out the opened window and waited.

It isn't Lela, I told myself. There was nothing familiar in the bird's eyes. I didn't have the words to tell Mom, and I wouldn't have told her even if I could. I simply sat there with her. Watching and waiting. But the robin never came. It had flown away. Just when Mom opened up her mind and heart, the bird was gone. Her untenable connection to Lela was gone.

Mom looked for the bird for days after.

"It's not a pet, Gwen. Accept it for what it was. For whatever reason, that bird was drawn to you," Lara consoled. "You know, robins are often depicted as guides in the wisdom of change and growth. Maybe that bird, whether connected to Lela or not, was telling you to let go of the past. Put it behind you, really behind you, and move on."

Mom thought hard about Lara's words, and she woke up one morning determined to put the past behind her. Maybe it was the sunny weather, or maybe she just realized it was time, 'cause when she opened her eyes, really opened them, she saw that her life was as it was meant to be. It was a good life filled with abundant blessings.

Mom stopped blaming Dad and tried accepting what she couldn't control. It was inevitable that Lela would die, and Mom knew the right job would eventually present itself. She practiced patience and her demeanor grew soft. She was learning to embrace each day, the challenges and the rewards. She thought about all of life's possibilities and began looking forward to the unknown.

Calmness returned her soul, and as if on cue, the robin reappeared. Its return was unexpected, and it came in a pair. It brought its mate. They nested on a ladder in the storage area under Mom's window. Mom didn't question their presence. She didn't ask "why." She accepted the experience for what it was, and it was beautiful.

We watched the robins meticulously craft a nest from the twigs, twine, and mud they collected. We counted as the robin laid her eggs. "She laid another one," the kids cried out enthusiastically. She laid an egg each day for four days, but we feared for the unborn babies when our neighbor's cat appeared. He snarled and growled beneath Mom's window. Mom sent Dad and me out to scare him away, but that cat was persistent.

"To hell with natural selection," Mom said. "I'm gonna give those eggs a fighting chance." She secured the ladder against the wall and surrounded the storage area with chicken wire. Logan and I peed along the makeshift fence, hoping our urine would keep predators away. We waited and worried for days thereafter. We vigilantly patrolled the fence's perimeter looking for signs of unwanted visitors.

It was a bright sunny day when Logan noticed

the first crack in an egg. We mindfully kept our distance from the nest. We inspected the fence before nightfall, and I kept vigil beneath the opened window. It was during dawn's early hours that the warm breeze carried the firstborn's faint chirp to my ears. My chest filled with pride when I heard the hungry cry. The mother robin quickly silenced her young.

Three baby birds soon rested under their mother's protective wings. The fourth egg had disappeared during the night. Google told us that a mother would remove an infertile egg from the nest. Though we were sad, we rejoiced in learning that our robins had already beaten the odds.

We watched as the parents brought food for their young. We marveled at how quickly the babies grew from naked, awkward fledglings to feathered adolescents ready to spread their wings and fly.

I reflected on my own passage from puppy to adolescent to adult. I was surprised at how quickly my own journey was moving. Amazed by how fast I was slipping into middle age.

I'll never know for certain if Mom believed the events of those few weeks were connected to Lela. She never said, but the robins' presence comforted her. They renewed her hope. She wasn't sad when the last baby chick was gone. Only disappointed that she hadn't seen it fly away.

I too felt disappointed when I peered into the empty nest. I searched the yard for a sign, any sign, that those birds were near and that they knew me. But there was no sign. I couldn't tell one robin from the next. My disappointment turned to despair. The depth of my feelings surprised me.

Everyone leaves. My mother, Gail, Lela, the robins, I reflected sorrowfully.

Lela said our paths would cross again. I believed her. I looked everywhere for her. Every day I'd sniff the air in search of something familiar.

Nothing.

My faith flickered and my stomach turned sour.

"You don't think he's sick, do you?" Mom voiced her concerns to Dad. "He's not himself. He seems so lethargic."

She lay next to me and rested her head lightly on my shoulder. "Don't you get sick on me," she whispered in my ear. "I can't lose you too." She buried her face deep in my fur. "I need you," she said faintly, stroking my side.

I closed my eyes and exhaled slowly. The warmth of her touch stilled my despair and quieted my fears. Her reassuring words soothed me.

It was as Lela had said it would be. Mom needed me. She would never leave.

~Sixty-five~

I was there when the shelter first called. The same shelter where Emi had once lived and where we donated Lela's belongings. They had a new litter of puppies. Young puppies, just weaned. They'd be ready for adoption the following week. We were welcome to stop by and look before then.

The message didn't surprise me. The kids had begged for a puppy since Christmas. But Mom and Dad didn't enter into serious discussions about it until early spring. Around the same time that the robins were nesting.

"I think it's time," Mom said. "A puppy will be good for all of us, especially Shamus. Besides I'm bound to find a job this fall. I can train the puppy before heading back to work. What do you think?"

"If you're ready," Dad said supportively. He knew Mom had needed time to heal. She had to know that she could love another dog without being disloyal to Lela's memory. She had to free herself of that guilt before she could bring a new dog into our home.

"I think I am," she said with a smile. "We both are. Right, Shamus?" She tussled my ears and scratched under my chin.

The simple truth was that while I enjoyed the extra attention I'd gotten since Lela's passing, I craved a canine companion. A playmate to chase and wrestle with. Another dog to share my secrets and the backseat with on long car rides. Besides I too sensed it wouldn't be long before Mom found a job, and I certainly didn't want to spend my days alone. I'd never been alone, and the thought of it still frightened me.

"Yes!" I yelped. I too was ready. My tail beat fervently against her thigh.

It was decided that night, shortly after the robins left. We would adopt another dog.

But what one? I wondered. I tossed and turned until dawn thinking of all the possibilities. I knew it wouldn't be a pure black Lab. Mom had already decided that. She wanted a rescue dog. One born into unfortunate circumstances. One in need of a home.

Ours was a good home. Imperfect but full of love.

Mom called the shelter the next morning and put her name on a waiting list. A week later, the shelter left the message about the newly received litter.

Mom and Dad took the kids to see the young pups.

"She's a cutie, Shamus. I thought it would help if you were familiar with her scent before we bring her home." Mom placed an old towel in front of me. It disappointedly carried the smells of many young dogs. I couldn't ascertain one pup from another.

"She's gonna keep you busy. You'll have to show her the ropes now. Can you do that?" Mom asked me earnestly.

Yes, I thought. *I'll help you teach the puppy just as Lela had taught me. I'll teach her about our family and tell her all about Lela. I'll warn her about chewing rugs and furniture and phones, and make sure she doesn't chase after Emi. She'll learn not to jump and where to pee. I'll introduce her to Ronan. I can do this,* I told myself. *But where do I start?*

Panic mixed with excitement. We were adopting a puppy!

The kids had already picked out her name. They decided on Shelby. Haley showed me the collar and leash they'd bought for her. The matching set was thinner than my own. *She must be small,* I worried. I was hoping for a medium-size dog. Like me.

Dad walked in carrying a big plush pillow. I stuck my nose deep into its fabric. It smelled new and unsoiled. I tugged at one corner trying to wrestle it from his arms. I couldn't wait to rest upon it.

"This one's not for you, big guy," Dad ribbed. He saw the disappointment on my face. "Don't worry. The kids picked out something for you." He rubbed my chest heartily.

"Here, Shamus," Logan called out. "We didn't forget about you." He carried a big peanut butter biscuit in his hand. *Peanut butter. My favorite,* I thought dreamily. I devoured the tasty treat in seconds. I swiped the crumbs from my muzzle and turned to the bits that had fallen on the floor.

"Shelby's lucky to have you, Shamus. We all are." Mom scooped my muzzle into her hands and rubbed her cheek against it. "You won't feel slighted, will you?" She gazed into my eyes, searching for an answer.

I wagged my tail and lapped at her cheek reassuringly.

The shelter called again. This time to tell us the

pups were ready.

Shelby was coming home.

~Sixty-six~

Lela and I watch a hummingbird dart about the garden searching for sweet nectar. It hovers around a large lily whose petals spread welcomingly, pointing the way to its fruits. The bird's wings tremble in anticipation. It's suspended in mid-air, seemingly weightless.

It moves suddenly, startling us both, plunging its long, narrow beak deep into the lily to claim the reward.

Its humming grows louder as it feasts.

Lela picks up a scent and races ahead.

"Where are you going?" I shout after her.

She pauses and looks back over her shoulder. Her big, dark penetrating eyes sparkle with mischief. There's nothing cloudy in them.

"Wait," I holler. "They'll be back soon. Don't you want to meet Shelby?"

She tosses her head back and lets out a long playful howl.

I know she's leaving. I'm not meant to follow. I fondly watch her run off. She stops along the way to frolic. Her hips no longer burdened with age.

The humming grows deafening and Lela's image fades.

The light turns to darkness and back to light again.

My eyelids separate.

Beeping. A familiar beep.

The gravel crunches under the weight of Shelly's tires. Her friendly horn beeps again, and I hear them calling me.

"Shamus, Shamus. We're home," Haley's voice rings out.

I shake my head and lick my lips. The sun's high over head.

A burp bubbles out.

"Shamus. Come meet Shelby," Logan hollers.

Shelby. Yes, Shelby's coming home today, I think, stretching my legs and back. I yawn and taste the fresh air filling my lungs.

A car door slams, then another, and another, and another.

The banging jars my senses.

It dawns on me suddenly. Shelby's here.

"Shelby's here NOW!" I shout, jumping up from my pillow.

I press my nose against the screen. *Where is she?* I wonder.

"Who has Shelby?" I bark eagerly. The window frame shakes under the weight of my shifting paws.

Then . . .

I see her.

The sun bounces off her new dog tags. Her light, soft-looking fur is radiant. Her ears and tail are long. Her paws are big, and she swaggers as all puppies do. She's gonna be big. *Someone I can wrestle with*, I think gleefully.

My welcoming bark rings through the house. My body quivers with excitement. I can't help whining.

Her ears perk up. Her tail beats hard and fast as she prances in place. "Hello," she calls to me. I'm surprised by the sound of the young bark. I thought it'd be deeper, stronger.

"Ready to greet her?" Mom asks.

"Of course I am!" I cry, charging past her.

Shelby meets me half way, and we run joyful circles around each other.

I sniff and freeze.

There's something familiar about her scent. Something I hadn't detected before. Too many undecipherable smells had mingled together on her towel.

I sniff again.

It can't be, I think as I turn to face her. *It can't be!*

She brazenly returns my stare. There's a twinkle in her eye.

I catch my breath.

A tiny, faint butterfly freckle.

My heart stops and my legs grow weak.

"I know you," I whisper.

The End

Discussion Questions

1. What is the significance of the book's title?

2. Why did the author choose Shamus to narrate the story? How would the book have been different if Gwen was the narrator? Lela?

3. Are the characters believable? Can you relate to their dilemmas?

4. How do the characters change or evolve throughout the course of the story?

5. What is the author's message about faith?

6. At what point did Shamus begin his succession? Can you identify specific examples that illustrate the gradual shift between Lela and Shamus? At what point do you think the transition was complete?

7. Did any part of the book make you uncomfortable? If so, why?

8. Why does Shamus refer to God as "Grammy's God"?

9. Why did Lela not show herself to Gwen after her passing?

10. Did the book end as you expected?

11. What emotions did the story evoke in you as a reader?

12. Do you look at animals differently as a result of reading this book?

13. If you could ask the author to change something about the book, what would it be?